The Black Sands of Hades

Halcyon Universe: Side Quests

Mindi Briar

Mindi Briar

Contents

Author's Note

There's no way *Bikini Vampires* is actually Nox's favorite show.

–Petrichor Blooms

[Miri] leans heavily against a holo-room door advertising that, inside, a fifth-season rerun of *Bikini Vampires of Black Sand Beach* is playing.

–The Invisible Bright

...I recognize the singer. I think I've seen her in music vids from that popular holo-drama. *Angelique Azalea, that's her name.*

–The Taste of Lies

The Black Sands of Hades is based on the fictional Halcyon Universe holo-drama *Bikini Vampires of Black Sand Beach*, which was intended as an homage to overdramatic, sexy TV shows like the ones popularized by the CW Network. It takes place around the same time frame as *Adrift in

Starlight, but other than the above quotes, it does not overlap with any of the other books in the series.

Get your popcorn ready.

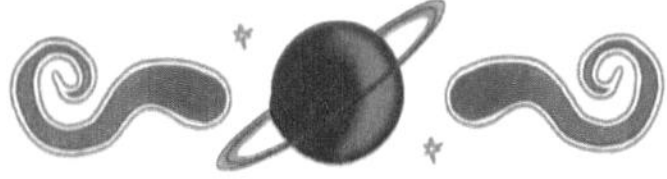

In my ideal future, there is space for everyone to find their happy ending. The Halcyon Universe series is queer-inclusive, and that means some of my characters have identities and lived experiences that I don't share. For this reason, I'm including a recommendation list at the end of the Acknowledgements section to shine a spotlight on underrepresented (and amazing!) voices in the queer community.

I also encourage readers to make informed decisions about the books they read, so please note the content information below.

- Violence

- Blood consumption

- Sexual assault (past)

- Character trauma/PTSD

- Stalking and emotional abuse

- Discussion of past suicidal thoughts/attempt

- Some mild body horror

- Explicit consensual sex (including f/f, f/m, and f/f/m scenes)

- Wild animal death

- Recreational drug and alcohol use

- Strong language

To the "Tempted" anthology squad, for giving me the audacity to write all this spice.

Pilot Episode

THE PLANET HADES

YEAR 3728 D.E.

Chapter 1

ANGELIQUE

Hades' sun blazes like it has a personal vendetta against my retinas. I reach across the ship's console and turn the viewscreen tint a notch darker.

I timed my arrival for the planet's sleep cycle, hoping to keep my presence here on the down-low. Descending to the planet's surface during the daytime hours, however, will be a punishing task. This planet's only settlement, a picturesque beach resort, is fully nocturnal. The blistering solar radiation forces all but a handful of native species to seek shelter underground during the day.

A life without sunlight was a hard sell when I took this job, but I wouldn't be here if I had anywhere else left to hide.

Even though I'd call myself a *modestly* successful singer at best, people snap pics of me anywhere I go. *Anywhere.* The previous planet I'd tried to make into a new home was practically a desert wasteland, and still some drunk glitch managed to plaster my image all over their uniweb profile, bragging about the fabulous Angelique Azalea paying a visit to their shitty excuse for a local saloon. That planet was so remote, I had a full day to pack my things before the syncships arrived and the upload hit the galactic uniweb to blow my cover.

I've had to start over so many times. Hades is an absolute last resort. But at least it *is* a resort, and they have a healthy budget for entertainment. The pay's not bad, though it's not enough to make up for the drawback of *having to live on Hades*. They were even (grudgingly) willing to accept my only non-negotiable: they get the voice of a popular singer, but not my name. I'll be hiding behind a mask for every performance.

Despite the extra interest they would have gotten by advertising Angelique Azalea, they barely argued. I get the sense this is one of those "always hiring" jobs that loses talent almost faster than they can book them.

Although my ship's atmo control works overtime, I'm still sweating by the time I set down on the landing platform. I relay my pilot license number and ship's registration to the air traffic control bots, and the platform sinks slowly into the ground. I sigh as cool shade swallows me.

The controller instructs me to taxi to an assigned parking space. It's hard keeping my eyes on the illuminated lines I'm supposed to follow, because the hangar is a gorgeous, high-ceilinged lava cave studded with mica that glitters in the floodlights. The walls are jagged with a mix of natural stalactites and gouges from the human tech that dug this cavern out. Taxiing past rows of parked starships, my jaw drops at the ridiculously expensive custom models among them. I'm comfortably wealthy, or I *would* be if I had access to all of my assets, but the people vacationing here make me look like a pauper.

I anchor my baby-blue two-seater, climb out, and rummage in the cargo hold for the sparkly handle of my costume trunk. I left almost everything behind on Monroe, and my possessions have only dwindled since. Now I'm down to a few new dress purchases—pieces no one's seen me wear yet—a scroll-tablet, and the vintage bedazzled blaster my dad gave me for my last birthday before he died. It's hard not to mourn the gorgeous wardrobe I left to gather dust in my old apartment. My throat tightens as

I picture the brightly colored walls and scintillating beaded curtains of my old bedroom.

Someday, maybe, I might be able to think about it without being consumed with fury that it was all taken from me.

After following the exit signs, I arrive at a brightly-lit lobby in front of the traffic control office. A cute dark-haired woman wearing a cropped, Hades-flag-orange jacket hits me with a stunner of a smile. "Welcome to Hades, home of the galaxy-famous Black Sand Beach. Is this your first visit—?" She consults the screen that must be scanning my ID as I stand in front of her. "Miz...Smythe?"

"Mm-hmm."

"Well, we are so excited to have you! What brings you here?"

"A job," I say shortly.

"Oh, wonderful!" The greeter has all the enthusiasm I'm unable to muster. "A longer stay, then?"

I shrug. *That all depends, doesn't it?*

The greeter—whose name tag reads *Gabrielle*—hands me a brochure. "You'll want to become familiar with these safety instructions. Do you need directions to where you're staying?"

"Uh, yeah." I flick through my scroll for the address my new employer sent.

"Ah! Entertainment block!" Gabrielle slides a map across her desk and points. "We're here. To get there, you go—" She traces a labyrinthine line with her fingertip. The underground dwellings on Hades may not be fully natural lava caves anymore, but their twisting and meandering shape makes their origin clear. I'll be lucky if I don't spend my first week here getting lost.

Gabrielle taps the approximate location of my new living space. "Did they send you the door code for your room yet?"

I scroll through my messages. "I don't see it here."

Gabrielle rolls her eyes. "They always insist on verifying ID before admitting a new tenant. But it's the middle of the day, so the housing coordinator's probably asleep. What do they expect you to do, cool your heels in Underworld until dusk?" She catches my raised eyebrow and clarifies, "Underworld is the resort's public lounge."

"Fitting, I guess. That'll be where I work."

"Oh?" Gabrielle searches my face. My pulse kicks up. What if she recognizes me? I'm placing a lot of trust in the expensive piece of tech-jewelry that rests weighty and warm against my throat. The glamour pendant is supposed to project a mask that subtly alters my facial features. But this is the first time it's being put to the test.

"Do they have you dancing, then? Tending the bar?"

No sign of recognition. I relax a fraction.

"Singing." I tug on my trunk. Its hovers need a charge—it's starting to sag toward the ground.

"Well, be careful," says Gabrielle, a wrinkle appearing between her eyebrows. "It can be a rough crowd in there during the daylight hours. You're safer staying in your room while the resort sleeps."

"I can handle myself." Even though my blaster is currently wrapped in a few layers of underwear, I'm not afraid to use it. Not anymore. "Just point me to this Underworld."

Gabrielle says lightly, "Your funeral, I guess."

This late into the planetary sleep cycle, Underworld is nearly empty. From Gabrielle's warning, I half-expected a bar fight in progress. Instead, a handful of bots whir around disinfecting surfaces and collecting trash. Off in the back corner, a tight cluster of sleepless black-clad patrons huddle in a booth. I can feel their eyes on me the moment I walk in, but I ignore them, not wanting to invite harassment. I find a seat of my own, order a drink from the screen at the end of the table, and unfold the brochure Gabrielle gave me.

Safety Information

(Compiled by the Hades Tourism Association
in collaboration with the Hades Ranger Academy)

Thank you for visiting our beautiful planet! We want you to enjoy your stay without accident, injury, or death.

I huff out a laugh. No shit.

Here are some tips to remember as you vacation on Hades:

1. *The sand remains hot even at night. Prolonged exposure can lead to burns. Protective footwear is recommended while walking on the beach.*

2. *Dawn alarms will sound twice. We recommend that you strive to be underground by the time the first alarm goes off. If you hear the first alarm and you are still aboveground, promptly make your way to approved, climate-controlled underground areas. **Do not** wait until the second dawn alarm.*

3. *Do not leave the fenced perimeter of the resort without a certified ranger present.*

4. *Swimming is permitted in designated areas. Do not swim outside of designated areas without a certified ranger present.*

5. *Wildlife attacks are rare, and extremely unlikely within resort boundaries. If the rangers do sound an alarm, please exit the water as quickly and calmly as possible and move to a safe location underground until the all-clear is given.*

6. *It is recommended that you keep your suite doors locked and bolted during daylight hours. Hades Resort Co. is not responsible for any thefts or assaults that occur during your stay.*

I raise my eyebrows. My expectations were already rock-bottom, but this place is somehow managing to dance the limbo under them.

The feeling of being watched is so oppressive that I finally lift my gaze to the group in the corner. They don't bother pretending they're not staring. I raise my hand to give them a sarcastic little wave. *Take a vid, it'll last longer.*

They snicker and go back to their drinks. All of them except one: the lanky man in the middle, the one with wavy, shoulder-length dark hair and a jawline to die for. His gaze doesn't waver. My breath catches, and warmth creeps up my neck. I came here to be invisible, and this is not an auspicious start.

Ugh, being in hiding sucks. Attracting the attention of the sexiest man in the room should be the goal, not a setback.

About two hours into nursing a series of drinks—not all of them alcoholic, because Gabrielle's warning made me nervous—nature calls. The entire corner group has gone back to ignoring me now, but even so, I don't think it'd be a good idea to leave my stuff at the table. I reluctantly hoist my dead-battery hovercase to drag it to the washroom. Neon signs point me down a hall to a series of single-stall cubicles. Predictably, the light at the far end of the hall is out.

I contemplate pulling out my blaster, but brush away the impulse as a childish fear of the dark. These stalls are lockable. Once inside, I'll be safe.

I dart inside the closest one, hauling the travel case with one hand. As I shut the door, the light flickers on.

And I scream as a figure in black lunges for me from the far corner, all glowing orange eyes and bared teeth. Instinctively, my hand shoots out to grab her by the throat, pushing her to arm's length.

She's a dirty-blonde, pale-skinned woman—one of the weirdos who was watching me in the lounge, I'm sure of it. I scrabble for the door button with my free hand, but with my attention split, she manages to break my grasp. She swings a clawed hand at my head and her fingernails snag in my hair. I try to duck away, but as I dodge, I trip over the blasted travel case and fall backward. My head cracks against the tiled wall. As pain shoots through my skull, I scream again.

Do not pass out, Angelique Azalea LaRue. Panic always brings Dad's voice back to me. *You gotta fight. Stay alert. Look for something you can use as a weapon.*

Well, given that I'm sprawled across the case containing my gun, my options are limited to a toilet plunger and my own oval-shaped, hot-pink nails. The former is out of reach, so I employ the latter, raking my assailant viciously across the arm when she grabs my leg.

"Leave me alone, creep!" I choke out. "I'm already calling the Authorities!" It's a total bluff. My keycuff does have an emergency-dial setting, but I haven't recalibrated it for this planet yet. It won't do me any good to call Susannah's Authorities; the call would take a day to even go through.

And even if they *did* show up, they probably wouldn't do shit to help me.

"What Authorities?" The woman snorts a laugh. "No Imperial peace-keepers here, sweetie. The rangers are all you got, and they're asleep."

Shit. I'm more screwed than I thought.

I suck in a breath for one more scream, but the woman pushes a cold, dry palm over my mouth. I snap my teeth, dig my nails in, but even scratching bloody marks into her arm doesn't deter this freak.

"Now hold still," she whispers, her eyes glowing with a strange orange light.

As the attacker presses me down, pushing my head to the side to lick my neck, I freeze. Memories roll over me: *Jude's weight holding me immobile against the mattress. His invasive fingers. A cry of pain tearing out of my throat. His loathsome whisper in my ear: "You're mine, only mine, forever."*

I failed to protect myself then. Just as I'm failing now.

The sharp sting of the attacker's teeth on my neck grounds me in the moment. *What the fuck? Why is this glitch biting me?* My urge to fight overwhelms the freeze response, and I try to kick out again. But my limbs are paralyzed. I'm only able to move the barest centimeter, a mere twitch instead of the shove I intended.

With the option to fight taken from me, I regret not allowing myself to pass out. At least then I wouldn't have another memory to haunt me when I wake screaming in the night.

I close my eyes and try to disappear into my mind. *Don't give up. Just wait for it to be over. Just survive...*

The door slams open. The paralysis evaporates as her weight lifts off me, but I force myself not to move. I only crack my eyes open a tiny bit, and my heart thuds at what I see. The handsome man with the wavy hair has my attacker by the throat, pushing her up against the opposite wall with her feet dangling.

"I told you not to touch her!" he growls.

"You're wrong." The woman has to rasp it past his choking grip. "She isn't bait. Just some quarkbrained tourist. Said something about calling the Authorities—doesn't even know we don't have any."

"Fuck!" He releases the woman, who drops to her knees, coughing. "We don't have any *yet*. I'd like to keep it that way. Get the fuck out of here, Vi."

"Aw, come on, Romeo," the woman whines. But she yanks the door open and leaves, slamming it behind her.

The man kneels next to me. I keep my eyes shut, hoping "play dead" will get rid of him, but I hold my muscles tense in case I have to lash out.

Gentle fingers explore the bloody wound where the woman—Vi—bit me. I hear the purr of a zipper. Something rattles inside a container. Then I feel the cool sting of disinfectant and the hissing, tickling spray of a liquid skin-patch. When he's done, he picks up my hand and begins wiping disinfectant under my nails where the attacker's blood is already caking, half-dried and tacky.

"I know you're awake," he says softly.

I open my eyes. He's bending over me, the first aid kit open on his lap. He's frowning, but the look in his eyes feels surprisingly kind.

"Who are you?" I choke out.

He ignores the question. "There's a bruise on the back of your head. Let me tend it."

How does he know? Feeling utterly helpless, I turn my back to him. His fingers slide through my hair, parting it at my scalp to rub sticky balm against the swelling.

He guides me to stand up. My head pounds, but the pain in my neck is already receding. The man looks straight into my eyes, his cool green gaze holding me captive. "Lock yourself in this washroom until dusk," he tells me. "Don't come out for anyone."

"I will."

"Did you call the Authorities?" he asks, lifting the wrist that has my keycuff.

"No. There wasn't time." Why am I telling him that? I should lie that they're already on their way.

"Good." He runs a gentle finger across my forehead and down my temple. My body goes all floaty, simultaneously out of control and hyperaware of its reaction to him. "I need you to do one more thing for me."

My lips say, "Anything," without me meaning them to.

"Forget," he whispers, his eyes flashing orange.

And I do.

Chapter 2

ANGELIQUE

My new living quarters are depressingly gray. I've seen the pics of lavish tourist suites on Hades, splashed in vivid sunset hues, furnished with huge soft mattresses and plush carpets. They didn't bother with the same quality in the apartments for hired entertainers. I get a gunmetal-gray sleep pod, a worn brown sofa, and carpet that might as well be cement, given how rough, cold, and colorless it is.

I turn to the hospitality coordinator, whose name tag says *Jayce*. They're in their late twenties, roughly my age, but they seem to consider me, a non-guest—*hired help* even!—beneath them. They turned up to Underworld just after sundown with a bedhead and the attitude of someone whose oatmeal had been pissed in. The whole five minutes it took to show me to my room, assign my ID cuff master access, and inform me of the rules (no loud parties after dawn, no pets, and don't punch holes in the wall), they acted like they were doing me a grudging favor instead of *their job*.

"There's no bed?" I ask, trying (and sort of failing) not to sound like I'm complaining.

Jayce's lifted-eyebrow side-eye accuses me of being a diva.

Well, sorr-ee if I don't want to live like a broke university student in this luxury resort!

"The couch folds out into a bed, if a sleep pod isn't good enough for you." They sidle toward the door. "If you'll excuse me..."

"Thank you," I call after them as the door swishes shut.

So much for the celebrity treatment. I'm not Angelique Azalea anymore. Now I'm Lea Smythe, random entertainer-for-hire.

With a sigh, I prop open the glittery lid of my trunk and begin unpacking. My costumes take up only half of the available wardrobe space. I'm going to need to do some uniweb shopping soon, or I'll end up—cringe—*repeating an outfit within the same week.*

When the trunk is empty, I carry it to the charging port and then survey the rest of the room. That shabby sofa could be much nicer with a pink cover. The pull-out bed won't be very comfortable, but with a mattress topper and a down duvet, I can make it decent. I probably shouldn't paint the walls, but putting up a few art prints will at least give me something to look at other than gray. And the washroom—maybe blue-and-green hand towels to go with my peacock-themed makeup case?

Yes. I can work with this.

I'm tempted to flop down on the ugly sofa and start scrolling the uniweb marketplace for interior decor, but my new employer wanted to meet with me this morning. (Evening?) So instead, I change out of my travel attire into a short, skin-hugging floral-print dress with a purple overrobe. I dab on some light makeup, curl my hair, and refasten the glamour necklace.

The full-length mirror on the back of the washroom door reflects back a vibrant silhouette and an indistinct, mysterious impression of a woman's face.

Perfect.

That group who stared at me all night is gone when I return to the lounge. The place is now packed with tourists enjoying a bite of breakfast and their first drink of the night on their way to the beach.

Up on stage, a distinguished elderly man plays a pensive tune on a piano module, largely ignored by the clientele. The table atmosphere is energy and excitement, but the pianist lives in his own little world, not responding to it at all.

Well, no wonder they hired me. They need someone to match the vibe.

My new manager introduces herself as Karina. She's a tall woman wearing a form-fitting black suit underneath a brown-and-black tortoise-shell-pattern robe. "This way," she says, leading me toward the stage. We skirt around the pianist, lost in his soulful plinking, and enter the stage door to his left.

Back here, there's a row of passcoded lockers in which performers can store their costumes and instruments. There's a washroom—"You can change in there if you're from a culture that mandates modesty," Karina says offhandedly—and a vending machine for water and coffee. Several of the lights are flickering and a few are out altogether. The floor is bare concrete. The lack of luxury compared to the public-facing areas of the resort is striking.

This is what it's like being a nobody again, working my way up with zero connections. When I'm Angelique Azalea, I get treated like a VIP. Even in the middle of the Susannah desert, I got free drinks and an apology that they couldn't offer me a *private* dressing room.

I peek into the washroom, a dingy but fairly standard layout with a waster, a sink, and a standing dry-disinfect station. My heartbeat kicks up, my breath suddenly coming short. Struggling not to hyperventilate, I back out and close the door all but a crack.

What a weird thing to trigger anxiety. *It's just a regular washroom that could use some cleaning, for fuck's sake. Nothing creepy hiding in there.*

Something tickles the back of my mind, an almost-memory that I can't quite catch hold of. I brace my hand on the doorframe, blinking fast as the anxiety fades along with the feeling of having forgotten something.

I roll my shoulders back, take a bracing breath, and shake my head when Karina asks if something's wrong. Complaining will only label me "difficult to work with." The pay's decent and they're letting me keep my anonymity. I can handle this.

"I'm fine," I reply, trying to project chirpy approachability. "Just a bit tired from waiting up all night." *In a washroom just like that one. Where I was totally safe and fine.*

"One more thing," Karina says. "The final performance slot of the night ends a little after daybreak. If you're working that shift, go straight home after. Walk with a buddy if you have one. Don't linger in the lounge, and definitely do not wander around the resort alone. The daytime is...dangerous here. People have gone missing."

I lift my eyebrows. "Oh?" is all I say, though I'd very much like to add, *I notice you didn't include that in the job description.*

Karina waves her hand, as if to brush away the heaviness of what she just said. "Most likely, they ran off with a vacation fling and didn't tell their spouse where they were going. But the rangers require us to have this talk with new hires. They're big on safety. Sometimes a little paranoid, if you ask me."

"I read the safety rules." I keep my tone light, as if to agree with Karina's assessment of the rangers as paranoid, but I have no intention of taking risks. People don't make up arbitrary safety rules for shits and giggles, as Karina seems to want to believe.

Karina shows me a wallscreen outside the manager's office, which displays a weekly schedule of performances, color-coded by performer. I'm delighted to see that they've highlighted my slots in magenta. *Very on-brand.* I have my first performance later today, a two-hour slot.

"What are the expectations for my off-stage time?" I ask.

Karina says, "At least for the first few weeks, you'll need to spend a few hours per day rehearsing with your accompanying pianist. Outside of that, as long as you're on time, sober, and well dressed when you're scheduled to come on stage, you're free to spend your time as you like."

I grin. I half expected some kind of arbitrary rule like "No going topside and risking your life in the dangerous outdoors! You must stay underground all night OR ELSE!" This means I can spend my time off warming myself on the hot black sand, swimming in bathtub-warm waters, and having a judicious cocktail or two. Maybe this gig won't be so bad after all.

Her "missing persons" warning squirms in the back of my mind, but I file it alongside the other safety tips. As long as I keep to the approved tourist areas and don't wander around alone, I'm sure I'll be fine.

With three hours to kill before my first show, I decide to explore the beach. It's been a long time since I had a reason to don my favorite neon pink bikini and the sheer silver overrobe that leaves little to the imagination. Scooping my hair into a high ponytail, I arrange the curls around my shoulders and adjust the glamour necklace. Its weight against my collarbone is still unfamiliar, but I'm starting to get used to it.

In the mirror, I notice a faint mark on my neck. *Weird. How did that get there?* It almost looks like a love bite, except I haven't had so much as a one-night stand for more than a year.

I cover the spot with my hair. *I'll worry about it later. Maybe get it checked out by a medic if it doesn't heal up.*

Following the signs for beach access, I find my way to a wide volcanic tunnel, thronging with tourists. The floor is paved in a mosaic of colored gems. Light shines from below them, creating an otherworldly stained glass effect that casts a shifting, multicolored glow on each person's skin. On either side of the corridor, windows are propped open, allowing vendors to hang out of their shopfronts hawking everything from skimpy, brightly colored swimwear to food to safety gear. I stop to buy a pair of Hades-approved beach shoes—the brochure said it was dangerous to go without them—and some extra skin protectant lotion.

Then the corridor gives way to an escalator staircase, and I inhale the scent of Hades' night air for the first time.

Maybe I was too quick to judge this place. The aggressive heat and radiation of daytime and the ill-repair of my underground living space had me worried. But as I crest the escalator, my jaw drops.

Hades at night looks just like the uniweb promotion images: alien plants in strange, curving shapes glowing vivid against the night sky. No, it's even better—because an image doesn't convey the *smell*. The spicy, humid, lush scent of a world come alive under the cover of darkness.

The heat of the black sand seeps through the soles of my protective booties. It's like there's an oven below the surface. I squeeze out a dab of lotion and begin swiping it onto my skin as I drink in my surroundings.

Rows of hammock-like beach chairs suspend tourists just high enough off the ground to bask in the warmth of the sand without being burned by it. There's a bar nearly every ten meters, and plenty of folks on the beach have already visited one; colorful cocktails are everywhere. Some of them even glow in the dark.

I might be more weirded out by light-up beverages if everything else wasn't bioluminescent here. A massive electrified fence separates Hades' forest from the beach resort, but the flora isn't what they're trying to keep out. Much of the light radiates from fringy fungi that line the pathways between the beach and the underground. Along the water line, the gentle glow of crystal-shaped solar lamps is answered by tiny darting shapes in the water. None of it, the resort's uniweb site assures me, is poisonous or radioactive…as far as they know. To be safe, they advise not ingesting any unfiltered ocean water or local plant matter unless—of course—a certified ranger tells me to.

Sparkly, reflective, and brightly colored clothing is popular here, so my style fits right in. Even the beach flyball tournament has a light-up ball and neon goalposts.

That's not to say *everyone's* wearing clothes. There are plenty of nude swimmers and sandbathers. The resort advertises an inclusive policy on attire or lack thereof, along with a zero tolerance policy on harassment. I wish I felt brave enough to ditch my bikini. I was raised in a culture with a nudity taboo, but these days, that's not what sends echoes of past shame reverberating through my brain at the sight of my nakedness in the mirror.

Maybe I'll work up to it. Maybe this will be good for me. *A growth opportunity,* my therapist would tell me, if I hadn't ghosted her after one visit when I left Monroe.

"Hey there. Can I buy you a drink?"

I jump at the sound of a voice in my ear and turn too quickly, almost knocking a sunset-orange cocktail out of the hands of a man with shoulder-length dark hair. My "hi!" comes out too high-pitched.

"My apologies. I startled you." The man's smile is devastating, dimpled and warm, his green eyes crinkling in the corners. His all-black ensemble—tank top, tight shorts, and calf-high boots—makes him an oddity among the brilliant beach fashionistas. Maybe he's trying to blend into the background, but I doubt those gorgeous eyes go unnoticed. I'm unprepared for the way my whole body hums with awareness, as if I'm syncing up to some subtle vibration he's giving off.

And why does he seem…familiar?

I try to remember where I might've seen him, but though it feels close enough to snatch, I can't quite recall. To cover my confusion, I laugh and say, "No worries. I didn't spill your drink, did I?"

He looks down at the syrupy orange liquid dripping down the back of his hand. "You did, but it was entirely my fault. Let me make it up to you by buying you your own?"

I hesitate. I wasn't planning to indulge before my show tonight, but one drink—and one conversation with one stunning man—couldn't hurt, could it?

"Why not," I say with a smile.

He guides me toward the nearest bar, gesturing to a table and asking what I'd like. I watch him carefully as he orders for me. It doesn't matter how hot a stranger is, I'm not going to turn my back on him while he's holding something I plan to consume. But he brings the drink straight to me, nothing suspicious, and sits across from me with another winning smile.

"My name's Romeo, by the way," he says.

I nearly tell him my real name, but catch myself just in time. "Lea."

"Pleasure to meet you." He bows like we're nobles on the Imperial Moon Palace, not a couple of scantily clad beach tourists. "So, what brings you to Hades? Vacation? Business?"

"The latter." I sip the cocktail he's given me. Sweet and tangy, with a pleasant burn at the back of the throat. "I'm the new singer for Underworld. My first show is tonight."

His eyebrows arch. "A singer? Interesting. Mind giving me a little preview?"

I smirk. "Sorry. You'll have to wait for tonight's show. Make sure to clap really loud—I need my new manager to think the audience is wild for me."

"Tease." Romeo's eyes sparkle, and his tone is playful, but I still tense up. The ghost of another voice hissing that word still wounds like a laser blast.

To his credit, he seems to realize that the flirtation hit a wrong note, and eases up. "I'd love to come see you tonight. What time?"

I tell him, and then sit in silence for a moment, struggling to ground myself in the here and now. *This isn't Jude. It's a handsome stranger who shows no sign of bad intentions.*

Why can't I shake the sense that something will go wrong? It's like, after Jude, I always expect the rug to be pulled out from under me. I miss the carefree woman I used to be, who could go home with a good-looking stranger and trust that they wouldn't hurt her.

And in the end, it wasn't even a stranger who harmed me. It was the man I was supposed to love.

Romeo starts up the conversation again, asking what I think of Hades so far, and I force myself to respond with casual lightness. His magnetic energy pulls me in again, and after a few minutes, the banter feels more natural. But a cold pit remains in the depth of my gut nonetheless.

Chapter 3

I can't get a read on this woman, and it bothers me more than I want to admit.

The second she walked into Underworld yesterday, all my internal alarms went off. Sparkly suitcase, pink catsuit, and a face-altering pendant I immediately identified as Imperial spy-tech.

She's an infiltrator working for the Imperial Authorities. I'd bet my last credit on it.

Stars, last night was a close call. I could strangle Violetta. The glitch heard "might be an Authority plant" and decided, without any discussion, to attack her. Never mind that the Authorities probably sent the so-called singer here to investigate the unusually high number of disappearances. If their undercover operative goes missing, it won't stay an investigation for long. It'll turn into a full-on invasion.

Approaching her on the beach was a test. I needed to confirm that my compulsion successfully buried her memories of Vi's attack. But that conversation produced more questions than answers. I thought she'd try to subtly question me, not flirt so convincingly I caught myself getting butterflies. Placing an undercover operative as a highly visible entertainer is an original move on the Authorities' part, to say the least—but I expected at least *some* hint that she's more than that.

There was only one thing I noticed: the way her eyes went distant and frightened at a couple of random moments. She was working hard to cover it, but "Lea," whoever she is, lives life on high alert.

Is it because she suspects what I am?

Or is it something else?

My keycuff vibrates gently against my wrist, alerting me to a new message. It's Benito. *<Did you talk to the redjacket yet? She remember anything?>*

<Nothing,> I type back. *<We're safe for now. But this woman is off limits, understand? You don't talk to her, you don't drain her blood, you definitely don't let her catch you on the hunt. Spread the word. Anyone who messes with her and blows our cover is kicked out of the gang permanently, and I won't hesitate to throw their quarkbrained ass right under the bus.>*

<Yes, boss,> Benito replies. I can almost hear the sarcasm.

<I'm dead serious. If the Authorities get an excuse to start hunting us down, we're cooked. So we won't give them a reason. Period.>

Benito replies with a little animation of a cat doing an Imperial salute. I roll my eyes. The gang might think I'm being an overbearing glitch, but this is for their own good.

They may have forgotten what kind of torture it takes for an immortal to die, but I haven't.

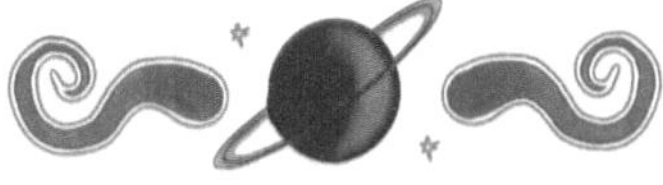

ANGELIQUE

I'm heading toward the escalator, drinking in one last look at the ocean, when someone behind me says, "I saw you talking to Romeo."

I whirl, surprised to see the greeter from last night. Now that I've seen a bunch of beach patrol personnel wearing that same uniform, I recognize it: a skintight white shirt and matching shorts with a cropped orange jacket over the top. The word RANGER is embroidered in black over the left breast pocket.

So she's one of the fabled rangers, the authorities on all things safety-related here on Hades. They also seem to be standing in for actual Authorities, since this planet has none. *Interesting.*

"Hello again," I say brightly. "Gabrielle, right? Thank you for the safety brochure last night. It was really helpful. Sorry if I was a bit grumpy. Travel stresses me out."

She cracks a smile. "Friends call me Gaby."

"Lea Smythe." I reach out to shake her hand.

"Nice to meet you, Lea. Word of advice?" Gaby leans in. Her black bobbed hair falls forward, wafting a fruity scent. The orange and white of her uniform make a stunning contrast to her light-brown skin. A shock of awareness hits me for the second time today. *Is everyone on the resort this blasted attractive? Or do I really need to get laid?*

"What?" I ask breathlessly.

Gaby cuts a look to the side before murmuring, "You might not want to make friends with the Midnights."

"Who?"

"The Midnights. Local gang, always wearing black," Gaby says. "I'd keep my distance if I were you. They're dangerous."

I suddenly realize that Romeo managed to keep me talking for a couple of hours straight without saying a single thing about himself. I'm definitely going to have to ask some questions on the next date.

If there *is* a next one.

"I know you'll be staying here for a while, so you deserve a fair warning," Gaby continues. "Don't go anywhere alone with them."

Don't worry, my PTSD won't let me. Out loud I say, "Should I not make friends with anyone?"

The escalator spits us both out in the crystal-paved corridor. I start walking, but Gaby keeps pace with me.

"I, um…would you like to have lunch with me sometime? Or a drink?" she asks tentatively.

Is she asking as a friend, as a ranger, or as a date? Either way…I wouldn't mind.

"That sounds nice," I say, feeling the corners of my mouth lift up involuntarily.

My first performance in Underworld goes about as well as I could expect. The pianist hasn't had enough time to rehearse with me, so I sing to a recorded playlist. I deliberately avoid the fan-favorite songs that Angelique Azalea is known for; my necklace can only do so much if someone recognizes my voice. Instead I play it safe with jazzy covers of Top 100 hits. It doesn't engage the crowd as well as a live band might, but at least more of them are paying attention than during Boris's set earlier. I certainly hope so; I wriggled into a skintight glittery red dress and diaphanous gold robe for the occasion, and I'd be offended if I didn't catch at least a few eyes.

I'd also be lying if I said I wasn't aiming for a *certain* pair of eyes. I feel them on me for the whole set, burning into my skin from across the room. I don't dare meet Romeo's green gaze for fear it'll put a hitch in the smooth honey of my voice.

I scan the crowd for Gaby's orange jacket, but no Hades rangers are present. I guess they have to be on duty. I'm singing the planet to sleep, after all. As I close out my set with a crooning, soulful cover of a second-millennium oldie, the dawn alarms blare topside. The lounge briefly becomes even more packed as people come in from the beach to seek refreshment in the resort below.

By the time I've taken my last bow, my crowd has doubled since the beginning of my set. I blow them a kiss over my shoulder and close the stage door behind me, taking a long breath as the cooler air washes over my flushed cheeks.

Stars, it felt *amazing* to perform again.

I change clothes in the washroom and gulp water from the beverage machine, wondering if the serving bots will make me dinner if I sneak into the kitch from the back door. I never eat much before a performance, so I'm always starving afterward.

Unfortunately, the kitchbots chase me out of the food prep area, but not before I'm able to snag a synthmeat sandwich that someone sent back for having too many pickles on it. I inhale it on my way out of the lounge, garment bag draped over my arm. There *are* more pickles on it than I like, but whatever, I'm starving.

The crowd outside Underworld is starting to thin out as sand-baked, happy-drunk tourists begin to hit their bedtime. I'm sure they've all heard the rangers' warnings about staying out past dawn. One particular pair of girls, one wearing a ruffled aquamarine one-piece and the other in a pastel orange bikini, weave down the corridor in front of me. They keep giggling about having forgotten which room number they're in.

Maybe I should let them know they're headed for the staff quarters, not the guest rooms. I take a half-step forward, opening my mouth to say something, when a blonde woman in a tight black dress and knee-high heeled boots comes around the corner and does it for me. "Ladies!" she exclaims. "I think you might be lost. Here, let me help you find your way back." Looping an arm through each of their elbows, she deftly steers them back the way they came, brushing right past me.

A chill shudders through me.

Why? Do I know her? Where would I have seen her before?

Blazes, the déjà vu I keep getting in this place! I'd better not be stuck in a time loop, like that shitty subplot in season twenty-six of *Starship Days*.

I don't know what compels me to turn around and follow the trio, but I do. I remain at a distance, always waiting for them to turn the next corner first. I even slip off my heels, which were hurting anyway, to muffle my steps. Their voices echo down the hall, both drunk women laughing at whatever the woman in black said.

I remember Gaby saying, *The Midnights. They always wear black. They're dangerous.*

What if those women are about to get robbed? I should call the Authorities. They'd probably say they can't do anything unless they see someone actively getting stabbed, but...

I lift my keycuff to dial before I recall that this planet doesn't have any. It's the rangers or no one.

And I only have one ranger's call code. The one Gaby typed in earlier today, her capable, steady hands gently cradling my wrist as I held it out for her to enter the number. I was meant to message her tomorrow about setting up a time to meet on her day off.

She'd want me to report this. Right?

I press my back to the wall and dash off a quick message. <*Hey, sorry to bother you, but a woman in black just grabbed these two drunk girls and I'm worried. Can you come check it out?*>

As soon as I hit *send*, I want to take it back. What if nothing's actually wrong? Gaby's going to think I'm paranoid. Maybe I can flirt with her and play it off as wanting to see her again. I just hope I don't embarrass those poor women by having a ranger bust down their door.

Gaby responds lightning-fast. <*Where are you?*>

Stars, I have no idea. I scan the numbers on doors as I pass them. <*I just passed room 370.*>

I get another instant response. *<I'm on my way. Stay safe.>*

By which she probably means to *not* keep following the woman in black. But I'm committed now. I follow them all the way to room 331, then lurk around the corner trying to eavesdrop as one of the bikini-clad women taps her keycuff to get in. The woman in black follows, and the door closes behind them.

Not five minutes later, Gaby sprints up, sweat dewing the fine hairs at her temple. Three more rangers straggle behind her. "Where?" she pants, unholstering and extending the electrified baton I didn't notice her carrying before.

"Whoa!" I hold my hands up, then point. "They went in there. I don't want anyone to get hurt—"

Gaby dashes to the door, tapping her keycuff against the lock. Rangers must have universal access, because the door slides right open. I shiver, hoping I'm never on their bad side.

Or in need of their intervention.

The rangers pile into the room, shouting indistinctly. I hang back, wondering if I should go home. But I'm too blasted nosy.

After a couple of minutes, Gaby comes back out. Her face is set in grim stone, but she softens a bit when she sees me. "Hey, Lea. You did the right thing calling me over. You might have saved those girls' lives." She rubs her forehead. "You didn't see the Midnight leave, did you?"

"The woman in black? No, she and the two other women went in there and no one came out."

"That's what I thought." Gaby lets out a long sigh, her shoulders slumping, then calls over her shoulder, "We're gonna have to search the vents, Jareth!"

One of the rangers still inside the room responds with a distant, "*Fuck!*"

"You mean she's not in there anymore?" I ask, jarred.

"Nope." Gaby folds her arms. "Her victims are still alive, though. If you'd waited any longer to call me, they might not have been."

"V-victims?" I can feel the blood draining out of my face, my stomach lurching. "I thought she was just going to rob them…"

Before Gaby (or my own better judgment) can stop me, I step to the open doorframe and peer through.

Lying on one of the room's two luxurious mattresses, I see the two swimwear-clad women sprawled, limbs tangling. Bright red blood stains the white duvet, seeping from twin bite marks in the sides of their necks.

Second Episode

Chapter 4

ANGELIQUE

*H*ow are you doing?> Gaby messages me the next day. Dusk has just fallen, we've gotten the all clear for beach access, and I'm getting ready for my early show at the lounge.

My fingers pause above the holo keypad. How do I respond without telling the truth, which is, *I cast up twice last night and only got about four hours of sleep?* Something about the bleeding bodies of those women shook me to my core; it doesn't even help knowing that they're going to make a full recovery. It's probably residual trauma from what happened with Jude, but blast if it doesn't feel *immediate.* Like I'm in danger *right the fuck now.*

Which I guess I still am. Gaby tried to dance around saying it, but they haven't caught the woman in black yet. She did a stellar job of disappearing into the void. I hope she didn't notice me following her, but when she led those women past me, I know she saw my face. It's Lea Smythe's glamoured, false face—but enough to paint a target on me.

<I'm fine,> is the answer I go with.

My keycuff dings. *<If you have time today, I'd like to talk.>*

I'm supposed to be at Underworld in fifteen minutes to begin warming up, but I *do* want to talk to Gaby. *<Maybe this afternoon?>*

<I have beach patrol duty all afternoon,> Gaby responds. *<But if things are quiet up there, I can patrol and chat at the same time.>*

Suddenly, my morning doesn't feel quite as shitty as before. Yes, I'm currently dabbing on an extra coat of concealer because my dark circles are so obvious that my necklace was picking them up and adding them to my fake face. And yes, nausea and hunger are warring in my belly like a pair of rival pirate gangs. But going to the beach yesterday was the highlight of a confusing, exhausting night. Having an excuse to go back gives me something to look forward to.

Still, I tuck my rhinestone-studded blaster into a hidden inner pocket of my robe before I head to work. I've had enough of feeling helpless.

GABRIELLE

Chief Ranger Korrie Han steeples her hands and watches me pacing in front of her desk. "Ranger Lopez, you do realize you're starting to sound paranoid?"

"I'm not making any of this up, Chief Han. I've been documenting the evidence for *years*. Witnesses put 'figures dressed in black' near the last place where at least five victims were seen. And last night, we had an eyewitness *proving* one of the Midnights was behind the attempted murder and exsanguination of—"

"Ranger Lopez."

"Chief, I'm begging you to listen to me. These people don't pay rent to the resort. They have no assigned rooms, not in the staff quarters, not in the guest rooms. They have no jobs. They functionally don't exist, and yet I've fucking *seen* them every day for the last six years. Something is weird here! Why will no one at least look at the evidence I've gathered?" I fling the memory chip down on her desk. "It's like they've bewitched you all to forget you've seen them the second you turn away!"

"Forget who?"

When my eyes widen, Chief Han's bland face breaks into laughter. "It's a joke, Ranger Lopez. I'm aware that the Midnights are essentially squatters here. I really don't care what they do, as long as they stay out of the way and don't bother the tourists, and so far that's all I've seen. To accuse them of the murder or kidnapping of dozens of missing persons over the past fifteen years, you're going to need a lot more evidence than a gut feeling."

"Which I have." I gesture at the memory chip. "Please, Chief, just look at what I've compiled. If you don't think there's anything to it, I'll shut up. But just *look*. Please?"

Chief Han sighs and pulls the chip toward her. "Fine, Lopez, but only because I like you."

"Thank you." I press my palms together. "Let me know when you're ready to discuss."

"I'll do that," says the Chief Ranger. "Now, don't you have a patrol to be on?"

ANGELIQUE

If...no, *when* I leave Hades, I need to bring the scent of the beach with me, bottled as a perfume. I breathe it in greedily as the escalator lifts me to the surface. That dark sky, the warm sand underfoot, the steady glow of fungi and lanterns, the audacious flash of glittery beachwear...I've fallen faster and deeper in love with this beach than I've ever fallen for another human.

I drift along the edge of the water, letting it lap at my protective booties, as I scan the beach for ranger uniforms. There: a gray-haired man in the white shorts and orange jacket, telling off a group of saurian-humanoid tourists for lying directly on the sand. ("Just because you've got scales doesn't mean you can't burn!") Another ranger, a dark-skinned, pink-haired woman, is stationed on a tall lifeguard stand. She scans the water with night-vision binoculars, a whistle held between her teeth.

Now that I'm looking for them, the rangers are everywhere, involved in everything. They're watching the bars, making sure no one gets too drunk. They're cruising through the swimming area on paddleboards. I even spot a couple of them patrolling the perimeter wall, probably to make sure no quarkbrained tourists attempt to climb it.

And then my eyes catch and hold on Gaby. Her chin-length black bob frames a brilliant smile as she laughs at something another ranger said. I'm momentarily dazzled.

She notices me staring—another embarrassment to add to my growing collection—and waves the other ranger off, heading my way.

"Lea! You look like you're feeling better."

"Oh, good," I say with a self-deprecating smile. "The makeup is working."

Gaby chuckles. "Really, though, I'm sorry you had to witness that last night. Despite all our warnings, that kind of thing isn't common. You did good, calling me for help."

I catch myself blushing and hope the necklace won't pick it up. "Thanks for getting there so fast. You were the real hero."

She doesn't deny it, just says modestly, "All part of the job."

"Did you catch the woman who did it?"

Gaby shakes her head. "We had teams searching all night, but she disappeared. The Midnights have hiding places the rangers have never found. The worst part is, we don't have the staff to keep searching. Beach safety is our priority."

My jaw drops. "But you…the rangers are basically the Authorities here, aren't they?"

"We are," Gaby confirms. "This whole resort—the blasted planet, for that matter—is privately owned by some offworld bigwig who only visits when he wants a vacation. He won't let the Authorities patrol here because it'd be *'upsetting to the guests,'* but without them, there were deaths and disappearances every single week." She catches my eyes widening and hastens to explain. "This was, like, fifteen years ago, right after the resort opened. Galactic newsies started calling Hades the *Death-tination Vacation.* That was when the vendors pooled their resources to fund a safety patrol. The pay is shit, but there are enough folks stuck in poverty on mining colonies or whatnot that some of us consider it a good deal. Risk your neck to keep rich tourists alive, and in return, you get to live…here." She gestures at the vibrant beach life around us.

Funnily enough, this history didn't show up when I searched Hades on the uniweb. I bet the resort's owner tried to bury it so he could make the rangers look like his idea. Typical.

"Is that where you come from?" I ask. "A mining colony?"

Gaby gives a small, sad smile. "I was born to a couple imprisoned on a penal colony when my mother's birth control implant failed. It wasn't a great childhood. Children of convicts are legally considered innocent, freeborn citizens, so they weren't allowed to force me to work in the mines. But they also weren't required to give my mother any extra food to support me." Her eyes grow distant for a moment, then she shivers and returns to the present. "Anyhow. I signed on for Hades ranger training as soon as I turned sixteen, and here I am."

A lump forms in my throat. It's easy to forget, having lived on wealthy Monroe since I was twelve, that deprivation and hardship are a fact of life for poorer worlds.

"What about you?" Gaby asks, in a transparent bid to change the subject. "What made you decide to take a job on Hades?"

I weigh my words carefully. I don't want to lie to her, but at the same time, I can't trust *anyone* with my true identity. "My career was getting stagnant," is the angle I decide on. "I wanted to explore the galaxy a little. Sing for people who haven't heard of me."

Gaby laughs, a high, bright sound; I want to compose a melody around it. "Well, if adventure's what you were after, you'll certainly find it here. Whatever else people say about Hades, there's never a dull moment."

As if on cue, a deafening horn blast startles me into clapping my hands over my ears. It's so deep I can feel the vibration in my chest as it pulses for three long beats.

Gaby's already tapping an alert on her keycuff. "Perimeter breach," she yells, taking off toward the water. "Everyone out now!"

Swimmers are already rushing for the shore, the water churning into a froth around their frantic limbs. The underground escalator bottlenecks with tourists shoving each other.

I know I should follow them, but I linger for a moment to watch Gaby and the other rangers. They're all jumping onto a fleet of small watercrafts that I hadn't noticed parked along the edges of the perimeter fence. The fence extends into the ocean to close off the swimming area from the water beyond.

But there's something in that water now.

A fin.

Jagged with spikes, the fin has to be nearly the size of a bedsheet. Its owner stays just below the surface, but the way it's circling is universally recognizable as predatory.

The rangers speed out onto the water, only a handful of them remaining behind to usher the tourists to safety.

"Miz." I turn to see one of them shaking my frozen arm. "You need to get inside. The beach is closed."

Part of my brain wants to rebel, to stay here and watch Gaby's team round up this monstrous alien fish. To see her return to safety. But the smart thing to do is to follow the rest of the crowd underground.

So, after casting one more anxious glance at the churning water, I flee.

The gem-paved, vendor-lined beach access corridor seemed spacious when I walked through it an hour ago. Now, it's jammed with tourists standing shoulder to bare shoulder, everyone buzzing about the emergency. I hear a few people who say they saw a fin, just like I did—some of them embellishing that they saw the creature leap out of the water and eat someone. And then there's the folks who saw nothing, but won't let that stop them from making something up.

"I heard it was a huge spidery thing climbing the walls from the jungle."

"There was a creature in the sky, didn't you see it? I know it's dark, but there was still a *shadow*…"

"What's going on?"

I whip around, recognizing the voice. Romeo is a few meters away from me, his handsome profile only visible when the crowd ebbs a little. I crane to see who he's talking to and stumble on the hem of a stranger's skirt.

"A sea monster got into the swimming area," a woman's voice responds. I can only see the back of her head: rose-gold beach waves and a flash of diamond chandelier earrings that seem a bit much, even for Hades' glitter-forward fashion scene.

"Again?" Romeo groans. "The rangers said they reinforced the barrier two weeks ago. With what? Sticky tape?"

If he'd said that to me, I might have giggled just like the other woman does. Overhearing the words, though, my knee-jerk reaction is defensiveness on Gaby's behalf. The rangers are trying their best to protect people, and if Gaby's version of their inception is true, they don't have a ton of resources to work with.

"Well, while we're stuck down here, would you be interested in getting lunch with me?"

My jaw drops. *What a player. Does he say that to every woman he meets on the beach?* I'm more hurt than I have any right to be. *And here I thought I was special.*

The woman tosses her hair. "I might be, if we don't have to wait in line for an hour."

"I know the good spots," Romeo says, winking at her. Winking! If he tries the same routine on me, I'm going to throw a drink in his face. Gaby was right to warn me away from him.

The memory of her words stops me short. *The Midnights...keep your distance...they're dangerous.*

The last time I followed someone wearing black who was trying to get a tourist alone, it ended in bloodstains and nightmares.

I don't want to believe Romeo is the same, but...

Without consciously meaning to, I start weaving through the crowd to follow them. Romeo is tugging on the woman's hand, and she's laughing as he pulls her along, shoving a path through the crowd.

He turns down a far less crowded side corridor. The signs tell me that this area houses Hades' public services like medical care and staff support. Further down the street, I see a big orange sign with the word RANGERS in black.

That means this area is well-monitored, right? I don't need to follow them around. I'm totally being a creep. I should just...stop.

But I don't. I edge along the street, slower now, watching Romeo lead his conquest down a narrow alley between the healer's office and the ranger headquarters.

That doesn't seem a likely place for a hidden restaurant.

In Dad's voice, my survival brain whispers, *If you see something, say something. Tell the Authorities.* That's the smart thing to do. I quicken my pace, heading for the door underneath the RANGERS sign.

But I have to pass the alley to get to the door, and I can't resist a quick glance. What I see freezes me in place.

Romeo has the woman backed against the wall of the healer's office, his face in the crook of her neck. It looks like he's kissing her. But her face is crumpled in agony, not blissed-out. Her hand goes to her throat, futilely trying to push him away.

Her fingers fall away, dripping red.

Adrenaline zings through my body. I take a step toward the ranger headquarters and trip over my own beach shoes. My sharp gasp is quiet, but enough to draw Romeo's attention. His mouth is bloody when he raises his head, eyes glowing orange in the dim light. My next breath is a choked sob as I realize: *he's not human.*

Not that I'm bigoted against nonhumans; the realization hits me more in the archaic sense of "human" as "sentient being that can be reasoned with." Romeo's luminescent eyes are wild, feral, hungry.

A phantom pain spikes in the nearly-gone bruise on my neck. I clap a hand to it, realizing that it's in the same exact place from which the woman slumping in his arms is now bleeding. Right over the vein.

I force my feet to move, stumbling in the direction of the ranger office. I'm too slow. Hands, slick with smears of blood, clamp around my upper arms.

I scream.

Chapter 5

ANGELIQUE

R omeo's hand slaps across my mouth. I taste iron and gag.

But to quiet me, he had to let go of my right arm, so I reach into my robe and free my blaster from its inner pocket. I disengage the safety and shove it against his chest. I feel him hesitate as I push the muzzle hard into his ribcage.

"Let go, or I'll shoot." It comes out as a mumble against Romeo's fingers. He lifts his hand, and I repeat the words clearly.

His grip loosens and he takes a step back, holding up his bloody hands. "Knew you were a redjacket," he growls. The glow is fading from his eyes, but he still looks murderous.

"You think I'm an Authority?" I laugh and turn the blaster briefly to the side, letting him appreciate its glittery glory. It's an old-fashioned design, barely larger than the palm of my hand. Short-range, not terribly effective against armor, and it needs recharging after about five shots. No Imperial soldier would be caught dead carrying something this frivolous, but it'll put a hole in a man.

"Aren't you?" Romeo takes another step backward. "That bauble around your neck is spy-tech. Knew it the minute you walked into our lounge. I'm not a fool—I know the Authorities have their eyes on us. The rangers are doing a piss-poor job of keeping the Hades death rate down."

"While you're doing your best to make it go up?" I spare a glance for the woman he'd been...*biting? Ugh. What the fuck is wrong with these people?*

His eyes dart toward her as well. "I'm not—shit! I gotta tend her wound. Can you not shoot me for a second?"

"No promises," I mutter, holding the gun steady on him as he walks backwards toward his victim.

He kneels at her side and pulls a little orange first-aid pouch from his pocket, the kind that tourist shops sell for a few credits. With practiced ease, he dabs at her neck with gauze, sprays disinfectant, then applies the liquid skin-patch that will seal the wound.

The bruise on my neck gives a phantom throb and the blaster trembles in my hand. *Whoa. Déjà vu again.*

"Is she going to be all right?" I ask.

"Why do you think I lured her to the doorstep of the med center?" Romeo uses a wet wipe from the kit to clean his hands and face, then tucks the first-aid kit back into his pocket. "She'll come around in a minute, stumble in, and they'll treat her for blood loss. She won't remember any of this."

The temptation to touch my neck becomes irresistible. "You've done this before."

His green eyes hold mine steadily. "Yes."

"To me?" It comes out as a question, but the random trauma responses I've been experiencing since I got here have started to make a lot more sense.

"Listen." Romeo stands up, his hands raised in front of him. "I can explain, but we have to go somewhere else. Cambots patrol this area."

"Only if it's somewhere public," I counter.

"Whatever makes you feel comfortable."

I make him lead the way back to the Underworld lounge. Partly because I don't trust him to walk behind me—I keep my hand on the gun inside my pocket, just in case—but also, to be quite honest, because I've gotten turned around and don't remember how to get back there.

With the beach still closed, the place is packed. I manage to snag a booth just as another couple is standing up to leave. I fiddle with the table privacy options and a transparent sound barrier surrounds our seats. To any outside listeners, our conversation will sound muffled at best.

Romeo says, "Are you planning to buy me a drink, or are you going to shoot me first and save yourself some credits?"

I glare at him. "You've had plenty to drink already, seems like."

He sighs, running a thumb across the corner of his mouth as if to catch an invisible drop of blood. "Swear to me you're not an Authority?"

"I'm not a soldier," I scoff. "Have you *seen* me?"

"Then what's with the spy-tech?"

I let my fingers explore the shape of the glamour necklace. I'm surprised he recognized it; it's supposed to disguise itself as an unremarkable gold chain. "Let's call it witness protection."

He cocks an eyebrow. "Now I'm even more intrigued. Did you rat on a pirate gang or...?"

My mind starts running through a half-formed collection of potential lies. Then I pause. Why bother making something up? I've got leverage on him.

"You can't tell anyone what I'm about to show you." I keep my voice low and fierce. "If I find out you blew my cover, I'll make sure there are more Authorities on your ass than fleas on a dog."

Romeo waves a hand. "Trust me, I'm no snitch."

I find the switch on the underside of the glamour pendant and turn it off.

For five seconds, I let him see the heart-shaped, sleepy-eyed, dimple-cheeked face of Angelique Azalea. Singer and songwriter of five original albums, plus a bunch of popular song covers that went viral on the uniweb. Lead actress in the musical *The Empress and I*. Resident performer at the ultra-exclusive Highball Lounge for two years in a row.

Then I flick the glamour pendant back on and wait for him to say something.

The last thing I expect to hear is, "Am I supposed to know who you are?"

I stare at him, unsure if he's serious. Then I burst out laughing. "You don't recognize me?"

"If you're some holo-drama actor, I'll tell you right now, I don't go on the uniweb a lot. So I'm not really caught up on who's who in the celebrity world."

The giggles are threatening to turn into hysterics. I force myself to breathe.

Romeo folds his hands on the table. "So you're famous. And you, what, had some kind of scandal that forced you to drop the unbelievable number of credits that black-market spy-tech costs? And you decided to go into hiding on *Hades*, of all places."

I shrug. "Plus or minus a few details...yeah. That's the gist of it."

He rolls his eyes and groans. "The Midnights are going to kill me when they find out. I swore up and down you were an Authority spy."

"The Midnights...are you really in a gang? Gaby told me to avoid you." *Seems like she was right.* "Do you know the woman who attacked those two tourists last night?"

"Know her? She's a fuckin' thorn in my side." Romeo runs a hand through his hair. "Vi's never been great at self control. Blazes, she nearly *killed* you that first night you were here."

The words jolt something deep inside my brain, a memory I can't quite reach. I wrinkle my brow. "Why can't I..."

Romeo sighs. "Here, look into my eyes real quick." When I do—trying to ignore the smolder of attraction that still curls in my belly at the intense green of his gaze—he says softly, "You can remember now."

His eyes flash orange, and it all floods back in an instant. The woman—Vi—attacking me in the washroom. Romeo stopping her, patching up my throat, and warning me to stay locked in the stall until morning.

Tears form in my eyes. The memory has been buried since that night, keeping the trauma as fresh as if it happened five minutes ago. My heart thunders in my chest. My hands shake. My breath comes in gasps.

Romeo reaches across the table and puts a hand over my wrist, rubbing gentle circles into my skin. "I know it's a shock," he says. "Honestly, I think we do people a favor, making them forget."

"H-how…" I can barely form words. "How about not attacking us in the first place?"

His eyes slide away.

"No, seriously." I turn my hand up, grasping his wrist and digging my nails in. "What the fuck is your sick little Midnight cult doing? *Blood drinking?* Do you think you're *vampires?*"

Romeo meets my gaze again. He doesn't have to say anything. I see it in his face.

"Oh, stars, that *is* what you think." The hysterical laughter is back. "Vampires…on a planet where people can only go out at night, and the daytime burns you up."

"It's not delusion," Romeo says quietly. "It's a medical condition. A parasitic infection."

I raise my eyebrows, skeptical.

He gently removes my fingernails from his wrist, putting my hand palm down on the table and resting his heavy, pale hand over it. "I was one of the construction workers who helped build this resort," he explains. "There were some preliminary inspections of the environment before we came, so we knew this place was going to be dangerous. Carnivorous trees. Giant hungry monsters. And, of course, the sun. But there were hazards that no one had discovered yet."

"Hang on a sec." I scrutinize Romeo's face. "This resort is, like, fifteen years old. How old were you?" He can't be more than thirty.

"We started building closer to twenty years ago," Romeo says. "And I'm forty-five in Galactic Standard years."

Well. Older than I normally date, but not out of the question—wait, NO. Get a grip, Angelique! He literally wants to eat *you!*

"You were saying about hazards?" I prompt.

He nods. "We spent a lot of our time underground at first, carving out the tunnels and setting up the living spaces. But at some point, we had to go back topside and build the resort perimeter. And that's where things got weird." He closes his eyes. "The first murder happened a week in—we woke up in the tunnels one morning and found our buddy Henley with his throat ripped out. Everyone thought it was an animal that had gotten underground, so we did a full search. Nothing. Then Frieda turned up dead a couple of days later. That night, Benito tried to hang himself. We cut him down and he confessed. He'd never felt anything like it before, he said. Uncontrollable blood-thirst. We figured, hey, Benito's gone a little wacky from the radiation, and we locked him up while we tried to figure out what to do.

"Then another guy came forward and said he was starting to feel the same. Next, it was me. Our work crew was only about twenty people, and by the time we had the perimeter wall up, nine of us were battling the thirst, and five more had been murdered by the ones who lost control."

"What was causing it?" I ask, breathless. The idea of some contagious murder bug in the air is chilling. *Am I at risk?*

"Well, at the time, we had no idea. We knew that if we reported ourselves to the Authorities, we'd probably find ourselves jailed or killed," Romeo says. "But we wanted to get to the bottom of it, so we called in a medic. Told her we were worried about the effects of radiation, didn't say anything about the thirst. But she caught it right away. Tiny parasitic creatures in our blood. Tried a bunch of cures, but they're pretty near impossible to kill. Turns out they make *us* hard to kill as well. Our wounds heal within minutes. Greg once tried to ex himself by going outside in full sunlight—he didn't enjoy it, but he lived to tell the tale, and doesn't even have scars anymore." Romeo gestures to his face. "You'll notice I don't look forty-five? That's the parasites too. Mercedes got infected in her seventies and actually aged *backwards* for a while."

"But *how'd* you get infected?" I press. *Tell me what I need to avoid.* "Clearly, not everybody gets it, or someone would have shut down the resort by now."

"Almost every native life form is infected with the organism," Romeo says. "If you have an open wound that contacts infected blood, that's it, you've got it too. Us construction guys had to chop down a whole bunch of alien plants to build that perimeter wall. We get a little cut, the sap gets on our skin, and...oops."

"But...there's all those plants inside the perimeter." I stare at him, my thoughts racing through the possibilities. "Do the rangers know about this?" If they did, wouldn't they add *Beware of sudden-onset vampirism from touching plants* to the safety brochure?

Romeo laughs. "Sure, some of them. A couple of infected people *became* rangers. Because that's the other thing about the parasites—they seem to thrive on the radiation from Hades' sun. If an infected person tries to leave, they'll literally take over that person's mind and stop 'em from going anywhere. So all us vampires are stuck here for good. We gotta find something to do with our time."

Gaby? I don't even want to think about whether she's...

"Well, if the rangers know, why don't they warn people not to touch the plants?" I ask.

Romeo waves his hand. "Everything you see inside the resort perimeter has been grown in a lab and triple-tested to make sure it's parasite-free. Don't worry, we're not out here letting tourists infect themselves. That's part of the rangers' job. Any creature that gets in from outside the wall, they have to assume it's infectious and eliminate the threat."

I fold my arms. "I have another question. What's with the mind control stuff? You said the parasites can take control of your mind. Is that how they make people forget the attacks?"

He nods. "We need blood to live, just like the carnivorous plants. But drinking from Hades' wild animals gives us aliens a stomachache. Our solution is to take occasional sips from tourists. But I swear to you, we try to minimize serious injuries. We only take small amounts from healthy people, we heal them afterward...and we use the parasites' mind-control abilities to make them forget the attack so they aren't left traumatized."

"What happened with Vi the other night, hurting those two girls?"

Romeo shakes his head. "I assume she let her hunger get out of control because I stopped her from drinking her fill from you the night before. She must have taken two at once to sate herself, then the rangers interrupted her before she could heal them. I do think they're going to be fine, by the way."

"Good." My stomach still rolls thinking about them lying prone, covered in blood. "So when you say 'we,' is that the Midnights? You're a...vampire gang with rules about biting people nicely?"

"More or less." He leans forward, arms folding on the table. "Speaking of which, one of our rules is that we don't tell anyone about Vampire Club. So are you going to make me erase your memory, or will you allow me to put a compulsion on you to prevent you telling anyone?"

"Are those my only two options?"

"I could kill you instead."

It *sounds* like he's joking, but I'm not willing to risk it. I grimace. "If you wipe my memory, I'm just going to go looking for the truth again. I'm a stubborn glitch. Can't I just promise not to tell?"

"Of course you can promise not to tell," Romeo says. "I'll make sure you keep the promise." And his green eyes catch mine, his hands holding mine in a gentle trap.

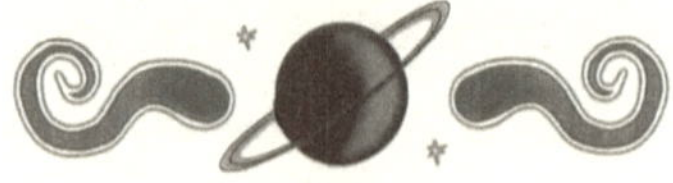

I spend the evening onstage, crooning slow love songs with a racing heart that won't settle. No matter how desperately I scan the crowd for her face, Gaby doesn't show. I sincerely hope she's alive and uninjured after the wildlife attack, but more than anything, I need to *talk* to her. I'm furious that Romeo's compelling me to keep the vampires' secret. All I want is to say the words out loud to someone else. To have their reaction determine whether it's all real or if I should admit myself to the healers for a mental evaluation.

Romeo promised that now that I know everything, he won't let anyone attack me, take my blood without consent, or mess with my memory anymore. He says it's like that with lots of the staff who live and work on the resort. Once they figure it out, the Midnights leave them alone as payment for their silence.

How do they all sleep at night?

With their doors locked, presumably.

I wonder if any of the resort staff have gotten together a "living with vampires" support group.

After the final notes of my last sultry love song, I barely linger to enjoy the applause before fleeing the stage. The back room feels sinister, dark and empty as most of the non-robot staff has already gone home for the night. I gather my things as quickly as possible and dash for the exit, practically sprinting for the safety of my room.

Even with my door barred and all conceivable hiding spots checked twice, paranoia grips me tightly. Vi escaped through a vent when she attacked those women. Could she crawl through a hidden tunnel to my room? I imagine her dropping down from the ceiling like a black-clad spider, leaning over my sleeping form, sinking her teeth in...

Stars. I'm going to need to go to the healers tomorrow and get a prescription for insomnia patches. Otherwise I'm not sure I'll ever sleep again.

Lying awake, huddled under the safe tent of my covers, I send a message to Gaby. *<Hope you're all right. Did you catch the creature?>*

I don't expect a response this late, but my heart thuds at the chime of my keycuff's new message notification.

<You doubted us?>

There's a goofy smirk on my face. *<Never. Just fishing for details. Ha. Get it?>*

Gaby responds instantly. *<Terrible joke. Get off my planet.>* She adds a winking animation.

<You're stuck with me for now,> I type back, although I've spent the last few hours debating whether I should cut my losses and flee while I still can. *<So? Details?>*

There's a longer pause. *<We caught it in a net and threw it outside the wall. Believe it or not, that was the easy part! The hard part was figuring out where it came through. Took us almost four hours to find the crack and patch it up.>*

<Do creatures get through the wall very often?>

<More often than we'd like,> Gaby answers, *<even though we inspect the upper wall every single day, and a dive team checks the underwater wall at least once a week..>*

If she'd told me all of this on day one, it might've kept me awake in terror. But the other disturbing Hades facts I've learned today are already ruining my sleep, so I find myself fascinated instead. *<Is there a guidebook on local wildlife? If I'm going to live here, I want to be prepared.>* In particular, I'm curious if the vampire parasites affect more than just the plants. I doubt that information is publicly available, but maybe I can nudge Gaby into telling me what the rangers know.

<Careful, that's how you end up joining the rangers,> Gaby jokes, as if she read my mind. *<Most of that info is off-limits to tourists. But since you're staying here, I can grant you access to the Hades biodiversity database. You'll have to use my login at the public library to look at it. They don't let anyone download it to personal devices because some of the information is classified. But it has tons of anatomy drawings and holo-captures.>*

<Thanks! That sounds super interesting. I'll go take a look tomorrow.> Classified information might include details on the vampire parasites. If it weren't the middle of the day—which I now know to be peak vampire hunting time—I'd be heading to the library right now.

<I have tomorrow off. I could meet you there,> Gaby offers. *<Make it a date? What time do they let you offstage?>*

A smile tugs at the corner of my mouth. *<Come to my next show and find out.>*

As my eyelids get heavier, I wonder what it is about Gaby that dispels my anxiety. Just the thought of spending time with her makes me feel so...safe.

Third Episode

Chapter 6

Romeo

Once all of the Midnights are back in our hideout, I shove down my embarrassment and relay the details of my conversation with Lea.

"What do you mean, she's not an Authority?" Benito crosses his arms, frowning at me. "You were all but a hundred percent sure."

"I'm still not totally ruling it out," I say, "but she, uh, accidentally caught me in the act of biting someone and the whole truth came out, and she didn't try to arrest me. Just threatened to shoot me with this tiny glitter blaster that probably wouldn't've even hurt. She claims she's some celebrity going incognito because of a scandal."

Gillian laughs. "So you wiped her memory and drank her half dry, right?" When I don't respond, she narrows her eyes. "*Right?*"

I sigh. "I compelled her not to say anything, but I let her keep her memories."

"*Romeo.*" That's Violetta, perched on an old supply crate we've been using as a gaming table. "You're always on our ass about safety and secrecy. Even if she's under a compulsion to keep quiet, knowing about us makes her a liability."

"You're one to talk about being a liability." I hate how defensive I sound—like I have to justify myself. "Who got herself stuck in a vent the other night and had to have me and Benito yank her out?"

"Which was your little *celebrity's* fault in the first place. I owe her one for calling the rangers on me."

"No," I snap. "No one is touching Lea. She's still off-limits until we figure out what else is going on with her."

The Midnights start a chorus of grumbling and protests. I hold my hand up to stop them. "Authority or not, she's high-profile enough that there'd be scrutiny if she goes missing. There are enough tourists around. None of us are starving." I glare at Vi. "Let's all be more careful, yeah? I really don't want us to have to disappear anybody again."

At the word "disappear," the group goes tense. We all remember what happened to Wright when he almost exposed us.

Sometimes, when I can't sleep at night, I wonder if all the separate parts of him are still conscious and experiencing pain, or if the parasite allowed him the sweet mercy of death.

After a long interval of awkward silence, Vi breaks the ice by pointing a black-booted toe at me. "Whatever, I think Romeo's just sweet on this girl. You all saw him eyeing her up across the lounge. Is that it, huh, Boss Man? You got a little crush?"

I flash a deadpan look at her, determined not to react. Any denial would only incriminate me.

Because, yeah, much as I hate to admit it, I think our new possibly-a-spy, maybe-a-celebrity, definitely-a-nosy-pain-in-the-ass is cute. Especially now that I've seen her real face, which is even prettier than the fake one her necklace generates.

What can I say? I guess I'm a sucker for a woman who threatens me with a blaster.

As soon as the Midnights start talking amongst themselves, I slip away and slide the partition closed over the entrance to my sleeping cave. Flopping onto my bed, I start composing a message.

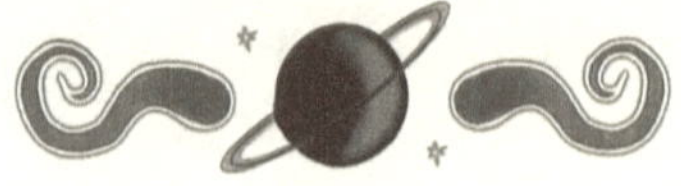

ANGELIQUE

I expected the nightmares. Bloody teeth, parasites wriggling through veins, monsters dragging swimmers below the waves.

But what I didn't expect was Romeo's crimson smile morphing into Jude's leering face as he leans close to sink his teeth into my skin.

I jerk awake, a hoarse scream ripping from my throat. My room is empty and silent, the lights still in day mode. My keycuff shows that it's barely dusk in the world above. The resort won't be fully awake for another hour.

Going back to sleep is out of the question. Groaning, I shuffle into the washroom and stare blearily at my reflection. The bruise on my neck is almost gone now, nothing left but a faint yellow smear.

The bruises Jude left faded quickly, too. The physical ones. I don't know if I'll ever be rid of the ones he left on my soul.

After showering off the sleep-sweat clinging to my skin, I use the washroom's hot water dispenser to make myself a strong cup of instant coffee. It's far worse than the brew I'd get from Underworld, but I need something to jumpstart my brain function. I burn my tongue on my first gulp as I check my scroll for messages.

Nothing from Gaby since her flirty *<Sweet dreams>* six hours ago. There's an automated reminder about my work schedule for the day, and...

An unknown call code. My heart stutters, my mouth going dry. *Who could it be but him?* There's only one person who makes new accounts every time I block him. I thought this time, with the extra privacy protections I put in place when I forged my new identity, I'd be safe.

How the blazes did he find me again?

My finger hovers over the message alert. It's better to know what he knows, right? Deleting it without reading would be foolish. Yet the very thought of reading whatever evil shit Jude wants to say to me makes the horrible coffee in my stomach threaten to come back up.

I tap into the message anyway.

<I hope this is the right Lea. I had to sweet-talk Karina to give me your call code. She doesn't like me for some reason, even though my friends and I are her best customers. I probably should have just asked for your call code in person, but after dropping that bombshell on you yesterday, I wasn't sure if you'd give it to me.

This is all coming out wrong. Stars, I'm a glitch. If you don't want to talk to me, that's fine. I just wanted to let you know that if you have questions, you can ask me anything. I'll be around. But if you want me to leave you alone, say the word, and I'll fuck off.

Yours, Romeo>

I let out a long, slow breath. *Not Jude. Thank stars.* Despite my brain equating the two of them in that nightmare, I'd let Romeo and his vampire friends drain my arteries dry before I'd let Jude even talk to me again. The bloodsuckers at least don't *like* hurting me.

But I need to think for a while before I respond to Romeo's overture. So I close the message and turn my attention to the comforting, time-consuming routine of curling my hair.

Despite the persistent nausea from anxiety and lack of sleep, my insides bubble with warmth when I look out from the stage to see Gaby leaning against the bar, sipping coffee.

The bubbling turns dark and sulfurous like a swamp when I notice Romeo and the other black-clad Midnights at a table near the back. Vi, my attacker, is conspicuously absent, and the group is acting like regular lounge patrons: drinking, talking, and mostly ignoring my performance, except to halfheartedly clap when a song ends. But I *know* Romeo's watching me out of the corner of his eye.

I can't decide how I feel about it. So I ignore him and imagine I'm singing to Gaby instead. The small smile on her face is all the encouragement I need.

When my set ends, I change hurriedly in the back room, waving hello to the pianist, Boris, on my way out. He's not such a bad guy, Boris. We've been rehearsing together. His music taste is stuck in the 3600s, but he's a quick study when I hand him a new score.

"Have a nice date," he calls after me.

I turn around, fire rushing to my cheeks. "How did you—?"

"You sang your entire set staring into that ranger's eyes." He flashes me an indulgent, grandfatherly smile. "But you young people always think you're playing it cool, don't you?"

I clear my throat, hoping my glamour necklace is hiding my blush, but knowing it probably isn't. "We're just getting to know each other."

"As you should. Don't let me stop you." Boris makes a "go on, get" motion. "Miz Lopez is a very nice young lady. I approve."

I don't know what to say to that, so I dart through the door into the main lounge area.

Romeo and the Midnights have disappeared, their table now claimed by a group of saurian tourists who are complaining loudly that the chairs in this lounge aren't designed for people with tails. I try not to examine my pang of disappointment too deeply.

"Hey, you," Gaby says. She's chewing a tooth-cleansing tab to wash away the coffee breath—I can smell the minty freshness. "You were stunning up there. I had no idea you were *that* good. Your voice reminds me of…I don't know…someone."

If she's even slightly more acquainted with the uniweb than Romeo, she might have heard my voice before. A moment of panic paralyzes me. Why did I think I could do this? Sooner or later, even with the necklace, someone's going to say, "Hey, doesn't that random lounge singer at the resort sound a lot like Angelique Azalea?" and people are going to get suspicious. I should have taken a job doing *anything* else. Selling swimsuits. Unloading cargo ships. Even a job as a ranger might be less dangerous.

Except I can change my name and face, but I can't make myself not yearn to perform. Even though it was the thing that blew my cover each time.

"Hey," Gaby says again. She reaches out to stroke my shoulder, the smile fading from her face. My skin tingles under her gentle, callused palm. "I meant it as a compliment. I'm sorry if it was rude to compare you to someone else. I've never talked to a wildly talented singer before."

"Not your fault," I say, forcing a smile. "I just got lost in my head for a second. Ready to go to the library?"

Gaby nods. "Also, I brought this for you." She holds up a to-go container from one of the resort food stalls. I crack the lid open and the sweet aroma of fresh pastry rises to meet me. "You were up so late and on stage so early, I figured you wouldn't've had time to eat."

I nearly kiss her. She's right—now that I'm offstage, I'm *starving*. "Thank you," I attempt to say while taking a huge bite of the warm, soft bun at the same time. *Ohhh, it's filled with custard. I'm in love.*

Gaby walks and chats at my side while I stuff my face. "You'll be relieved to hear the rangers did a full sweep of the resort walls this morning. All the vulnerabilities have been reinforced. No more wildlife incursions today."

The wildlife isn't what I'm worried about. I focus on chewing instead of saying it out loud.

The library is close to the ranger station—and the alley separating it from the med center. The place where I saw Romeo bite someone yesterday. My heart rate spikes and I avert my eyes. On a signboard out front, a smiling model shows off his arm bandage as he advertises a blood drive.

That woman didn't die, I remind myself. *She's going to be fine, and so am I.*

It's funny how you can believe something with your brain, but the rest of your body treats it like a lie anyway.

The windows of the library are ablaze with animated, neon-colored ads for new holo-dramas, graphic novels, and music albums. Once we step inside, though, the clean white walls are blank except for a large screen cycling through another ad reel. One wall is taken up with a bank of charging lockers full of rentable tablets, another has six doors leading to private holo-viewing rooms, and the middle space is all media-download stations.

Gaby misinterprets the look on my face and says apologetically, "I know our library is small."

"It's not that!" I spin in place. "It's just been years since I was in a library." In fact, I haven't set foot in one since I was a child. When I moved to Monroe as a teen to book my first few singing gigs, I suddenly had the credits to buy my own devices and unlimited subscriptions to any entertainment I wanted. It was all too easy to forget my younger days, when borrowing a tablet to read the latest adventure serial was a luxury that I only got when my parents brought me to town once a month.

Once I've secured a borrowed tablet, Gaby motions toward the seat in front of one of the download ports, dragging a second chair over to join me. She logs in with her own credentials and navigates to an obscure corner of the database that seems intentionally designed to look boring. None of the entries have cover images. The description blurbs are written in such a dense, dry academic style that my eyes cross when I try to read them.

"What do you want to know about?" Gaby taps at one of the nondescript entries. "This one is all about local wildlife, but there are thousands of entries, so..."

"Can I look at the pictures first?" My face burns. I sound like a teen in Gen Ed who doesn't want to do the coursework. This is the first time I've found myself wishing I was smarter so I can impress someone.

Gaby doesn't seem bothered. "Oh, yeah, I think I can do an image-only view. Hang on."

She toggles a setting, then sits back and lets me start flipping through pics and short videos depicting the lifeforms that call Hades home. The ones in the ocean are predictably terrifying; deep water dwellers from any planet have always scared the daylights out of me. The fungi, carnivorous plants, and creatures with various numbers of legs that populate the land are only slightly less nightmare-inducing.

I pause to examine the descriptions under some of them, scanning for a mention of the vampirism parasites, but there's nothing obvious. Most plants come with a warning not to touch them, but that doesn't mean much; at least half of them are poisonous. One type of tree, extremely common in these parts, has lure vines that apparently smell like honey and lilac. They creep up silently, lulling prey with their sweet scent, before swallowing creatures whole. They then dissolve their catch in a pit of acid inside the tree's trunk.

Delightful.

I cut a glance sideways and see that Gaby has scooted over to the download port next to mine. She's not looking at Hadesian wildlife. In fact, she seems to be scrubbing through security cam footage.

"What are you working on?" I ask.

Gaby jumps. "I...nothing. Just work stuff."

"Aren't you off duty?"

"No such thing, for a ranger," Gaby quips. Then she lets out a sigh. "If you must know, I'm still trying to track the woman who hurt those girls the other night. Some of our local vendors identified her as a regular named Violetta. She's been staying at the resort for *years*. But she doesn't have a registered residence, no job, nothing. According to the resort's records, she never has."

I open my mouth, but the words stick in my throat. Romeo's compulsion makes it impossible for me to spill anything about the vampires to Gaby, who clearly doesn't know. Swallowing, I try again with careful wording. "Do you think she's with the Midnights?"

"Oh, I *know* she is," Gaby says bitterly. "They're all like that, you know. No record of existing here. No one knows where they came from, where they sleep, how they get the credits to pay for food...but the Chief Ranger refuses to investigate, and I don't have the resources for a solo investigation."

My throat physically hurts with the desire to tell her what I know. Romeo's a bastard for tying my tongue like this. It feels like betrayal to keep Gaby in the dark. And yet I'd be betraying Romeo if I told her. There's no winning.

The compulsion doesn't seem to mind me asking questions, at least. "Do you think Vi—Violetta—has hurt people before?"

Gaby lowers her voice. "Don't spread this around to any tourists, but in addition to a bunch of accidental deaths, we've had at least a dozen people go missing in the past decade. Or, at least, that's how many times we've had the Authorities show up, claiming the Hades resort was the last place those people were seen alive. Maybe none of them died—maybe they ran off with a lover they met here or something—but it's happened enough times that I'm pretty sure the Authorities think we have a resident serial killer."

"And you think it's the Midnights." I swallow, my throat feeling thick and swollen.

She might not even be wrong.

Romeo took great care to sell me the good side of the Midnights. Healing people's wounds, never taking too much blood, dropping them off right next to an infirmary. Maybe Vi's vicious attack was, like he said, a one-off accident caused by her going too long without blood.

Or maybe he's lying to keep me from digging any deeper.

I push away from the download port, no longer interested in wildlife. I lean back in my chair and lift my arms to stretch, pretending not to notice the way Gaby's knees brush my thigh.

"Ready for a break?" she asks. "We can go up to the beach and get drinks. Or one of the surface shops does a fantastic seaweed wrap I think you'll really like."

"That sounds amazing." I push my chair back and turn toward the door as Gaby logs off the station—

And see Jude sitting two stations down from us.

My kneecaps turn to water. Spots dance in front of my vision as my throat constricts, each breath a battle.

He found me. So soon. I've only been here three days.

I was a fool to think I'd ever be able to stop running.

Chapter 7

ANGELIQUE

I grab Gaby's sleeve, wondering if Jude's already seen me. Can I hide behind her all the way to the door—?

"Lea? Are you feeling well?" Gaby puts a tentative hand on my arm. "You look like you're about to faint. Can you breathe?"

"I saw—I saw—"

I turn to point him out, but the man at the computer has heard my wheezing and turns to stare at me. He's not Jude after all. He has a similar haircut, and the width of his shoulders makes him look almost identical from the back, but...

"P-panic attack," I choke out. "Flashback. S-sorry. I'll be all right in a minute."

Gaby nods. "How can I help? Do you like to be touched or not?"

"T-tight hugs sometimes help." I count my breaths. *In, two, three, four...*

Gaby's strong arms encircle me and press against my back and shoulders. The scent of her hair fills my nose as I inhale. Seconds ago, her touch was making my pulse race. Now the pressure of her embrace calms me, reminds me that I *am* safe. *Jude isn't here. Even if he was, he wouldn't recognize me. Breathe in. Hold. Breathe out.*

It takes several minutes before I'm calm enough to stand shakily and, with Gaby guiding me, walk out of the library.

"I think I'm gonna have to postpone the drinks," I tell her with real regret. "I need some time alone."

"Of course. I'll walk you home." She keeps her arm around my waist as we meander slowly down the corridor.

She breaks the silence first by saying, "You don't have to answer if you don't want to, but...did something you saw in the database set off the panic attack? I just want to know so I don't accidentally trigger you again."

I suck in a long breath. The one time I saw my therapist before I left Monroe, she told me that talking about my experiences with a trusted friend might help me process them. But I don't think I've trusted a single person I've met in the past two years of planet-hopping.

Maybe now's a good time to start?

"It wasn't the database," I tell her, my voice sounding thin and weak to my own ears. "Please don't think it was your fault. I saw someone who reminded me of my ex."

I feel her stiffen slightly at my side, but she just says, "Mm?" and gives me space to find the next words.

"His name was Jude." I cringe to say his name aloud. "I was...I am..." How much can I tell her? Unlike Romeo, I don't have dirt on her to threaten her into silence. Nor do I really *want* to do that to her. But something about Gaby makes me feel safe enough to give her a vague outline of the truth. "I was kind of famous back on Monroe. You might recognize my name if I said it. I...this isn't my real face." I finger the pendant at my throat, but I can't turn it off, not while we're in a public corridor. "I got invited to a lot of parties with up-and-coming celebrities. Dated a lot of them too, but never for long. And then, one night, there was Jude."

As soon as I start talking, the rest of the story spills out like water through a broken dam.

Jude was a friend of a friend's manager. Not a celebrity himself, but definitely connected. We hooked up at my place, and in the morning, I was ready to send him on his way.

But Jude didn't take the hint. He stayed, made me breakfast, even did the dishes. Cuddled me on the couch. I thought, *Maybe this is what it's supposed to be like.* I'd been singing about love for years—this grand, all-encompassing emotion that sweeps in and steamrolls people's plans—but I'd never given anyone enough of a chance to go deeper.

So I gave Jude the chance.

And *did he ever* take it.

He was suddenly at my place every day, even when I wanted to be alone. He hated it when I asked for space. At first, it was puppy dog eyes and "Don't you like me?" It was doing so many nice things for me—flowers, chores, coming to my shows, posting lovey pics of us on his uniweb profile—that I felt horrible for pushing him away. He was such a good man and I didn't deserve him. *I* was wrong, because I wasn't appreciating him enough.

Slowly, as I forced down my own needs, Jude took up more and more space in my life. Now it was him *telling* me I was broken, a bad person, rather than simply implying it. *Cold-hearted, selfish glitch.* He pointed out every flaw in my performances. He told me he couldn't post that pic of me because it made my nose look too big. I was miserable, but I told myself I deserved it. That if I could just do what I was *supposed* to do and fall in love with him, he'd be kind to me again.

And then there came the night when I just couldn't bear his hands on me anymore. When he came to me in my bedroom—which he'd somehow turned into *ours*—I told him I didn't want him to touch me. *Not tonight.* I was starting to understand that maybe I meant, *Not ever.*

But he didn't take "no" for an answer. And I couldn't stop him.

I heard Dad's voice in my head as it happened. Dad teaching me how to target an attacker's weak spots and fight them off, how to fire a blaster if I had to. Dad had been so scared when I moved to Monroe at seventeen, so worried that this exact thing would happen to me. He prepared me so well.

But at the critical moment, I froze. I didn't defend myself.

I wanted to die.

Instead, I waited until Jude fell asleep, then snuck out and left him inside the apartment I had paid for. I ran to the Authorities to report him, but they just sent me to the hospital. The healers cleaned me up, asked if I needed a safe place to stay. They told me the Authorities would likely drop the case because Jude was my live-in partner.

"Fuck those glitches," Gaby bursts out at this point in my narrative. "Stars, the redjackets are so blazing *prehistoric* sometimes. It's gotta be something to do with that bastard Emperor and the way he treats his thousand wives."

Despite the dark emotions that have me by the throat, I almost laugh. "There's only around thirty of them, I thought?"

"Well, yeah, because he keeps killing them all...don't give me that horrified look. I can say what I want; there aren't any Authorities here." She makes a rude gesture to the ceiling, directed at the Emperor on his faraway Moon Palace. "So? What'd you do? I assume that, because you're here and not there, you ran for it."

"Not right away," I murmur, residual shame pinking my cheeks. "I stayed with friends for a week or two. Talked to a therapist. Tried to get the Authorities to help me kick Jude out of my apartment so I could go home. But then he started showing up at my friends' place instead. And he didn't just politely knock. He stole weights from the downstairs gym and threw them through the windows. When he tried to set their apartment building on fire, the whole group collectively told me they were sorry, but no one could let me stay with them anymore until the Authorities arrested Jude. But they kept saying there wasn't enough evidence, which was *bullshit*. So I got on the next starship back to my home planet."

We've arrived at my door, but Gaby's still invested, her eyes fixed on my face with a mix of sympathy and outrage. "And?"

"And with everything that happened, I'd forgotten that my mom had just moved in with my stepdad and his five kids. I was there for about ten minutes before I realized I couldn't stay. Jude knew where I grew up. It was only a matter of time before he'd find me there and ruin the nice life my mom had built with her new husband. If he hurt my step-siblings and it was my fault, I couldn't live with myself. So I hugged Mom goodbye and told her I was going to have to disappear for awhile, but not to worry about me. That was two years ago."

Gaby's brown eyes are tearing up. "Oh, Lea…"

"Jude has found me on every fucking world I've run to," I say bitterly. "He found Lila in the Esperanza slums, Ani on Susannah…he even found Jelli in an off-the-grid pirate waystation. I got rid of every single one of my belongings he's ever touched, in case he planted a tracker. Changed my ID. Re-registered my ship. The last time he found me, I went and bought this necklace that changes my face, because I finally realized that was the problem. People kept recognizing me and posting pics on the uniweb, leaving him a trail of photos to follow like breadcrumbs. When I thought I saw him today…" My breath hisses out shakily, the fear of being hunted still fresh. "I felt like I was dying all over again. I don't know what I'll do when he finds me this time. I have nowhere left to go."

Gaby takes me by the shoulders. "Listen to me, Lea," she says, low and serious. "If Jude comes here, you tell me *immediately*, got it? Hades isn't your average Imperial world, and the rangers aren't Authorities. We take assault and stalking *very, very seriously* on this world. Do you want to know how many pervs I threaten with gonad removal on the daily because they can't keep their hands to themselves on a nude-friendly beach? We are dedicated to keeping this resort safe. From sea creatures, from carnivorous plants, and from human monsters as well."

The rush of relief, of feeling protected, goes straight to my head. I lean in and kiss her.

The spark between us is instant and powerful. Her lips go soft under mine and she lets her palm cup my face for just a moment too long. Then she gently but firmly pulls away, holding me at arm's length.

The rejection stings. I drop my hands, ready to disappear into my room and curl up into a ball of abject mortification. Gaby brushes my arm and says, "It's not that I'm not interested. I like you a lot, Lea. I do want us to…keep getting closer. But I think we both know your head's not in a good place right now." She leans close and presses a soft kiss to my cheek. "Go get some rest."

It's only after the door is closed behind me, sealing me into my room alone, that I burst into tears.

The dawn performance is not my best. It's easy enough to disguise swollen eyes and a red nose with makeup, but I can't hide that my voice is still scratchy. Even though I drank so much honey-lemon water that I have to hold my pee the entire time I'm on stage, it's like fighting for my life trying not to let my voice crack.

Thankfully, Gaby doesn't show up. If she witnessed this, it'd be one humiliation too many.

I rush offstage as soon as my set ends. Gargling warm water in the washroom soothes my throat slightly, but the tightness from the panic attack hasn't totally gone away. That wasn't Jude earlier, but my instincts are braced to see him around every corner.

It's late, but I know I won't sleep again unless I take a trip to the med center. I slip out of the lounge and set a quick pace. *The med center is safe. The dawn alarm only just sounded. I'll be fine.*

Still, I can't shake the feeling that I'm being followed. I glance over my shoulder several times, and once or twice I think I see a shadow darting behind a corner, but...

Maybe it's my imagination?

I arrive at the med center in record time, practically jogging the last few steps into the safety of their waiting room. The healers on staff don't ask too many questions. All it takes is one look at my face, and not only do they hand over a week's worth of sleep patches, but they throw in some anti-anxiety meds, too. Apparently I look so wrecked that even a full face of makeup *and* a glamour necklace can't hide it.

I stuff the meds in an inner pocket of my robe. "Thank you," I say fervently.

"There aren't any therapists practicing on Hades," says the healer, "but maybe you should look into messaging an offworld one, honey. Pardon me saying, but you don't seem well."

"I'll think about it. Thanks."

I rush out the front doors, already ripping open one of the anti-anxiety packets. Halfway down the steps, I look up and freeze. Romeo is leaning against the handrail, failing to look casual.

"Oh, hey, Lea."

Stomping down the last few steps, I set my arms akimbo and glare at him. "Was it you who followed me?"

"I wasn't following you." He meets my gaze for a few seconds, then his eyes flick away. "Oh, fine. I was. But only because I wanted to see you home safe."

"Safe from who? People like you?"

He sighs. "I made you a promise, Lea. The Midnights won't harm you."

"What if I don't trust you?"

"I suppose I deserve it. But I want to earn your trust."

Arching an eyebrow, I ask, "How do you plan to do that?"

"By keeping my promises."

I frown. "You realize that strategy's going to take some time."

"Of course." Romeo clasps his hands behind his back, looking painfully earnest. He lowers his voice. "I'm immortal, remember? I can wait."

I grunt in response, pulling the anxiety patch out of the packet and rolling up the sleeve of my robe.

His eyes follow the movement. "Nightmares, huh?" I hate how his voice goes all honey-smooth and gentle. I can't stand pity.

"Guess why?" I lob back sarcastically.

"Those patches are garbage, you know. Lowest possible dosage. They're so afraid of people coming here to score mind-alts that they barely medicate people who really need it."

I crumple the packet in my hand. "Well, it's all I've got, so if you'll excuse me…"

"What if I could offer you something better?"

It takes a moment for that offer to filter through my brain. "Are you…trying to sell me mind-alts?"

Romeo snort-laughs. "I suppose, in a way, I am. I've…made a hobby of testing the medicinal properties of local plants and fungi, since it's a low-risk endeavor for me. Let's just say I know exactly which mushroom you can eat to get the best night's sleep of your life, with some colorful euphoric dreams as an added bonus."

Eyeing him suspiciously, I ask, "Would that infect me with the parasite?"

He shakes his head. "These mushrooms don't carry it. I did a bunch of tests before I introduced it to anyone outside our circle."

I groan. "You *are* an illegal mind-alt dealer." That answers one of Gaby's questions: how the Midnights earn their money.

"Not for everyone." Romeo's eyes twinkle in a way I can only interpret as flirtatious. "Tourists don't get the good stuff from me, and certainly not for free. But you're a Hadesian now. Special privileges."

The lure of a good night's sleep, plus dreams that don't include rehashing my past trauma, is awfully tempting. Is it worth ingesting something potentially dangerous? Right now, my exhausted, overstressed brain says YES.

"All right," I shoot back at him. "I'll take whatever you've got."

The grin that lights up his face is unbearably sexy, in part because it seems so earnest. "Come with me."

"You'd better not be about to lure me off somewhere and murder me."

"Earning your trust starts here," he says with solemn sincerity.

So I let him lead me down an unfamiliar maze of tunnels marked with KEEP OUT: CONSTRUCTION IN PROGRESS signs. But, when his back is turned, I message Gaby where I'm going and with whom...just in case.

Chapter 8

ANGELIQUE

We've been walking for about fifteen minutes when Romeo suddenly stops, turns to the wall, and...disappears into it?

I yelp, rushing forward to find that he's fit himself through a narrow crack hidden in the textured wall of the lava tube we're walking through. It's dark inside, none of the resort corridor's lighting in there, but Romeo flips on a torchlight attached to his wrist, illuminating the way through.

"Come on," he calls. "It's less of a tight squeeze back this way."

I balk. "Where exactly are you taking me?"

"Home," Romeo replies, his voice imbuing the word with fond warmth.

"I thought you lived in one of the resort rooms."

Romeo chuckles. "Are you kidding? The rent for a permanent resident is astronomical. We built our own home outside the rangers' jurisdiction, so they don't breathe down our necks."

"I thought you said lots of rangers are infected, too."

"Oh, they are. And the ones who took jobs with the resort think us Midnights are shiftless freeloaders. I suppose that pretty ranger you've been seeing told you to stay away from us?"

I splutter, but he just smirks. "That's their favorite line. That we're dangerous. Killers. Really, I think the rangers are just jealous we don't have rent to pay."

Somewhere in his monologue, he's managed to catch my hand and ease me through the crack in the wall. I follow the beam of the torchlight, then stop to admire the cavern we emerge into. The black rock glitters with flakes of mica, reminding me of the glorious scintillation of the starship hangar when I first flew in. It's more damp here than in the temp-controlled resort areas. Short stalactites drip from the ceiling. A trickling sound hints at an underground stream somewhere nearby.

"Come on," Romeo urges. "We're halfway there."

I quickly send Gaby another message describing the crack in the wall. This may be beyond the rangers' jurisdiction, but I still want someone to know where to look for my body if I go missing.

This new branch of the underground maze has an unfinished air to it. Instead of one long corridor, it's more a series of caverns connected by narrow openings. We have to leap across the stream a few times; in the clear depths, I glimpse pale, fat creatures with fluttering fins and firefly-esque lights slowly blinking on their undersides.

"When we were building the resort, we abandoned this section of cave because of the water," Romeo tells me. Even his low murmur echoes loud. "There was some talk of using it for sewage, but it turned out the stream flows into the source of the resort's drinking water. It would have taken too much engineering to divert the flow somewhere else, so we closed it off and left it pretty much as it was when the construction crews first got here."

It's an odd place to live, but I can see why someone might choose it. The sparkling caves have an eerie sort of loveliness to them. I could do without the lumpy cave fish and the constant drip-drip of moisture, though.

We arrive at a cavern that branches off into several tunnels. In the center is a circle of crates mixed with mismatched sofas and armchairs, with a tent made of a tarp suspended over them to keep the drips from the stalactites off.

Romeo reaches for a string woven with bells dangling from the framework that supports the tent. He gives it a shake, and the high chimes bounce back and forth, lingering in the echoey space.

"What?" calls a grumpy voice.

"I have a guest." Romeo's words carry nearly as well as the bells. I hear stirrings, footsteps. A figure appears in one of the tunnels. Then two people emerge from another. I vaguely recognize their faces—I've seen Romeo sitting with them at Underworld. His gang of vampires in black.

I glare at Romeo. "Is this necessary?" *I came here to get drugs, not to meet all your friends.*

"I think it might be," says Romeo mildly. "Let me introduce you."

There are about a dozen Midnights who come out of the tunnels to meet me. "This isn't everyone," Romeo explains apologetically. "There are twenty-four of us total, but...uh...dawn is our prime hunting time."

Great. Really comforting to know that somewhere, a bunch of tourists are becoming snacks.

I almost expect the vampires to go mask-off and reveal twisted, fanged, feral faces now that I know what they are. But they remain distressingly normal. Benito is brown-skinned and crinkle-eyed, his hand rough with calluses when he shakes mine. Muscular, golden-haired Julia stands close enough to him for me to assume they're partners. Mercedes has hair that's permadyed silver—or maybe it's natural, because she's the one Romeo mentioned who aged backward from seventy.

And then there's—

My heart stops.

Violetta.

The blonde woman steps forward, eyes cast down, and my mouth goes dry. "*You.*"

"I'm sorry for attacking you," Violetta says, sounding like she's reading it from a notecard. "I promise not to hurt you again."

I ignore her offered handshake. "What about what you did to those girls?" I challenge her. "If I hadn't followed you, if the rangers hadn't gotten there to help them, they could have died."

Violetta rolls her eyes. "Yeah, because you interrupted me mid-feed. I would've healed them afterward. Those are the Midnights' rules." She recites the last part in a mocking sing-song.

She might be telling the truth, but her attitude makes me bristle. I take a step back to put Romeo in between us.

"I don't want to talk to her," I tell him in a low voice.

His gaze is concerned as he turns his back on her to focus on me. "I thought maybe if you talked it out with her, it would help with some of the anxiety."

"Well, it hasn't." My heart is already racing, my palms clammy despite the anxiety patch on my forearm. Romeo was right. Whatever dosage they gave me is useless.

He casts a look around to all the other vampires. "Sorry, friends. As you were," he says, and leads me into one of the dark openings.

Motion-activated lights brighten as we pass. Romeo ducks his head under a low archway and pushes aside a curtain.

Inside is a dead-end cavern, dry and warm, draped in black fabric. Three crates lined up in a row support a mattress piled with flannel blankets, and more crates stacked against the wall have their sides open to reveal a motley collection of knickknacks, including two books printed and bound ancient-style on paper pages, and neat piles of folded black garments. String lights illuminate the space just enough to be cozy.

"Have a seat." Romeo motions at a maroon bean bag chair in the corner. I move aside the blanket rumpled on top of it and catch the spicy sandalwood scent of Romeo's soap. Or maybe something he puts in his hair?

He pushes his mattress off to one side, exposing one of the crates underneath. He tips the lid back and rummages inside, glass tinkling and plastic rustling.

"Here." He pulls out a small jar and hands it to me before closing up the crate. It's labeled with a scientific name I can't pronounce and is half full of dried dusty-blue lumps.

"Is that whole crate full of Hades plants you tried to eat?" I ask.

Romeo grins. "Only the ones that turned out to have recreational value. Not all of them are safe for non-vampire consumption, so don't get any ideas." He gestures at the jar in my hands. "You'll want to take only about a thumb-sized piece at a time. Might be safer to start with half that amount, in case you're extra sensitive."

I begin to unscrew the lid, but he puts a hand out to stop me. "Also, you'll want to be safe in bed first. Your *own* bed. If you take it here, well, not that I wouldn't mind sharing my bed, but I think *you* might." His crooked smile makes something flutter in my stomach. "I'll walk you home."

There's a tiny little corner of my brain that *wouldn't* mind sharing his bed, but it's strongly overruled by the majority that would mind a lot. "Thanks." I push myself up out of his chair. Against all expectation, he's lured me into the heart of his secret lair and...has chosen to be a gentleman.

If he's trying to prove I can trust him, it's kind of working.

"Next time, come here during the night, and I'll show you our secret passage to the planet surface," he promises as he leads me back to the common area. "The rangers would pass out if they knew we had access, so don't tell your girlfriend...but once you've seen the glorious Hades jungle, you'll never be impressed by that boring beach resort again."

Clutching the jar of dried fungi to my chest, I reply, "I think the beach resort is plenty for me."

Romeo shrugs. "Give it a year or two. The tourist glitz will get old."

I envy the ease with which Romeo predicts a year in advance. Since leaving Jude, I haven't stayed anywhere longer than a few months. My brain stalls when I try to think about any future past my next few scheduled shifts at the lounge. Half the time, surviving to the next moment is all I can do.

The Midnights have settled into the chairs under the awning, pouring drinks that look suspiciously home-brewed. The unlabeled containers are my first clue; the second is the fact that the beverage is a viscous orange concoction with chunks of fruit still floating in it. Despite its hideous vomity appearance, the smell is mouthwatering, a sweet fruity tang. I've been to a lot of bars on a lot of planets, but I don't have a name for this recipe. I have a strong suspicion it's native to Hades—and might not be safe for human consumption.

"Hey, Lea," calls Julia, holding up the sloshing jar. "Want a sip?"

"She's going home, Jules," Romeo replies, saving me from having to come up with an excuse. "We'll terrorize her with your brew next time."

Julia sticks out her tongue at him. "This batch is my best yet, I'll have you know!"

"Hey, Jules, get back over here," Benito says. "If Romeo's going to be busy, I need someone else to beat at vertical chess."

This all feels...oddly comfortable and familiar. Actually, the tableau reminds me of my parents' friends having game nights and getting drunk in our living room. I suppose I was expecting coffins, bats, and torture racks. My suspicion lingers that this is all a ruse to lure me into a false sense of security, but...the Midnights are *people*, aren't they? The blood-thirst is simply an unfortunate disease. I wouldn't hold cancer or slime flu against someone.

If I wasn't absolutely exhausted, stressed to my limit, I might consider staying for awhile. Getting to know them. Hearing them out. But that's going to have to wait until after I've had several good nights' sleeps.

"I need to go," I whisper.

Romeo offers an arm. "You're not looking so steady. Let me help you."

I want to refuse his chivalrous gesture. But I'm swaying on my feet. Leaning on him isn't going to kill me.

The comfortable laughter and chatter fade into an echo behind us as Romeo leads me through the cave toward the main resort. Mercifully, he doesn't try to talk to me. My own thoughts are loud enough.

Until we hear footsteps approaching from up ahead.

Romeo tenses. "Who's there?" he calls out.

Silence, but the footsteps quicken. Romeo pulls me behind a protrusion in the cave wall, whispering, "Stay here a moment."

"Who is it?"

"I don't know," he replies in an undertone, "but the Midnights always yell back."

He steps out from behind the rock, holding a loose, fight-ready stance...

Just as Gaby comes around the corner, pointing a stunner at his face.

Chapter 9

ANGELIQUE

I jump out of hiding to stand between them. Well, I *intend* to jump, but it's more of a stumble. Romeo catches my shoulder to stop me from overbalancing.

"Don't shoot," I blurt out. "I'm fine. I'm safe."

Gaby lowers the stunner a fraction, her eyes narrowing. "Romeo," she sighs, in a tone that implies, *I should've known.* "If you've hurt her, I'm putting you in lockup for a week while I convince her to press assault charges."

"He never hurt me," I tell her hastily. "He was just—"

Gaby's eyes drop to the jar in my hand. "Giving you untested narcotics?"

"Oh, pull the stick out, Gabrielle," Romeo says with an eyeroll. "You know dreamspice is safe. I don't hand it out like candy, but your girl here is having a really hard time. In case that escaped your notice."

Up until now, I hadn't considered that Romeo and Gaby might *know* each other. But I've only been on this planet for under a week. They've lived here in the same community for *years*. Of course they've interacted before. And from the sound of it, this isn't the first time Gaby's caught him peddling mind-alts.

"I'm well aware, thanks," Gaby says, tense as a guitar string even with her stunner lowered. "Which is why I came immediately when she messaged that you were luring her outside the resort boundaries."

Romeo's eyes narrow. "Are you sure you weren't just scoping out where I live so you can stalk me later?"

"Thanks for coming, Gaby," I interject, desperate to defuse the situation. "I was maybe a little paranoid to message you. Romeo was just about to take me back to my apartment." When her eyes narrow, I add, "So I can go to sleep. Alone."

"Great," she says, with a smile that's faker than my identity. "Then you won't mind if I escort both of you...right?"

If she was angling to flare Romeo off, he doesn't give her any satisfaction. "This place is dangerous after sunrise. I'd welcome the safety of a ranger's company." If there's any sarcasm in his tone, it's subtle enough as to be imperceptible.

"Wonderful." Gaby's own sarcasm, on the other hand, is impossible to miss.

This posturing between them irritates the blazes out of me, though. I just want to *sleep*. Shouldering my way past Gaby, I start walking without waiting for them to follow me.

Gaby catches up quickly and links her arm through mine. "Sorry," she murmurs. "Maybe I shouldn't have come, but you sounded scared, and I got worried."

I can't stay angry. "It's sweet that you wanted to rescue me," I say, flashing her a quick smile.

There's a soft touch on my other elbow. Romeo's taking my other arm. At first, I'm annoyed at the obvious maneuvering for possession, like I'm some kind of tug-o-war rope. But...I'd be lying if I said it wasn't somewhat flattering to see two gorgeous people vying for my attention.

Together, they guide me out of the tunnels, through the resort, and back to the safety of my apartment. At my door, Romeo hangs back.

"Remember, just a small piece," he says, tapping the jar still clutched in my hands. "Don't you dare overdose."

Gaby guides me into my room. "I'll make sure she doesn't."

Romeo looks like he's bitten a lemon as the door slides closed in his face.

I kick off my shoes and go into the washroom to change out of my street clothes. When I come back, Gaby is sitting on the edge of my bed, the jar of dreamspice fungus in her lap. "I'm not staying," she promises. "I just want to be certain you don't do anything foolish. Whatever that man says, any mind-alt can be dangerous."

"I know you don't trust him, and I don't blame you," I say, sliding under the covers. "But he had every chance to attack me tonight, and he didn't. He says he wants to build trust."

Gaby's eyes narrow. "So he can strike when you least expect it?"

She's voiced the very fear I'm grappling with in the back of my mind. I shrug, wishing I had the faith in Romeo to jump to his defense.

"Be very careful, Lea, please. Even if his crowd aren't murdering people, they're still dangerous. Handing out untested substances in back alleys and sneaking off to unpatrolled areas are not things that trustworthy people do."

Cautiously, I say, "He seemed sincere when he promised not to hurt me."

"Oh, I'm sure he was." Gaby sighs. "The Midnights do seem to have local favorites who they consider 'under their protection' for one reason or another. Striking up a friendship might guarantee you safety for now. But you're only as safe as their word is good."

I shiver. "May I have the dreamspice now?" I hate how plaintive I sound. But I desperately need to be unconscious.

Gaby slowly unscrews the jar, removing a piece of the fungus and tearing it in half. She places the small morsel in my palm and drops the other piece back into the jar. "Chew it well," she says. "And if you have an allergic reaction, don't say I didn't warn you."

The fungus doesn't taste great—kind of like kale mixed with a bitter floral, and the aftertaste of dirt—but I manage to swallow. Almost immediately, lassitude pulls me down onto the pillows. I snuggle in.

Gaby gets up to put the jar on my nightstand, then leans over me to kiss my forehead. "I'll stay to make sure you don't react badly, then I'll let you sleep."

"Thanks," I slur.

After that, I remember nothing.

*H*ands trail down the sides of my breasts, igniting fire under my skin. I arch, begging without words. His lips close around one of my nipples. A flick of his tongue, and I cry out, almost sobbing with need.

Patience, love, *he whispers. Then he's licking his way down, palms brushing against my thighs as he parts them. He's savoring every slow, purposeful movement. It seems he enjoys putting me into a state of exquisite, pleasurable torture.*

*When his tongue finds the center of my torment, an ecstatic curse tears from my throat. I'm babbling—*yes, there, please, more—*and I feel his smug, throaty chuckle against my hypersensitive flesh.*

She'll give us away, *he murmurs into my folds.* Keep her quiet for me?

Gentle fingers turn my head to the side, and soft lips capture mine in a scorching kiss. I roll my hips, whimpering as they work together to wind me up. Her fingers pinching my nipple, his tongue circling, her lips behind my ear, his hands gripping my thighs hard enough to leave a mark—

Pleasure bursts over me like fireworks in my blood, and I wake with both their names on my lips.

The dream lingers as I slowly return to consciousness. I roll over in the sheets and reach out for a body that's not there. Still coming down from the blissful high of a very real orgasm, I sigh my disappointment. My eyes flutter open.

Euphoric dreams, he said? Well, that's one way to put it...

Another way is that Romeo gave me a whole jar of a mind-alt that induces sex dreams. I hope he didn't do any mind-tricks to ensure said dreams would be about him.

Though I can't imagine that, if he did, he would've included the part about Gaby.

I lie in bed awhile longer, savoring the afterglow of the dream. I feel better than I have in...not just days, but *years*. With my anxiety held at bay for once, I feel cherished and safe. I honestly can't remember the last time anyone made me feel like this—not even Jude in the early days of our relationship.

Slowly rising to a sitting position, I stretch luxuriously and kiss my fingers, pressing them to the jar on my nightstand. "I think you and I are about to be best friends," I tell the dreamspice.

Tragically, the pleasant, anxiety-free glow wears off as I get ready to report to work. As reality returns, embarrassment comes with it. How am I supposed to look Romeo *or* Gaby in the eye today?

Worse, what if I start mistaking the feelings from the dream for real ones, and they don't reciprocate? I've already tried to jump Gaby once. I might actually sink through the floor if she rebuffs me again.

Maybe the dreamspice will take pity on me and rotate the cast of characters in my erotic dreams. If I spend an hour thinking about that hottie Xander Bose from the *Hovercycle Gang* holos, could I convince my brain to star him in my next one?

Despite the fading high, I still feel much better than yesterday as I head to Underworld. A good night's sleep did wonders for my fried nervous system. The world is in sharper focus today, and when I start doing my vocal warmups, I'm pleased that the rasp from last night is entirely gone.

With renewed purpose, I step out on the stage to Boris playing the opening notes of our first song of the morning...

And meet the eyes of my worst nightmare sitting at the closest table.

Jude.

He found me.

Fourth Episode

Chapter 10

*I*t's fine. It's fine. I'm wearing my glamour necklace. He can't see me.

I can repeat the words all I want, but my brain won't believe them. My breath comes short, flubbing the first line of the song. It comes out a barely audible whisper.

I close my eyes tight, waiting for my brain to register its mistake. Surely this is a hallucination, a flashback, just like when I saw the man in the library. But when I open them again, nothing has changed.

Fuck. He's really here.

Jude is staring intently at me, face expressionless. He has to know who I am—but what if he doesn't? What if I'm giving myself away by my reaction? I rip my eyes away from him, trying to focus on anything else, to recover my composure. But I can't stop looking back at him, the way an arachnophobe tracks a spider on the wall, terrified that looking away will allow the creature to escape or attack.

My voice trails off again. Boris gallantly keeps playing flourishes to cover my mistake, but it's no use. There's no recovery. There's no going forward after this.

I've run to the ends of the galaxy to escape, and Jude found me anyway.

Drawing on every reserve of professionalism in my body, I rally. I let the rest of the song come out breathy and emotional, as if the choked-off bits in the beginning were intentional. I step off the stage and saunter through the crowd, putting distance between myself and Jude. I brush my fingertips teasingly along tabletops, make eye contact with entranced strangers, and croon seductively through the tightness in my throat.

With a toss of my hair, I flick my gaze along the back wall, looking for a brooding figure in black, or a sharp bob cut and orange-and-white uniform. Neither of my allies are here. *No,* I think frantically, *Gaby works this time of night, and Romeo...*

Actually, I have no fucking idea what Romeo does all day. Hangs out in his cave smoking plants he found in the jungle? At any rate, he's not here.

One quick "SOS" message to either of them would bring them running, but I can't send it without interrupting my own show. I've already flubbed the start—I can't start typing in the middle of a song. Karina would not be happy with me.

Anyway, I should handle Jude myself. He's my mess to clean up.

The hour passes in a blur as I weave between breakfasting tourists, doing my best to disguise the rough edges in my voice. Finally, I make my way back to the stage, feeling Jude's eyes on me the whole way. I perform my last number, take my bows, and Boris and I slink into the locker room.

As soon as the door shuts behind us, the pianist turns to me with raised eyebrows. "You don't sound like yourself today. Are you feeling ill?"

I fake a cough. "Y-yes, my throat is a little sore this morning. I'd better rest before tonight's show."

"If you need to call it off, I can deal with Karina," Boris says. "Take care of yourself, angel."

The casual endearment tightens my throat more. I don't think Boris meant anything by it, but it's what Jude used to call me when he was sweet-talking.

My hands are shaking so hard, I can barely open my locker. *Blast it. He hasn't even said a word to me, and I'm already a wreck.* This mess might be too big for me to clean up alone.

Maybe taking care of myself means asking for help when I need it.

I hastily change out of my show dress into a swimsuit and coverup. Then I text Gaby, *<Are you on the beach? I need to talk to you.>*

She responds right away. *<Yes, I'm topside on patrol. Come find me. Was it the dreamspice? I should've warned you. The dreams can be a little...surprising if you're not ready for them.>*

<Not that,> I respond. *<Remember yesterday when I thought I saw someone? I saw him again. For real this time.>*

I hold my breath, worrying her next message will question my sanity. Instead, she asks, *<Are you safe?>*

<I don't know. I just came offstage.> I swallow against the terrified nausea churning my gut. *<If you don't see me an hour from now, you might want to call the Authorities.>* If they wouldn't arrest Jude for stalking me, maybe they'd at least help find my body.

<Fuck them, they'll take days to get here,> Gaby replies. *<I'm coming to get you right now. What're the rangers gonna do, fire me?>*

Even through my panic, I smile. Not everybody would care so much for a woman they just met.

Romeo flits through my mind. *He cared, too.* Enough to give me the dreamspice and walk me home, only to let Gaby close the door in his face. I wonder if I should message him too, then decide against it. He might go rogue and drink Jude's blood.

Actually...would that be so bad?

<I'm in the Underworld backstage area,> I tell Gaby. *<There's a side door I can sneak out. Meet me there?>*

<On my way.>

I go to stand by the side door, trying to steady my wrist so I can watch my keycuff for more messages from Gaby. When the door slides open, I gasp in relief, expecting the ranger to burst in full of righteous fury. But it's not Gaby.

It's Jude.

Still himself. Not a mirage.

Fuck, fuck, fuck.

Touching my glamour necklace to reassure myself it's still on, I stammer, "Excuse me, sir. This is a staff entrance. You can't be in here."

"I saw the sign." Jude plants a hand on the door frame, using his body to block my exit as the door slides shut.

"This is inappropriate," I choke out. "I'm calling the rangers." I fumble with my keycuff for my recent call log. If I can get a call through to Gaby, if she can hear what's happening...

"Cut the act, Angel." Jude grabs my wrist, unclasps my cuff, and tosses it behind him, far out of my reach.

"You're hurting me." I squirm in an attempt to break his hold. I aim a knee for his groin, but he avoids it with a twist of his hips. He presses in, using his body weight to immobilize me against the wall.

I could scream, but Karina's not in her office, and Boris is having a post-performance beer in the lounge. There aren't any cambots back here. My mouth goes dry as I realize Jude could murder me right now and no one would see.

Hurry up, Gaby.

I go limp. He always seemed to like it when I submit. "What do you want from me?" I whisper.

In response, he reaches up with the hand that's not pinning my wrist and rips the glamour necklace off my neck, leaving a painful stripe of scraped skin. "Clever, Angel. Look. I have one, too." He fishes out a matching pendant from beneath the collar of his shirt. "Defective, though. You nearly clocked me yesterday." Then he drops both devices to the floor and crushes them under the heel of his boot. He cups my chin and smiles. "There you are."

I turn my face away. "Why are you here, Jude? What will it take for you to realize we're over?"

"You don't get to decide that," he hisses, his breath hot and minty on my cheek. "Come on, Angel. It's time to stop running. Your fans on Monroe miss you."

With one hand still on my wrist, the other iron-tight around my waist, he drags me out the staff door and begins leading me down the corridor. "Don't struggle, now," he says in my ear. "You don't want to make a scene."

"Actually, I do—"

"Because if you do, I'll fucking shoot everyone in this resort, and you last." He presses his hip into mine deliberately, letting me feel the hard bulge in his pocket. *A blaster.* The old "happy to see me" joke runs through my head for whatever fucking reason. I swallow a hysterical giggle.

I have every reason to believe he's dead serious, though. He set my friend's entire apartment building on fire just to get to me. Why would he stop at shooting people? So I let him guide me out into the main thoroughfare, nudging a path between tourists on their way topside.

He's taking me to the hangar, I realize. Once he has me on his ship, he can take me anywhere in the galaxy. My friends on Hades will never see me again.

I have a feeling that no one else will, either. Despite what he says about taking me back to Monroe, I don't think Jude's going to risk letting me disappear again. I've led him on too long a chase.

This time, he'll kill me before he'll let me go.

The sparkling crystal cavern of the hangar feels ominously dark when Jude drags me in. His winning smile distracts the ranger on duty enough that she doesn't notice his hand clamped bruisingly hard on my arm, or the pained wrinkle between my eyebrows. She doesn't even recognize me as the Underworld singer—why would she? With my necklace gone, I'm a stranger to everyone on this planet. Except for Romeo, for whom I briefly let my mask drop.

And he isn't here.

My heart pounds as Jude hustles me to a flashy little green four-seater starship and shoves me through its side hatch. "Strap in," he demands, climbing in after me.

"You don't have to do this, you know," I murmur, keeping my voice low and submissive as I click in my safety belt. "I'm no one. I'm just some girl. You could have anyone. Why bother with me?"

He gives a harsh laugh, releasing the ship's anchor and starting it up. "Oh, believe me, there's a dozen women salivating to take your place." As the ship rises up the elevator toward Hades' night sky, he turns to look at me, his eyes cold and hard. "But that doesn't mean you get to drop me like you did."

"It wasn't your fault," I lie, desperately searching for something to say to save my own life. "Fame was just too much for me. I couldn't handle it."

"Then tell me why, whenever I tried to track you, all I had to do was look for some slut warbling pop songs in a sleazy lounge?"

My throat feels like it's going to close.

"Oh, yes, you thought your disguises were so clever, but I know you, Angel. I know you'd never willingly give up singing. You can't let go of the attention, can you? That's why you left me, wasn't it? You wanted other men's eyes on you, and when that wasn't enough, you wanted to go out and fuck them, too."

Fury rips through me like wildfire. "How dare you?" I hiss.

"No, how dare *you?*" He leans over and clamps a hand against the back of my neck, gunning the ship's accelerator with the other hand on the steering yoke. "I'm going to make you regret every second you spent away from me."

My heart thumps in horror as I recognize the sting of a patch against my nape. *He's tranquilizing me.*

Fighting a wave of drowsiness, I pretend to slump over. As soon as he makes a satisfied "hah" in his throat and relaxes his hand, I strike.

I grab the yoke and yank it hard toward me.

The last thing I hear before I pass out is Jude screaming and cursing as the ship spins out of control and takes a nosedive toward the dark jungle below.

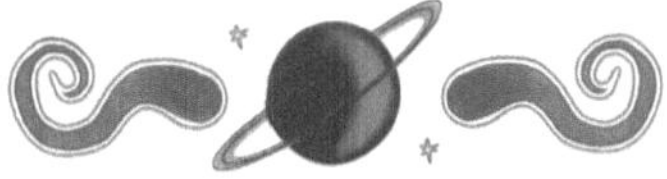

GABRIELLE

Chief Han, holographically projected above my keycuff, crosses her arms and frowns at me. "This pet project of yours is getting tiresome, Ranger Lopez."

"No, Chief, this time I don't think it's the Midnights." I'm briefly distracted as Ranger Voss approaches. I lift my eyebrows in question, and she shakes her head. They haven't found Lea yet.

Turning back to Chief Han, I say, "It's the new singer for Underworld. She and I have been getting...acquainted...and she opened up about a stalker who's been following her from world to world. An ex-partner who abused her. She messaged me in a panic hours ago, saying she thought she saw him again. And then she disappeared without a trace."

Chief Han sighs. "Well, at least your goose chases are gaining a little variety. I assume you've already finished searching the resort?"

"Everywhere we could. She's gone. That's why I need permission to look at the flight logs. A witness saw them heading in the direction of the hangar, and we think maybe he took her offworld."

"That would take them out of our jurisdiction," Chief Han cautions. "If you're going after them anywhere above our atmosphere, Lopez, you do it on your own time and credits, understood?"

"I already planned to, Chief."

"Fine." Chief Han taps something on her console. "I'm sending you temporary authorization to view the last twenty-five hours' worth of departures. But you can't waste any more of my rangers' time. We have enough problems cleaning up after that breach on Nighttwo."

"I'll only waste my own time," I promise, but my gut sinks. Finding Lea on my own will take at least twice as long, and the longer I wait, the less likely I'll ever see her again.

As soon as Chief Han clicks off the call, I unfurl my scroll-tablet to log into the air traffic control records. I run my finger lightly down the list, narrowing my search to everything after the timestamp of the message Lea sent.

There. A ship that took off maybe ten minutes later. I click into the control tower's autotracking, hoping to get an idea of its destination, and frown. The pilot registered a planned destination of some random uncharted moon, but the ship dropped away from its intended path before it left atmo. It took a nosedive and then lost contact with the tower.

As if it crashed out in the wilds.

Meaning Lea's still on the planet.

Heart pounding, I tap around in the database to see if there's any visual info I can access. But if the bots in air traffic control retain any vids, they're not stored here. And once the ship lost communication with the tower, the bots wouldn't have flagged that as a problem worth investigating; they would've assumed the pilot teleported the ship out of their range, same as most outbound flights.

I check the time on my keycuff. It's near midnight. Lea went missing around dusk. A handful of hours of night left—and if she's in the wilds by morning, it's certain death.

The only way to find her is to send out a search party and comb the jungle. The more, the better. There's no way I'll find her on my own.

But Chief Han's just forbidden me from getting help from my fellow rangers.

I bite my lip. I have only one other option, and I really don't like it. He might not even agree to help. But if he gives half a shit about Lea—and I kind of think he does—it's worth a try.

Chapter 11

Waking up to a knife at my throat isn't my favorite thing ever.

I'm still half-blissed as I swim back to consciousness, recognizing first the orange ranger jacket and then the dark eyes of the woman who seems to have appointed herself my nemesis.

"Gabrielle Lopez," I drawl, trying not to sound too sleep-fogged. "Why am I not surprised? You couldn't just take your win with Lea. You had to stick it to me, too."

"Do you actually care about her? Lea?"

The question isn't what I was expecting. "Sure. Yeah. She's cute. Thought she was an Authority for awhile, so I kept a close eye on her, but now I'm pretty sure she's just a lost celebrity who needs a buttload of therapy."

"And?" Gaby's knife is cold against my skin, but she's holding it so the sharp edge doesn't cut me. Nice of her. I'd have to put a stop to this real quick if there was a chance she could come in contact with my blood.

"And..." I sigh. "And she's sharp, and surprisingly tough, and did I mention cute? Yeah, I fucking like her. Don't rub it in. You're the one she's into. I'll deal."

"Shut up and get up," Gaby snaps. She retracts the knife into its handle, stowing it in her utility belt. "If you like her so much, you're going to help me rescue her."

"Rescue her?" I push myself upright. "What happened?"

"Near as I can tell, her ex showed up, kidnapped her, and then crashed his ship in the wilds. Time's ticking until sunrise."

"Shit, why didn't you say so?" I jump out of bed and start rummaging in my clothes chest. I don't miss the way Gaby's eyes flick up and down my body as I cast the covers off. This area of the tunnels doesn't get as much atmo control as the resort does, which means it's usually humid enough to sleep in the nude.

With a pair of black swim shorts in my hand, I pause. "Why aren't your rangers already out looking for her?"

"Chief Han says it's out of our jurisdiction since it's not within resort bounds. She refused to let me recruit other rangers for a search and rescue operation. But I can't do this alone." Gaby folds her arms, looking flared off at even having to say this out loud. "I need you."

"Oh ho ho." I grin. "You *need* me, do you? Which is why it's you waking me up with a knife at my throat, and not a bunch of rangers busting us for trespassing?"

"You're out of resort bounds, too. Chief says you're not our problem." Gaby huffs. Must've really ground her gears when the Chief gave us a pass.

She'd flip if she knew Chief Han is also afflicted with the vampiric parasite and has a long-standing deal with the Midnights wherein we stay out of each others' business. That shit with Vi is the closest we've come to violating the informal treaty in years, all because Lea couldn't mind her own. I've been telling Chief Han she should be straight with all her rangers, even the non-infected ones, about the situation here—but she thinks we're safer if it's need-to-know only.

I'm pretty sure Gaby needs to know. Otherwise she's not only a danger to us, but frankly, to herself as well. If she'd drawn my blood and happened to have a cut on her skin…well, then she'd *really* need to know.

First things first, though. "I'll ask the Midnights if they want to help find her. You understand, they aren't soldiers under my command. If they say no, then it's just you and me looking."

Gaby jerks a nod. "Thank you," she grits out. Must really hurt, having to make nice with a man she thinks is a murderer.

She's not even wrong.

After pulling on my heat-resistant topside boots, I lead Gaby to the Midnights' common area and jangle the bells to summon my fellow vampires.

Benito's the first one to emerge, grumbling, "Romeo, I'm going to kill you." He's a late sleeper, like me, but his groggy expression turns to one of tense wariness when he sees Gaby. "Or maybe she is?"

"Gaby's not here to kill anyone." I choose to ignore the fact that she was threatening me with a knife two minutes ago. As more of the gang trickle out of their rooms, I have to repeat the sentiment multiple times. Gaby's hand hovers near the weapons stored on her utility belt. This is starting to feel like a standoff from one of those Old Earth cowboy films in the Hades library archive.

Once the majority of Midnights have assembled, Gaby pitches them her request for a search party. Gillian raises her hand and asks if there's a reward.

"I'll stop trying to get you all arrested," Gaby offers.

Not everybody takes her up on it, but almost half do. By the time everyone's dressed and ready to go topside, Gaby's search party numbers ten.

"Do you have coordinates for the crash site?" I ask.

She shakes her head. "Rough estimate, that's all I could get out of the control tower. We head east and inland, probably not more than a few dozen kilometers away."

"Not to state the obvious," I say, "but that's a lot of ground to cover before dawn."

Gaby already has a plan. I can see it in the mischievous way her eyes light up. "Chief Han said I couldn't ask rangers to help us," she says slowly, "but she didn't tell me not to use our hovercycles. They just sit in storage all day, anyway..."

"Where are they anchored?"

"An underground garage. It has a tunnel leading outside the perimeter. I think I can sneak myself in—not sure about ten of you."

"That's no problem," I tell her. "We'll meet you outside."

The look she gives me says I haven't heard the last of her questions. She'll want to know where my access point to the outside world is, and if it's a security risk.

Maybe, if she's not a glitch tonight, I'll even tell her.

But there's no time right now. Somewhere out there, a woman with sad eyes, a voice like honey, and legs that look *stunning* in swimwear is in need of our help.

ANGELIQUE

I really didn't expect to ever wake up again.

Every part of my body aches, my head most of all. I wiggle my fingers and toes, then graduate to bending my knees and elbows. I don't think anything is broken, but when I lift my hand to my forehead, tacky moisture tells me that I'm bleeding.

Gingerly, I push myself upright. The ground underneath my palm is spongy and damp-hot. At first I'm afraid it's my blood soaking the starship seat, but as my eyes adjust to the dark around me, I realize I'm not inside the ship anymore. The mangled hull looms behind me, still smoking.

Dots and streaks of multicolored bioluminescence cast a faint glow, enough for me to make out the shape of my surroundings. Trees, ferns, and mushrooms cluster close, nearly blotting out the star-scattered sky above.

"Shit," I say out loud.

We crashed outside the resort's perimeter fence. And then, apparently, Jude just fucking *left* me here.

I hope a wild creature eats him. But I've got other things to worry about—like saving my own ass. I have no idea how much of Hades' night passed while I was unconscious, but the clock's ticking down toward sunrise, at which point I'll be incinerated if I'm still aboveground.

Standing doesn't feel like a good idea right now, but I force myself to do it anyway. My head pounds and I sway dizzily, but I can walk. Probably not run...although that might depend on what's chasing me.

I try to remember the highlights of Gaby's lesson on Hades' flora and fauna. Why was I so focused on the vampire parasite? Why didn't I pay more attention to things like, say, identifying which plants might try to kill me? I'm pretty sure there was at least one toothy predator out here, too. They weren't all ocean-dwellers.

First things first. I have to figure out which way leads back to the resort.

I don't trust the trees enough to climb one, but by stepping onto the crumpled nose of the starship, I'm able to drunkenly balance-beam my way to its uptilted tail-end. I can't fully see over the treetops, but I do notice a glow on the horizon. Praying it's the resort lights and not sunrise, I make a note of the direction in my mind and slide down the side of the starship.

I'm still in my beach gear. Not what I would have chosen for a jungle expedition. I peer into the wrecked cockpit, but Jude's taken the first aid kit, his blaster, and all the emergency supplies including the torchlight.

Asshole.

I select a sharp chunk of glass from the shattered viewscreen to use as a weapon, because I don't think I can face the jungle without one. Then there's nothing left to do but forge my way into the trees.

As I walk, I stay hyperalert for the slightest sound or movement, which isn't easy because the jungle is alive with the chittering of insects and other (hopefully) small creatures. The moons cast a little light for me to see by, but not nearly enough. A million curses on Jude for tossing my keycuff. If I had it, I could've called for help. Without it, even if Gaby's got the rangers looking for me, they won't be able to track my location.

I wonder if anyone even saw the ship go down. If not, they'll think we're on another planet by now. They'll give up the search before it even starts.

And why would I expect a woman I've known for just a couple of days to move mountains for me? It's her responsibility as a ranger to protect the peace in the resort, but once I'm off the planet, I'm not her problem anymore.

Deep down, part of me knows that this is how Jude trained me to think about myself. But the thoughts keep coming at me like missiles, a new one with every step...until each meter that I push forward feels like a "fuck you" to everyone not giving a shit about me.

Because I've been forging a solo path for years. I was alone when I was with Jude, alone after him, alone here on Hades, and I'm still alive. No one's coming to save me, but I blazing well won't give up and let anyone kill me.

If I'm going to die out here, I'll die fighting. If the sun roasts me, my baked skeleton will be flashing a rude gesture at the sky.

Angelique Azalea LaRue is not a quitter, my brain whispers in Dad's voice.

It doesn't matter if no one cares about me. *I want to live anyway.*

Somewhere in that internal monologue, my pace speeds up and a burst of strength propels me through a thick, waist-high cluster of fern-fronded fungi that glow blue at their tips.

My momentum nearly carries me directly into the wide-open jaws of a carnivorous tree's lure vine.

I stumble aside at the last minute, alerted by the tree's sweet floral scent. I'd read just enough of the text underneath the wildlife images to be forewarned: *If it smells too good, looks too pretty, or otherwise draws you in, run away. Evolution creates beauty because it attracts prey.*

The lure vine quests after me, its sightless, faceless mouth still open. Sparkling lights dance inside its throat, a jeweled tunnel leading to a pit of acid in the plant's belly, where anything swallowed will dissolve in agony. I grimace and scramble back, checking over my shoulder to make sure it's not herding me toward another of its species.

In my rush to get away from the vine, I realize I've lost my sense of direction. I need to get my bearings again.

I find a tall, lumpy tree that I think is benign, inspecting it thoroughly for sap ooze or lure vines before using its lumps as footholds to climb up its length. The glow of the resort feels just as far away as it was before, but now I can see a dark expanse lit with luminescent plankton lapping in gentle waves.

The ocean. If I can get to the beach, it will be much quicker to follow the coastline to the resort instead of forging through the woods.

My new goal in sight, I fumble my way down the tree, skinning my knee despite my best effort. I'll have to be cautious not to let any tree sap come in contact with my open wounds.

As soon as my feet hit the ground, I take two invigorated strides toward the direction of the ocean—

And run slapbang into the muzzle of Jude's blaster.

Chapter 12

ROMEO

Gaby wasn't kidding about the hovercycles not being used very often. These models aren't new, and mine has some kind of warning light flashing. It still flies, though, and that's all that matters.

I buzz between two lure vines, too quick for them to snap me up, then glance down to check my progress on the holo-map. The projection glows in a flat grid just above my keycuff, showing me where I am, where the rest of the searchers are, and the vast area we still have left to cover.

We're running out of night. The Midnights will be fine if we stay out past the dawn alarm—not happy, but also not dead. But Gaby won't be. If she gets a dose of that radiation, she's figurative toast. If she bakes in it for more than an hour, she's *literal* toast.

I lift one hand from the hovercycle's handlebars to tap my audio earring, connecting to Gaby. I'm strangely relieved when she answers it. Maybe because I've been trying Lea's call code for hours and getting no response, even though the comm satellites are supposed to ensure coverage anywhere on the planet's surface.

"Ranger Lopez, you need to head back."

Her voice is distant and muffled by her helmet when she responds, "Oh, it's *Ranger Lopez* now?"

"Fuckin'—*Gaby*. You need to head back. It's getting too close to dawn."

"Not until I find the crash."

"Don't be a fool," I growl. "There's nothing gained by adding another casualty to the crash. You need to go back."

"Just me? Not you?"

"The Midnights and I can keep up the search." *Now's as good a time as any, I guess...* "We're...special. There's an infection in our blood that makes us part of this planet. Sunlight hurts, but we won't die."

"I *knew* it," Gaby says, triumphant and sharp. "I *knew* there was something off about you."

"It's about time someone tells you the truth. Your Chief Ranger isn't going to." And I explain, as quickly and concisely as possible, what the parasite does. "So get back to the resort already. Trust me, I can handle it from here."

Silence on the other end. I almost worry we've been disconnected before Gaby finally says, "Chief Han knows about this?"

"Chief Han's infected, too. For years."

Gaby's voice goes hard and angry. "I'm going to chew her head off when we get back."

"You can't tell anyone else, though, understand? Our safety depends on it. If the Authorities get the idea that this planet needs to be quarantined..."

She's quiet a moment. "I still have a lot more questions," she says finally. "If you want me to swear silence, you're gonna need to promise you'll answer them."

"Deal." I glance nervously at the time on my keycuff. "Now will you turn back already?"

"Nope," Gaby says. "I'm leading this search. And I'm not calling it off until I absolutely have to."

"Gab—"

She clicks off the call on me.

Stubborn glitch.

As annoyed as I am, I have to respect her loyalty to a friend she just met a few days ago. Clearly, Lea means a lot to her.

I just don't want to see her get killed because of it.

I veer off my course, aiming for an intercept with Gaby's. If I have to knock her out and drag her back to the resort myself, I'm sure she'll forgive me...eventually.

That's when I spot the trail of broken trees and churned-up dirt. I slow down to call Gaby back.

"Head for my coordinates," I tell her. "I think I've got something."

ANGELIQUE

Jude digs the blaster into my stomach, his sneer just visible in the dim light. "Where do you think you're going, Angel?"

"Back to civilization, since you decided to abandon me out here!" I grip the top of his blaster and shove it away. "You do know that if we're out here at sunrise, we die, right?"

Jude gives a dismissive snort. "So say your darling rangers."

"If you want to test it, be my guest."

"Oh, we're both going to test it," Jude says, tapping his keycuff. "It's twenty minutes til sunup. You know as well as I do that we're not getting back to the resort that quick."

Panic floods my veins. I knew I'd been out for some time, but not *that* long. "I was unconscious *all day*?" I stammer. Then, narrowing my eyes, "And you didn't bother to go for help?"

"Oh, yeah, like the rangers were going to help *me* when you have them wrapped around your little finger with all your lies." Jude shoves me against a tree, his forearm against my collarbone. "But *I* found a cave where we can shelter. *I* was on my way back to get you. Because I *love* you." The way he growls it through gritted teeth, the pressure of his arm choking me, doesn't do much to convince me he means it.

A cave with Jude versus a painful burning death. Tough choice—and I mean that sincerely. "Show me the cave," I cough out finally.

"Good girl." With his hand at the back of my neck, he starts guiding me forward through the jungle.

Echoing in the distance, I hear the first dawn alarm. *Fifteen minutes until sunrise.*

Options for escape tumble through my head, but none of them are without consequence. Jude won't let me go without a fight, and I can't overpower him. Dawn's too close to do anything but sprint for shelter. My stomach rolls imagining what he might do to me if we're stuck in a cave for a whole day.

"Not much further," Jude mutters absently.

And that's when I smell it. Honey-floral perfume.

His grip on my neck prevents me from scanning the forest to spot any lure vines. I don't see any in our path, which means they're lurking out of sight somewhere.

If I can spot one before Jude does...

Movement in my peripheral vision. I nearly miss it in the gloom of the pre-dawn jungle, but my reflexes react before my mind has a chance to second-guess. I collapse at the knees, my drop so sudden that Jude loses his grip on my neck. And then I shove his legs with all my might, pushing him in the direction of the seeking lure vine.

It pounces.

Jude's scream cuts off abruptly as the vine's mouth closes over his upper half, whisking him off his feet. The vine's mouth curves up toward the sky, borrowing gravity to help slide its meal down the hollow esophagus into the belly of the plant.

On still-shaky legs, I back away until I'm far enough that the sweet smell of the lure fades into the earthy scent of the jungle. Only then does a laugh of pure adrenaline-fueled relief claw its way out of my throat.

I did it. I'm free of him. I'm *free*.

And that's when, in the far distance, I hear the second dawn alarm go off.

The horizon is already starting to get lighter, turning the liquid dark of Hades' night sky a brilliant blue-orange. Throwing caution out the airlock, I start racing through the forest in the general direction Jude was dragging me. *Where the blazes is this cave he was talking about? Glitch better not have been lying.*

I have minutes at most until the radiation spikes. The further I go without seeing even a hint of shelter, the faster my heart pounds in terrified panic. All around me, flowers are opening, strange acid-sweet scents announcing the coming sun. These plants are built to survive Hades' daylight. Me, not so much.

With no cave in sight, my skin already starting to feel hot, full survival mode kicks in. I'm not ready to die out here. If I can't find shelter, what else can I do?

I can...

Despite the heat, my blood runs cold.

I can become a vampire.

Romeo said the parasite keeps someone from dying if they're exposed to sunlight. I'd live through the day, would become permanently young and healthy...but I might never be able to leave Hades again.

Well. It's that, or die, so—

I lunge for the nearest tree and find a bead of sap oozing from a broken twig. I scoop it on my finger and smear it across my scraped knee.

My heart thunders as I stare at the mess of blood and golden sap. How long do the parasites take to infect a body? The sun is already almost above the horizon, the heat intensifying to sear my skin. It might already be too late for me.

Rather than wait for the sun to fry me, I stumble forward, blindly hoping Jude was telling the truth about this supposed cave he found. But if it even exists, it took him all night to find. What if I never—

A buzzing noise in my ear, growing louder. I wave my hand, wincing. I don't want to die sucked dry by a swarm of bugs, any more than I want to get fried to death by an alien sun.

But as it gets closer, I realize the sound isn't insect-related at all; it's the hum of a hovercycle engine.

"HELP!" I scream. What are the rangers doing outside the perimeter after sunrise? Are they suicidal—or already vampires? Either way, I can't afford to be choosy. "OVER HERE! HELP!"

The drone of the engine veers closer. And then, crashing through the trees, two hovercycles land in front of me, carrying two familiar faces.

Romeo.

And Gaby.

They vault off the cycles. Gaby rushes forward, eyes wild with panic. "Lea! Is...is that you? Wait, no way, have you been *Angelique Azalea* this whole time? I can't believe I—"

Oh, right. They can both see my real face now.

"We gotta go," Romeo calls, glancing at the horizon.

"Come on." Gaby pulls me toward her hovercycle, helping me on in front before jumping on behind me. "We have to get back to the resort fast. Just close your eyes and hang on..."

I grip the handlebar, my hands next to hers. Then I hiss as the scrape on my knee brushes the side of the cycle.

Romeo's at my side in an instant. He grabs my hand and turns it up, finding a smear of mingled sap and blood. "Oh, shit," he hisses. "You didn't..."

"Just a minute ago," I mumble. "I thought it was my only chance to survive."

"You did it on *purpose?* That was—" Romeo stops short of saying *stupid as fuck*, which I take as a personal favor. "The doctors might be able to reverse it if..."

He stops, glancing at Gaby. She wraps her arms around my sides and revs the engine. "Hold on, Lea, I'm about to break the speed limit."

"Don't get her blood on you!" Romeo yells as we accelerate.

I guess I pass out after that, because it's the last thing I remember.

Mid-Season Finale

Chapter 13

GABRIELLE

By pushing the hovercycles to their maximum speed, we make it back to the resort without a second to spare. The sun's already peeking over the horizon, burning my exposed skin and dazzling my eyes.

The other Midnights had more of a self-preservation instinct and returned as soon as the dawn alarm went off. They're waiting for us in the garage, eyes wide and worried as we speed through the access door and skid to a stop.

"The humans got burned!" one woman yells. "Get them to the med center *now*."

"On it!" Romeo's already lifting Lea off the front of my bike. She's been unresponsive for the whole drive, but I can see her eyes moving beneath her closed lids, as if she's dreaming. Her skin, flushed red like mine, is slick with sweat.

If Romeo told me the truth, then she's just given herself an infection for which there is no cure. If she survives, she'll crave blood for the rest of her life.

"Come on," Romeo says impatiently to me. "You got hit with the solar radiation too. Can you walk?"

I swing my leg over the side of the hovercycle, suppressing a roll of nausea. "I think so."

"Let me know if you're going to faint," he says, before basically sprinting off down the winding corridors.

There's no way I'm going to match that pace. I do my best to hobble along, but the feverish sickness is hitting me in waves now, and every inch of skin that wasn't covered by my uniform is on fire.

Two of the Midnights, a muscular blonde and a dark-haired man, come up behind me and catch my arms on either side. "Hey, come on, Ranger. Let us help you."

"Why would you?" I mumble. "You hate my guts."

"You promised to stop trying to get us arrested, yeah? And you just saved Romeo's singer sweetheart from a horrible burning death. I'd call us good now. Unless you'd rather walk by yourself?"

I kinda feel like I might cast up and then die, so no, I'm not refusing help. "Thanks," I slur, before the two of them loop my arms over their shoulders and drag me down the hall at double speed.

Thank stars, the med center is well-equipped with supplies to treat radiation exposure. Ranger training always underscores the importance of starting treatment quickly, before the organ damage gets too severe. As the healers pump me full of medications, they tell me that I got here just in time. I should be back on my feet in a few days.

"What about Lea?"

The healer's eyes slide away from mine. "We're monitoring her condition."

"Can I see her?"

"You both need rest," says the healer firmly. "We're taking care of her, don't you worry."

Then she presses a patch to my forearm, and sleep crumbles down on me like a cave-in.

ROMEO

T he next night

The healers know better than to waste their radiation-exposure treatment on me. The parasites in my blood gobble up solar radiation fast enough that it doesn't have time to do me any damage. All I get is a case of the sweats and a mild stomachache. By dusk the following night, I'm fine again.

When I visit the med center to check on Lea, the healers still have her in a drugged sleep and aren't allowing visitors. "She's fine, just healing," Healer Price assures me.

"What about Ranger Lopez?" I ask.

"She just woke up, if you'd like to go in and see her."

I'm probably the last person Gaby wants to see, but we left a conversation unfinished. I follow the healer to her room and let myself in.

Seeing Gaby out of her uniform is like seeing a shaved bear: surprising and kind of weird. I'm not accustomed to Gabrielle Lopez being anything but a confident badass. And yet, here she is in a hospital gown, her hair a frizzy mess, sipping a nutrient booster with a bendy straw.

She glances up as I come in and says, "Oh, it's you," though her tone lacks the animosity it once might've had.

"It's me," I agree. "How are you feeling?"

"A little better. They had me knocked out most of the night. Sounds like they're still keeping Lea—um, Angelique—asleep."

"Just call her Lea for now," I suggest. "That other name is a mouthful, and I still don't really know who she is."

That's a lie. I went to the library this morning and searched Angelique Azalea on the uniweb. But I'm not telling Gaby that.

"Stars, do you live under a rock?"

I glance up at the ceiling. "Yes, actually."

She snorts a laugh. "All right, bloodsucker, why are you here? To threaten me into secrecy again?"

"Something like that." I settle into the visitor's chair next to her cot. "You demanded answers first."

"Uh-huh." Gaby sets her drink aside. "Number one: what have I been investigating all this time? A bunch of people disappearing or being murdered—that's you, right? You and your gang...*eating* people."

I sigh. "You're half right. Some of the documented attacks *were* feedings that went wrong. I'm not saying none of us have ever hurt or killed anyone. But the majority of the 'disappearances' have been people who *joined* the Midnights. They slipped up, got some seaweed in their mouth while swimming, snuck outside the perimeter or whatever, and got infected. Now they can't leave. What else are they going to do? They pretended they died so their families back home would have some closure. Then they changed their names and came to live with my gang in the out-of-bounds."

"But there have been *bodies*."

"Like I said...some of them were real accidents." I'm not quite ready to tell her about Wright yet. That part of the Midnights' history is a nightmare we'd all like to forget. "But most of the ones without bodies are still alive. Some aren't even Midnights—a couple of them are rangers, like you. Or business owners, or service workers. There are maybe fifty infected people total in this resort, and only about half of them live in the tunnels with me."

Gaby looks stunned. "*Fifty?* And some are *rangers?* No way. I know you said that Chief Han's one of them, but I can't believe..."

"Do you want me to list the names? I know them all."

She holds up a hand. "Nope. No, I don't think I want to know just yet. I still need to get my head around the blood-thirst thing." Her expression twists into a grimace. "Have any of you ever...drank from me? You said you can wipe people's memories after..."

"I can't speak for everyone, just for the Midnights," I hedge, "but we don't go after rangers. We have an agreement with Chief Han. She doesn't bother my people if we don't bother hers."

Gaby rubs her forehead. "Except I've been on your ass for months now. No wonder Chief Han was so annoyed."

"Now you're getting it." I chuckle. "Hey, no hard feelings. I keep telling your boss that she needs to be more open with the uninfected rangers, but she thinks secrecy is safer. Maybe you can help me convince her otherwise."

"I'm certainly going to have words with her about it," Gaby mutters, glowering.

She has plenty more questions where that came from. Before I know it, an hour's gone by while I explain the mechanics and biological effects of vampirism. She's even more curious than Lea was. I'd be lying if I said I wasn't worried that she'll use this information to ruin my life somehow. But as we talk, I don't get the sense that she holds a grudge toward me anymore. Maybe, because we helped her rescue Lea, she's changing her mind about us.

I hope so. Because Gaby's smart as blazes, and I'm starting to think we could use an ally like her.

Chapter 14

ANGELIQUE

Three nights later

The next couple of days are a blur of bright-white med center walls and concerned faces. They keep me heavily sedated, hooked up to a bunch of machines, so my consciousness floats somewhere around the ceiling, only vaguely curious about whether I'm going to survive or not.

When they finally dial down the meds, the first thing I notice is how little pain I'm in. I feel...amazing. Possibly better than I've ever felt in my life.

Except I'm dying for a drink.

"Can I get some water?" I mumble when a healer comes in to check on me. Her look of concern feels like a bit of an overreaction. She steps out of the room and returns with a pouch of some viscous liquid, which squeezes out of a straw at the top. I can't place the taste—sweet, a bit acidic, like the scent that bloomed out of the flowers at dawn. Maybe some kind of fruit smoothie?

I'm still sucking it down, trying not to go too fast in case I get a stomachache, when another healer pokes their head in and says, "You have visitors."

A reflexive spurt of terror grips me. "It's not a blond man, is it?"

"No?" The healer looks confused. "It's Ranger Lopez and a man with black curly hair."

Gaby and Romeo. I relax. "You can let them in." *Jude is dead,* I remind myself. *His body's getting digested by your new favorite tree. He'll never be able to hurt you again.*

If I say it to myself a thousand more times, maybe my body will start to believe it.

As the healers withdraw, Gaby shoulders past them to barge inside my room. "Lea! We've been so worried. They wouldn't let us see you."

"I'm alive," I say. "Feeling great, actually. You know, you can call me Angelique now that Jude's out of the picture."

"Aw, I kind of like your nickname," says Gaby. "Feels like we get to know a part of you that your galaxy of fans doesn't."

I smile softly at her.

"Is he *really* out of the picture?" That's Romeo, peering in after her. "We never found a body. Just a crashed ship."

"A tree ate him." I take another sip of my smoothie. "He deserved it."

"He deserved worse," Gaby growls. "How did you manage to get away from him?"

I recount the whole story—getting drugged, crashing the ship, waking up alone—while somewhat enjoying the looks of horror on their faces. When I get to the part about the lure vine eating Jude, Gaby whispers a satisfied, "Yesss," while Romeo continues to look troubled.

"Those carnivorous trees don't fully digest a person-sized meal for weeks," he says. "Jude could still be alive in there."

"Yeah, but how's he getting out?" Gaby retorts. "Plus, even if he does, the sun will fry him. I don't think we're ever seeing that fucker again."

"You're sure?" The idea that Jude could potentially escape, however unlikely it is, sends creepflesh up my arms.

Romeo grins. "Even if you do, you're a vampire now. You could drink him dry. Or imagine he tries to shoot you again. What's it gonna do? Knock you out for a few?"

A tremor goes through me. "So I really did get infected?"

"Lea," says Romeo gently, "you've just drained most of a pint of blood."

I look down at the smoothie packet and, for the first time, notice the drops of dark crimson clinging to the straw. It should make my stomach churn, but instead it growls. "I thought it'd taste more like iron."

"If it tasted gross, the parasite would starve," Romeo reasons. "There are lots of biological changes that result from infection—altered taste buds are one of many things you'll start noticing."

"I don't feel any pain," I say tentatively.

"That too."

"But I'm *super* thirsty."

"Yeah," Gaby jumps in. "The change-over period, when the parasites are multiplying at the highest rate, is when an infected person is the most hungry. And dangerous. That's why they've kept you under sedation." She throws a look at Romeo. "See? I've been doing my homework."

Hurriedly, I squeeze the rest of the blood smoothie into my mouth. "I don't want to hurt anybody."

"And you won't have to," Gaby says. "The med center keeps a well-stocked blood bank. We're *always* running blood drives. Once the initial infection phase is past, you'll be able to drop by once a week and keep the hunger to a manageable level."

"A blood bank?" I frown at Romeo. "Why do the Midnights attack people if you could just—"

"Oh, here we go." Romeo rolls his eyes. "What Gaby's not telling you is that your little weekly ration is just enough to keep you from going full frenzy. It's not enough to make you feel *full*. To satisfy the parasite, you gotta supplement. But the Chief Ranger thinks we should just walk around half starved." Crossing his arms, he adds, "Also, the nurses are so fucking judgmental. They act all grossed out whenever they hand over a blood bag, as if I got infected on purpose so I could enjoy the sweet, sweet taste of someone else's vein juice. Not all of us were willing to put up with that shit. Especially not those of us who've been here longer than the resort."

"They're not being rude on purpose," Gaby retorts. "They're *scared of you.*"

"Who? Little old me?" Romeo puts on a fake pout.

Gaby rolls her eyes at him. "I think we should let Lea rest now. She's got a lot to digest."

I settle back against my pillows. "The blood *is* kind of making me sleepy."

"I meant *mentally* digest," says Gaby dryly, "but food naps are good too."

The next time I wake, it's the middle of the day, and everyone's asleep. My stomach growls urgently. I'm gonna need at least two of those blood smoothies.

I press the call button for a healer, but minutes stretch by with no response. Either they don't keep healers here during the sleep cycle, or the on-duty staff are busy.

With a groan, I push myself upright and swing my legs over the side of the cot. The scannerbot beeps anxiously, so I peel off the sensors connecting me to it. "Just gotta go find the blood bank," I tell it. "I'll be right back."

The bikini they rescued me in is long gone. The med center provided a soft white robe to cover me on my trips to the washroom. I wrap myself in it and belt it tight before heading out the door.

The med center's hallways are still brightly lit, but I don't meet a single soul as I wander around. I reach a passcode-locked door labeled STAFF ONLY and turn around, but the only other exit leads to the med center's lobby. I approach the desk, hoping the receptionist can help, but then realize that the shape behind the check-in station is a bot.

"Please scan identification," it intones. Then, once I've done so, "Patient Angelique Azalea LaRue. Are you requesting discharge?"

"Um, not yet? Listen, I need…" I check over my shoulder to make sure the waiting room is completely empty. "I'm hungry," I whisper. "I need blood."

"Please wait. Staff will assist you shortly."

I flop down in one of the waiting room chairs, but after another ten minutes, I feel like my stomach's trying to eat itself. I'm ready to start chewing on my own arm. "Excuse me," I call. "When do you think someone will be coming to help me?"

"I'm sorry. All currently available staff are working to stabilize an emergency patient. Time of service unknown."

I groan. Maybe I should just go to Underworld. Their cookbots can make drinks and food around the clock. It might not satiate my blood hunger, but it'll at least be some kind of fuel my body can run on. I'm, like, ninety percent sure my stomach can still digest regular human food. I forgot to ask, but I've definitely seen Romeo drinking alcohol. Soup would be safe, right?

"If they ask where I am, tell them I went to get some food," I tell the receptionist. "I'll be right back."

"Patient Angelique Azalea LaRue requesting discharge. Granted. You are free to go."

"Actually, I don't know if I should be discharged yet…?" The bot isn't paying attention, so I sigh and continue out the door. I can always check back in when I've gotten something in my stomach. Hopefully their blood bank will be staffed by sundown.

The Underworld lounge is quiet, too. A single pair of tourists, obviously very drunk, giggle at a table in the corner. The other seats are empty, so I sit down and tap my order into the table's screen. I'm so hungry it's actually starting to hurt. I massage my cramping belly and pray the bots won't need too much time to heat up a quick bowl of noodles.

Without fully meaning to, I get up and start pacing the room. My steps veer closer and closer to the drunk couple across the room from me. Do they have any leftovers I could snag from their table? What if I really quick just grabbed and downed one of their drinks? What if I sank my teeth into the juicy vein in one of their—

Whoa, whoa, whoa. This is what Gaby meant when she said I'm dangerous right now. I reel back, rubbing my temples. My conscious mind is still very much disgusted by the idea of attacking a human and drinking their blood—but to my subconscious, it feels no different than stealing a half-eaten basket of fries off their table to sate the worst hunger I've ever felt in my admittedly privileged life.

The scary part? I don't think my conscious mind is winning the fight. Even as I hear a bot wheeling toward my table, bringing a steaming bowl of soup, I know it's not going to be as satisfying as gulping thick, tangy blood.

I step closer to the tourists.

And then there's a yank on my wrist and I'm spinning into Romeo's arms. He and the Midnights must have just walked in—out of the corner of my eye, I see his friends settling into their favorite booth. But Romeo is focused entirely on me, his hands firm on my shoulders. "What are you doing?" he growls. "You shouldn't be out of the med center."

"No one was there," I protest. "I'm *starving*."

"I bet you are." He glances around the room. "Come on. I'm taking you back to your room."

"*Noooo*." I'm nearly crying. "I need to eat. Please, please..." I try to lunge away from him, meaning to go for the steaming bowl that still sits, untouched, on my table. Somehow my body turns it into a lunge toward the drunk bystanders' table.

Romeo grabs me again, this time tackling me into a booth seat. Flat on my back on the plush seat, with him straddling my waist, I wait for the panic to kick in. For my body to remind me of all the times I've been hurt before.

But this time it doesn't happen.

Because I'm a predator now.

I surge up, grabbing Romeo by the shoulders, and bite hard into the curve of his neck.

The trickle of blood against my lips is heaven. I suck, sinking my teeth deeper, needing more. Romeo groans, but rather than push me away, he pulls me closer. "Yes," he mumbles. "Take what you need. *Yes.*"

I didn't know it was an option to take blood from another vampire, but the evidence that they do *have* blood is flowing into my mouth at this moment. And, stars, it tastes better than I could have imagined. It's reminiscent of the thick, fruit-smoothie tang from the bagged blood, but warm and laced with an addictive sweetness that makes my favorite candy seem sickly and artificial. I greedily drink for a full minute, until finally my stomach is full enough for my conscious brain to regain control.

I unlatch my teeth from his flesh and pull back, wiping my mouth guiltily. "I'm sorry. Are you all right? Did I take too much?"

Romeo takes a couple of deep breaths, then pulls an adhesive bandage out of his jacket pocket. He slaps it over the wound. "I'll live. Gonna need an extra feeding today, though. Might have to swallow my pride and beg the healers for a ration." He peeks out of the booth, checking if anyone saw us. Hopefully, the tourists I almost ate thought we were just making out.

"I'm sorry," I say again.

"Don't be." Romeo reaches out, his thumb brushing the corner of my mouth and coming away red. "It's not you, it's the parasite. But we need to get you out of here before everyone wakes up. You're not safe to be around right now."

He takes my hands and helps me to my feet, and I don't know why, but his face is right there, and...

I kiss him.

It's a starving kiss, mimicking the way I just gouged into his neck. I drink his surprised gasp, then his raspy "fuck it" against my lips as he dives in with me. I grind my hips into his and discover that he's already hard.

Right, then. It wasn't my imagination. Biting him was...*hot*. Way hotter than it had any right to be.

Across the room, one of his friends whistles at us. Romeo breaks away and says, "You. Room. Now."

"Yes, sir." I bite my lip, hungry for another taste. His lips or his blood? *Is both at once an option?*

Romeo scoops me up and begins carrying me toward the door. I giggle and protest, but he keeps me cradled firmly to his chest.

"I just sucked half your blood," I murmur in his ear. "If you faint while carrying me, I'm going to feel bad."

"Fair point." He puts me down, then takes my hand and says, "How fast can you run?"

"I...don't know."

"I'll give you a hint," he says with a smirk. "Faster than you ever could before." And he takes off, pulling me behind him.

Before my transformation, I probably couldn't have kept up. But I find my feet punching the ground in time with his, speeding us toward my room.

Chapter 15

I've barely even broken a sweat by the time I'm keying in my passcode at the door. "This is amazing!" I gasp, tugging Romeo inside. "What else can I do now?"

"Remember what orgasms were like before?" He nibbles the outer shell of my ear, sending a tingle down my neck. "*Double* it."

I slam the door shut and lock it behind us. "Oh, now that you're going to have to prove."

"Ready and willing." He pauses. "That is, if you are?"

"If I don't have your clothes off in the next five minutes, I think I'm going to explode." I shove him toward my pull-out bed, which, thankfully, has relatively clean sheets.

Still, he's hesitating. "New vampires are always thirsty and horny," he says. "You might...not want to take things further, after it fades. And I want you to know that it's fine if this is just blowing off steam. I won't be upset if it doesn't mean anything."

Now I pause, too. This *meaning something* hadn't even occurred to me; the drive to fuck is nearly as strong as my hunger was.

"Friends with benefits," I tell him. "Does that work for you?"

His eyes, dark with lust, meet mine as he nods. "For now."

Then he leans in to kiss the side of my neck and my knees go liquid. We fall together on top of my pink duvet, me sprawling across his chest, our legs tangling. It suddenly feels like a life-or-death emergency that I get his clothes off.

Romeo flings off the white hospital robe I was wearing, but takes his time with my unders. He unhooks my breastband and takes his time sliding the straps down my arms before flinging it over his shoulder. As it hits the floor, he takes one of my nipples in his mouth as he begins to slowly inch down the waistband of the plain white briefs the med center put me in.

Frenzied with need, I reach for his waistband, too. My hands just get in his way, neither of us able to achieve what we want. Finally, he rolls me under him, pinning me to the mattress with his knees tight against my waist as he strips off his black tank top. My mouth waters at the sight of his toned abdomen, dusted with black hair that trails down into his shorts.

I squirm, convinced I could come on the spot without him touching me. "Please," I beg.

"Please what?" He leans down to nip my bottom lip, flicking his tongue against it teasingly. "Tell me what you need, Lea."

"You naked." I blush, but the burn of need between my thighs is too intense not to say it. "And...eating my pussy."

The wicked grin on his face tells me I'm about to have all my dirtiest dreams come true. "That can easily be arranged."

Seconds later, his shorts join my panties on the floor. I get one glorious glimpse of his long, pale, nude body, his cock standing stiff against a patch of black curls, before he crawls onto the bed and buries his face between my legs.

Even the teasing brush of his nose against the inside of my thigh nearly sends me over the edge. My back arches, and without meaning to, I'm begging.

He takes pity on me and draws a long, slow lick across my opening before circling my clit with his tongue. I fall apart in seconds, the orgasm tearing through my body so hard that I shudder and come close to blacking out. Romeo wasn't kidding—it's *incendiary*.

Romeo waits out the tremors with me, slowly working two fingers into my pussy as it clenches. He kisses my thigh, his breath hot against me, and then says, "How did that feel?"

I moan incoherently, a boneless puddle.

He chuckles. "Intense, isn't it? You'll get used to it."

"*How?*" I can't imagine that consuming pleasure ever becoming commonplace.

"All your senses are going to slowly heighten," he says, laying more kisses against my belly between words. "Eventually, you'll become accustomed to a new baseline of sensitivity. But I will admit, most of us vampires spend half the time we're not hunting on fucking. When orgasms feel *that* good, why wouldn't we have as many as possible?"

"Why indeed," I say breathlessly. "Um, should I be worried about diseases or—"

"The parasite can kill pretty much any disease," says Romeo, "but we can use protection if you're worried about pregnancy."

"Will my implant still work?"

"It should. The Midnights all have one."

"So I *could* still get pregnant?" I ask, aware that this is veering into less sexy territory, but too curious to shut up. "What would happen to the baby?"

"It'd be born infected, but fairly normal. A couple of the infected rangers have had kids." Romeo traces a finger down my hip. "You should know that body fluids may also carry the parasite. It doesn't seem to be as easy to contract the parasite through sexual contact as it is through blood-sharing, but the possibility isn't zero."

Gaby. My heart drops. This thing with Romeo aside, I'd been hoping...

Romeo sees the look on my face and crawls up my body to put his arms around me. "There are plenty of ways to protect a partner. Don't sweat it too much—just keep it in the back of your mind when you're with someone, and be safe."

I'll talk to her later, I decide. Now that Gaby knows about the parasite, I don't have to lie to her. She can decide what she's comfortable with.

My stomach twists with nerves. *What if she decides she doesn't want me after this?*

I don't want to dwell on that possibility, so I nuzzle into the warmth of Romeo's embrace, which is surprisingly comforting. For a few minutes, we just cuddle. I can feel the pressure of his erection against my leg, but he doesn't move to take anything further.

As I come down from the high of that first peak, desire ignites again, and I make the first move, turning my head to capture his mouth with mine. Romeo responds hungrily. Chest to chest, we make out like horny teenagers, hands roving down backs and cupping asses. His cock leaks between us, and I know he must be aching with need. When he reaches down and thumbs my clit, I find that I'm right there with him. I haven't had more than one orgasm in the same session since...

Well, since before Jude.

"I want you inside me," I whisper, biting his earlobe for good measure.

"Fuck," he moans. "Do you need me to get a—"

"You just said you can't give me diseases and my implant still works. Do I have to beg?"

He flashes that smirk. "I do like hearing you beg."

"Then fucking *please* get in me, Romeo, stars, please, I need your cock *now*—"

He lines himself up and thrusts. I'm soaked enough that he glides right in with no resistance. I wrap my legs around his hips, opening to him. He groans into the crook of my neck. "I want to go slow, but I—"

"Don't," I say. The bandage where I savaged his neck is right under my nose. I kiss him open-mouthed next to it, wondering what it would be like to drink his blood while he's inside me. "I need it hard and fast. We can go slow later—ohhhh—"

I trail off as his hips slam into mine, the friction striking my clit like lighting a match. I grind up into his thrusts, even as the weight of him pressing me down is almost too much...

With a burst of strength that surprises even me, I flip him over onto his back, rolling with him without breaking our connection. And now, oh, now it's even *better*, because he's looking up at me with that wrecked expression, his eyes glowing orange as if he's about to bite me. My thighs don't burn like they used to in this position, letting me set a frantic pace as both of us chase release. Romeo leans up to grab the back of my neck, pulling me into a messy kiss, his other hand on my ass urging me faster, and I'm so so close...

"Bite me," I say into his mouth.

He groans. "Are you sure?"

"*Please.*"

The instant his teeth sink into the meat of my neck, I come again. It's just as intense as the first time, maybe even more so as I clench around his cock, the pain of the bite transmogrifying into pleasure. He groans and bucks up into me, and I hope my neighbors aren't trying to sleep, because I'm screaming his name loud enough for the whole block of rooms to hear me.

Romeo lifts his head from my neck, teeth dripping red, and collapses back onto the mattress. "Blazes, Lea," he says, chest heaving. "You're going to ruin me."

I lift the duvet to catch the blood from his bite. *Hopefully this'll wash out.* "The feeling's mutual," I say, before tucking myself into the crook of his arm.

Chapter 16

JUDE

The inside of the carnivorous tree is dark, hot, moist, and full of a choking stink that gags him with every breath. His skin is on fire as the digestive acids eat away at him.

But he isn't dead.

By now he should be. He's been in blinding agony for enough time that his body ought to have melted around him. He can't take a breath without gagging. But for reasons he can't explain, he is still conscious.

With instinct-driven, animal strength, he claws at the tree's stomach, trying to rip his way out. He's despaired of ever truly escaping this hell when, at last, his hand finds the cool metal of his laser pistol, which he thought he'd lost in the journey down the lure vine's throat.

He aims it at the wall of the stomach and fires again and again, not caring that the stomach clenches and squeezes around him. Not caring that he might kill the thing and trap himself inside.

The pistol falls from his hand as another retching cough wracks his body. And then he feels rhythmic waves pushing him up, up, into the tight tube of the lure vine...

The tree vomits him onto the ground in a spill of acid.

Jude sits up, gasping for air. The sun has just gone down. Bioluminescent creatures are glowing brighter as the sky dims. He inhales fresh air and groans at the sharp pain of the ground under his raw skin. His clothes are half disintegrated and every part of him is blistering red.

Except...

He watches as, before his eyes, the skin begins to scab over and heal.

Blazing suns, he thinks, *I'm thirsty as a motherfucker.*

He pushes himself to his feet and staggers away from the lure vine, just in case it gets any ideas. Every step is agony. *Must find water.*

A low growl sounds in the bushes. Jude turns, locking eyes with a many-eyed, sharp-clawed predator beast.

"Nice kitty," he says, showing it his teeth.

The creature hesitates, then slinks backward. But Jude, acting on pure instinct, leaps forward. He gets an arm around the thing's head, then straddles its back, holding it in place with his knees as he sinks his teeth into the back of its neck.

Blood bursts onto his tongue, sweet and tangy, like the juiciest fruit he's ever bitten into. He drinks greedily as the creature yelps and writhes beneath him, until at last it subsides into futile twitching as he drains it dry.

He lifts his head, licking blood from his chin. His mind is clearer than ever, sharp and focused. The pain has all but disappeared. His skin is still raw, but he can already feel the itching of scabs forming.

It must be this planet. Some kind of healing property.

His stomach twinges sharply. Drinking so much blood at once, healing or no, might have been a bad idea. He groans and shambles toward the direction where he remembers finding the lava caves. He'll need somewhere protected to hole up while his skin heals. Then...

Well, he doesn't see Angelique's body anywhere. That means the glitch must have survived, too.

But she'll wish she didn't, when I'm done with her.

Deleted Scenes

Chapter 17

ANGELIQUE

One week later

It's time. I've been putting it off, because it feels so terribly final, but now that word of my Hades residency has hit the uniweb, I need to tell my family. Better they hear it from me than from some fanpage.

The interplanetary call relay is expensive to set up, but I have access to my old accounts again, so I can afford it. I sit cross-legged on the bed in my room, staring at the holo-capture, waiting for my mother to pick up.

She doesn't make me wait long. Her head and shoulders appear above my tablet's projector. She sounds a little flustered when she exclaims, "Angelique, sweetest, it's wonderful to see you!"

"Mom." That's all I can get out before I burst into tears. It's been two years since I dared to contact my family, just in case Jude might monitor the call.

Mom reaches out, as if she could hug me through the lightyears. "Is everything all right? Are you safe?"

I struggle to get ahold of myself enough to speak. "I'm good. I'm on Hades now. And...Jude's gone."

"Gone?" Mom raises her eyebrows. "He finally left you alone, you mean?"

"No." My voice hardens. "*Gone* gone. He came here and tried to abduct me, but...it didn't go how he planned. There was an accident. He's dead now."

Her hands fly to her mouth. "Oh, Angelique. Thank the stars you're safe now. We worried for you after he came here."

Ice pools in my stomach. "So he *did* come to see you?"

"A long time ago. Right after you left. He told us that you were having a psychotic break and might be a danger to yourself, then tried to get us to tell him where you were. But you hadn't told us anything, so we couldn't help him. Once we said that, he got really intense and strange. Your stepfather asked him to leave."

I shudder. "I'm glad he didn't try to hurt you to get to me. That was why I left, Mom. I knew he wasn't going to stop."

"Oh, baby." Mom's eyes well up with tears. "I wish you'd told us everything. We could have helped you."

"I didn't want you to get involved." The tears are falling fast again. I grab the corner of my sheet to wipe them away. "You have your new family now. How's John? How are the kids?"

Mom starts telling me about my stepsiblings—the oldest one is almost done with Gen Ed, and wants to be a xenozoologist—and I let myself cry as I listen. I've missed so much of their lives, first by being a performer with a packed schedule, and then by going into hiding. And now I'll never have the chance to experience the rest of it with them. Not unless they move to Hades.

Finally, Mom asks the inevitable question: "Now that you're safe, when can you come see us?"

I suppress a fresh wave of tears as I take a deep breath and lie.

"My residency contract with Underworld Lounge means that I have to stay on the planet for the foreseeable future, Mom. I can't come see you. *But*," I add hastily, seeing her face crumple in disappointment, "just tell me a date, and I'll pay for you to come to Hades. The whole family. Travel expenses, too. I want to see you so bad."

"Oh, Angelique, you can't do that. It's too much."

"My music sales have been depositing royalties into my account for two years, totally untouched," I tell her. "Jude, no matter how hard he tried, couldn't access that money. It's all mine again. I can't think of anything better to do with it than spoil my family."

"Sweetie..." Mom sniffles. "Thank you. I love you so much, baby. You don't know how good it is to hear your voice after all this time."

"You'll be hearing a lot more of it," I promise. "I'll call you every week. You're going to get sick of me."

She gives me a watery smile. "Not possible."

After the call ends, I curl up around my pillow and sob for a long time. The gross and cool biology of being a vampire distracted me for a while from the long-term, big-picture effects. Now, grief for the life I've lost hits me full force. I'll never set foot in my mother's house again. Never attend my stepbrother's graduation ceremony. Never see my siblings get married, unless they choose a Hades destination wedding.

And I'll never perform on a Monroe stage again.

My career as a pop star is over. I can put out new songs, sell albums, but I can't go on tour, audition for musicals, or star in holo-dramas. And it's going to get increasingly hard to explain any of that, unless I just...allow myself to fade into obscurity until nobody cares.

I let myself wallow until all of my tears are cried out. Then I reach for my tablet again and open a message to my legal representation back on Monroe. I need to tie up any loose ends I left—contracts unfulfilled, debts unpaid. It's also time to stop pretending I'll ever return to my apartment in the city. I don't know how much of my stuff is still left there—maybe Jude destroyed it all—but if any of it is left, I'll get someone to pack it up and send it to Hades.

My old life is over. It's time to start the new one.

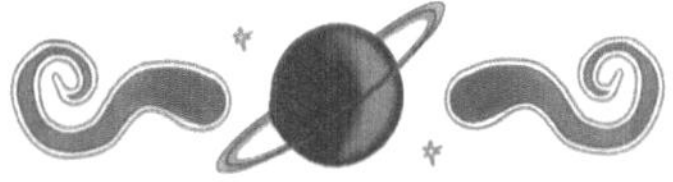

GABRIELLE

"No, really, I'm feeling a lot better," Lea promises.

We've been trying to get time alone ever since she was released from the med center, but Romeo (and Chief Han) have repeatedly warned me to be careful around her. It's only now, after a week of recovery for both of us, that we've been able to schedule a date.

"You, um, had blood today?"

She nods. "The med center gives me as much as I want, after that incident last week. I haven't been needing it as often, though."

I roll my eyes, trying to pretend that the mention of said incident doesn't still set off a storm of weird feelings for me. Lea told me everything the day after it happened. She'd gone too long without feeding, gotten a little hunger-crazed, almost eaten some tourists, and then fallen into bed with Romeo.

It should be the first part that bothers me more than the latter. But for some reason, it hasn't been hard to accept that the woman I'm dating needs to drink blood to survive. I'm even pretty chill about the fact that she's *Angelique Azalea*.

It's the part where she slept with Romeo that I can't stop thinking about.

"Are you sure you'll be safe for the next couple of hours?" I ask. "Because I don't want to be your only snack option down there." I reach out for her hand to help her down the last few steps into the damp cavern where the rangers keep our submersibles.

"Pretty sure," Lea says. "I shouldn't need to eat again until after my show."

She just started performing again yesterday, and according to her, the Underworld was packed with the biggest crowd they've seen in years. Word's started getting around that the mysterious Angelique Azalea has come out of hiding. There's been an influx of fans booking with the resort just to sneak a peek at our resident pop star.

I'm sure Karina's over the moon about it. Lea, not so much. All the attention seems to kind of freak her out. She called me after last night's show, and even though she said she was super excited to wear her real face again, I could hear her voice shaking.

Even now, at the offhand mention of tonight's performance, I can feel her hand go clammy in mine.

I quickly change the subject. "Here she is! The sub we'll be taking out today. What do you think? We call her Fishy McFishface."

Lea chokes a laugh. "You do *not!*"

"I'm serious. There was a break room poll for what we should have stenciled on the side." I point at the letters in bold blue against the sub's yellow paint. "Chief Han swore she'll never put anything to a vote ever again."

"Are you sure it's fine for us to use this sub?" Lea asks nervously. "Isn't it special ranger equipment? You don't usually let civilians on board, right?"

"Not usually, no." I smirk. "But I'm not the first ranger to use it to impress someone they're dating."

Lea gives me a blushy little smile. "Oh, you're trying to impress me, are you?"

"That depends. Is it working?"

"I'll let you know," she says as we climb in. The sub is just big enough for two, with a huge curved viewing window at the front. Once we're in the water, the backside of the sub will sprout the propellers and fins that prompted its name.

The sub's main use is patrolling the underwater portion of the perimeter wall and finding areas that need repair. But we only have to do that once a week. The rest of the time, using it for joyrides is a "don't get caught, and we won't tell" sort of perk amongst my colleagues.

The sub rolls toward the airlock at the end of the cave. I double-check our pressure shields before the portal closes around us and water begins to pour in.

Then the lock opens, and Lea gasps in awe. I steer the sub forward, sneaking a glance at her face.

Looming dark in my periphery, the perimeter wall holds strong to keep large, dangerous sea creatures out. But the filters still allow tiny organisms like coral polyps through. And here in the shelter of our manmade cove, free of large predators, the smaller creatures are thriving.

Glowing branches of coral crisscross the base of a sheer underwater cliff. If we were to follow the rock face up to the surface, we'd run into the beach's designated swimming area. But swimmers aren't allowed this far down. The coral is lovely but sharp, and the tiny, jewel-bright piscines that live in the reef are known to bite.

It's a good thing that tourists don't know this undersea garden exists. We wouldn't be able to keep them away from a view like this.

I position the sub toward the best view of the reef and anchor us in place. Then I turn to Lea. "Well? Are you impressed yet?"

"Yeah," she says faintly. "It's...wow. I thought the beach was fantastic, but this..."

"If we hold really still, sometimes the waterweed will open its flowers." I point to the dark clumps clustered nearby. "It's shy, though. Won't do it unless there's no big predators around, and it's not smart enough to know that Fishy McFishface is a machine."

Lea snorts. "I still can't believe that's its real name."

She unstraps her safety belt and leans into my shoulder, sighing. I breathe in the floral scent of her hair.

"There's something I've been wanting to talk to you about," she says, sounding a little shy.

My breath catches. "Is this about Romeo?" I manage to say. I've been dreading The Talk for days now. *Sorry, Gaby, but Romeo and I are together now, and I have to stop seeing you—*

"No! Well, not directly. Though we should talk about that, too." Lea pulls away a little, folding her arms around herself. "He's been really helping me through all this. The vampire stuff. I don't think I could do it without him, and I...well, I *do* kind of...like him. But I really like you, too, Gaby. Is that all right? If we...keep things open right now?"

Part of me wants to say no. To demand her attention all to myself, or let me move on.

But move on to where? I've lived on Hades long enough to know all the local prospects way, way too well. The most I'd ever want from any of *them* is no-strings casual fun.

Lea is the first person I've met in a long time who makes me want more than that. And I'm not ready to shut the door on exploring that feeling.

"Yeah," I say finally. "We can be open for now. But can we talk about it again after a few months? I want to make sure we stay on the same page. Because this isn't casual for me, even if we see other people. I really like you, too. I'm serious about this." Ugh, I feel hot all over. This is so embarrassing to say out loud. "That is, if you are."

She nods, her eyes shining even as her cheeks flush. "On that note...I really think we should talk about what a future between us could look like."

"All right." My heart is suddenly racing. *I'm as nervous as a teenager.*

"Romeo told you about the parasite, didn't he? About...what it does to us?" She licks her lips. "So you know that I won't age. I might never die of natural causes. We don't really know for sure."

"He did mention that," I say. "Honestly, I get why Chief Han wants to keep the vampire disease a secret, if it does stuff like that. Can you imagine? People would be coming here trying to get infected, thinking it's the Fountain of Youth."

Lea shudders. "It comes with fine print, though. Not just the blood-drinking. I can't ever leave Hades. This place is my home now, whether I like it or not. And...if you ever wanted to leave...you'd have to understand that I can't go with you."

Ah. She's afraid all this is a deal-breaker. That I'd leave her behind, one way or another—either by going offplanet or by growing old and dying.

"Counterpoint." I reach for her hand. "What if I want to stay here? What if we give ourselves some time to see where it goes? If you decide you can't stand me, well, then, no hard feelings, I'll just get old and die. But if we really like each other, maybe enough to give forever a try..." I shrug, trying to sound casual as I say it. "You could turn me."

"*Infect* you?" Lea sounds horrified. "You'd want that?"

"It doesn't sound so bad. Other than the blood stuff." I squeeze her hand. "Hades is already my home. I don't have any family offworld, and no plans to leave. I'm not in a huge hurry to become a bloodsucker right now, but I won't say never."

She lifts her eyebrows like she doesn't really believe me. Honestly, I'm surprised how reluctant she seems about the whole thing. She did infect herself, after all.

"So, then, the other thing we have to consider is..." She gets all red in the face, biting her lip. "Romeo told me that body fluids can carry the parasite. It's harder to catch that way than by blood contact, but it could happen. If we...get intimate, I want you to know that going in. We can find ways to protect you."

"I'm not that worried," I say immediately. "I like a little danger. Gives it a bit of a naughty thrill."

She jerks her head up, blushing harder. "Gaby! I'm serious! This is literally life or death stuff!"

"Life stuff, maybe. Stuff that will change my life. I'm still not seeing where 'or death' comes into it."

"Well, what about biting, then?" Lea challenges me. "Do you want to be bitten? Because I'm going to be really careful and try not to get too hungry, but…I've already seen how easily accidents could happen. Romeo's teaching me stuff like how much blood we can take from a person without hurting them, but I'm terrified that I'd lose control and take too much from you."

I run my thumb over her cheek. "Oh, sweetheart. No, I don't really want to be bitten, but even if you did, I know you wouldn't kill me."

"You're so sure?" Moisture gathers on her lashes. "I wish I trusted myself the way you trust me."

Gently, I brush a kiss over her lips. "You've only been infected a week. Give it time."

She sucks in a breath and slides her hand around the back of my neck, pulling me in for a more thorough kiss.

My heart races as I lose myself to the sensation of her tongue stroking mine. Lea moans softly, ending on a slight whimper as she tries to pull me closer. Then she breaks off to catch her breath.

"Blast it," she mutters. "Romeo told me all my senses would be heightened, but I don't know how to stand being this turned on all the time!"

Her words send a spike of desire to my core. "How turned on all the time *are* you, exactly?"

"Ugh, it's like I'm on *fire*." She presses the back of her hand to one flushed cheek. "I'm trying not to make it everyone else's problem, but…"

Before I can stop myself, I'm climbing into the passenger seat to straddle her lap. "Want to make it my problem?"

Her chest heaves, like she's close to hyperventilating. "Gaby, fuck, yes, but are you sure? We literally just talked about…"

"So don't drink my blood, and I won't drink yours." I slide my hand up her thigh, lifting the fluttery little skirt she's wearing. She's got nothing but a thong underneath. "Too bad there's no room in this sub. The things I'd do to you if we had a bed…"

Lea covers her eyes. "Wait, we're in a sub with a huge glass window. Someone's going to see us!"

"We're too far down. No one's scheduled to do a dive today." I lean in and suck on the side of her neck, making her moan again. "And Fishy McFishface has easy-to-clean waterproof seats."

"Oh," she pants. "Well, if you think we won't get caught…"

Her hands find the waistband of my shorts and slide under to squeeze my ass. I catch her lips in another kiss, letting my fingers trail over her inner thigh to the hot, moist center.

Lea sighs into my mouth and spreads her thighs, allowing me a better angle as I rub her with my thumb. "I wish you could feel this like I do," she whispers between ragged breaths.

"Mmm. Heightened senses, you said?"

"Blazes, yes. It's almost torture." She moves her hand around my hip into the front of my shorts, and I buck involuntarily when she finds my clit.

I pause my circling thumb. "Should I stop torturing you, then?"

She whimpers. "Fuck, no. Stopping is worse."

So I keep up a steady pace, watching her writhe under me as I ride her hand. When she falls apart, her ecstatic cry fills me with a sort of triumphant pride at making someone so beautiful feel so good. It stokes my own building orgasm until I'm shaking and collapsing onto her.

"Look," Lea whispers, her lips brushing my cheek.

I turn my head in time to see the bright burst of color and light as a waterweed flower opens, its tendrils waving as it searches for microorganisms to feed on. The whole waterweed patch begins to bloom. They light up the ocean floor with stunning bioluminescence.

"I've never seen anything so gorgeous," Lea says softly. But when I look at her, she's looking at me.

We kiss again, slow and lazy. I should be getting us back to the dock before the sub is missed, but I selfishly draw out the moment, wanting it to last forever.

Sixth Episode

Chapter 18

ANGELIQUE

Two months later

I've never seen such bright stars. Monroe's light pollution was considerable, and every other area I've spent time in was touristy and well-lit. Including the Hades resort.

The first time I found myself outside the resort perimeter, I was way too stressed to look up. Romeo's trying to rewrite that experience for me with these little hiking dates outside the perimeter wall.

"Isn't it stunning?" he whispers in my ear. A pleasant shiver snakes down my spine. "Most resort guests will never see the planet this way."

"Because the jungle would probably kill them," I say dryly.

"Precisely." There's a note of laughter in his voice. "But you and I, Lea? The wildlife would have to work pretty hard to put us down."

"I mean, I'm not in any great hurry to get chewed on by a plant," I say. "The parasite didn't take my pain receptors."

"Solid point." Romeo laughs. "I've been foraging the wilds for so long, I've developed a sixth sense for detecting lure vines and predatory movements. You'll learn too."

"And then test my new running speed?"

"Fight or flight. One of the two." Romeo gives me a contemplative look. "I see you as a fighter."

He turns away before he sees my flattered smile.

We've just come through a thick stand of trees into a clearing. Laid out before us, shining with reflected starlight and luminescent blue algae, are a series of small pools.

"Springs," Romeo says. "Not volcanic, but they're definitely hot. The sun boils them during the day. At night, they cool down just enough for us to use them like hot tubs."

"Resort tourists would go feral for this!"

"Yeah, they would." He smirks. "So the rangers absolutely forbid us from showing people, or even hinting it exists. As I'm sure you can imagine, they already encounter the best and most creative idiocy that humanoid society has to offer."

I snort. Gaby said something similar, though she was a hair more diplomatic about it.

"Come on." Romeo starts pulling his black sleeveless top over his head. "What are you waiting for?"

"I—wait. You didn't tell me to dress for swimming." I have my beach booties on, but I wore plain shorts and a sleeveless top when I heard we were hiking.

"Sweetheart," says Romeo, his voice dipping low with a teasing lilt, "I would never recommend someone *dress* for swimming."

He peels his clothes off and wades into the pool, stepping down off a ledge to submerge up to his waist. I try to cover the sudden wave of shyness that brings heat to my cheeks as I strip out of my shorts. I hesitate at the unders before pulling off those, too. This doesn't feel like a seduction—and despite our rocky start, Romeo's always respected my boundaries. He won't pounce on me unless I want him to.

And, today at least, I'm feeling conflicted.

Romeo and I have hooked up a couple of times, but it was mostly in the heat of my transition. Now that the parasite has stabilized, I haven't made a move on him in a few weeks. He seems to be waiting for my cue.

The thing is, every time things get heated between me and Romeo, I feel a surge of guilt about Gaby. She hasn't pressured me about closing our relationship, but it's weird being torn in two directions. It feels like I'm putting distance between us that doesn't need to be there.

On top of that, there's all the implications of my new infection. Like the fact that if things don't work out with Romeo, he and I will still be stuck in the same resort forever. At least Gaby can leave—not that I want her to. But I'm haunted by the idea that I might infect her accidentally and take that choice away from her.

I take a deep breath. That mental spiral is for another day. The hot spring waits, invitingly steamy, for me to sink in and relax.

"Is it—safe?" I ask. "There's no fish that try to swim up your butthole or—?"

"Oh no," Romeo deadpans. "Those live in the inland lakes, not these little puddles. Fish need a lot more space to look for buttholes."

I shove his arm with my toe.

He throws his head back and laughs. "Get in here, will you?"

The water is scalding hot. I hiss through my teeth, yanking my foot back, then easing in again. My skin begins to acclimate as I sink deeper, encountering an underwater ledge that seems to drop off sharply to a much deeper pool.

"Careful," says Romeo. "There's a hole in the middle that goes down way over your head. Speaking from experience, you don't want to fall in."

"Hot water in your ears?"

"Mysterious grabby tentacles in the deep."

I can't tell if he's serious or not, and to be honest, I don't really want to know.

I sit down on the ledge, submerging myself up to the collarbones. It's a little weird putting my bare ass on algae-slimed rock, but I deliberately don't think about it too much.

Romeo settles onto the ledge next to me, close but not touching. He tilts his head back and takes in the sky with its dense scatter of stars. Shrill cries drift down from a flight of winged creatures soaring overhead. The jungle is alive with rustles and chirps and howls. Before becoming infected, it would have terrified me, being naked and barefoot among so much life that may or may not be hungry for humans. Now I'm slowly opening up to the beauty of it all.

It's starting to sink in that this place is my home for the rest of what could be a *very* long life. After the initial rush, the first eight weeks of my new vampire existence have been defined by grief for what I'll never see again. But now I'm beginning to imagine the possibilities of what I *could* have.

"Do you ever think about building another settlement?" I ask. "One that's not connected to the resort, just for us vampires to live in?"

"Oh, all the time," says Romeo. "There are some obstacles, though. One, we'd have to source blood from somewhere. A livestock herd, maybe—no, I'm not talking humans, don't worry. Other mammals taste just fine. We just can't rely on Hadesian wildlife unless we want endless indigestion."

Ah, yes, I remember him mentioning that. I'll have to avoid drinking from animals here. Shouldn't be hard; I'd have to catch one first. "What's the other problem?"

"The resort owner actually owns the whole planet. The Emperor named him governor. He doesn't do much in the way of governing—just sits back and collects the profits. But unfortunately, he has to approve any building projects on Hades, and he's refused any non-resort proposals made by us lifers. If we aren't actively making him money, he doesn't want a competing city."

I give a furious huff. "Typical. Isn't there anything we can do? Petition the Emperor?"

"The Emperor doesn't listen to anyone but his bootlickers." Romeo heaves a sigh. "We could try building something underground without him knowing, but it'd take a lot of coordination. We'd have to get the machinery here under the radar, hide the mess from any satellite scans, and we'd have to do a lot of the work—and fund the efforts—ourselves. Then we'd have to keep it a secret potentially forever. No uniweb access, no trade with the resort, and very limited traffic in and out. It'd be more of a prison than a community. Much as I'd love to make it happen, we're gonna need to get a different governor first."

"I guess all we have to do is wait, then," I say. "We'll outlive him eventually."

Romeo turns to grin at me, his teeth white in the darkness. "That's right," he says. "Now you're thinking like one of us."

ROMEO

It's scaring me how easy it is to like Lea.

Flirting comes naturally to me, always has, but I'm careful not to get attached to any of the tourists I seduce for blood. Spreading the parasite by accident is my worst nightmare.

But this situation has felt different from the start.

Lea's new, both to vampirism and to Hades, and I'm trying hard not to mistake novelty for irresistible allure. But the shine's not wearing off as I get to know her. Quite the opposite. As she comes out of her shell, no longer terrified of being attacked, I fall more under the spell of Angelique Azalea's star power.

(Yes, I searched her on the uniweb. Yes, I listened to every recording. Yes, I joined her fanclub forum. Yes, I've fallen asleep looking at photoshoots.)

I'm also gaining a fresh hatred for her asshole ex, may he rest in pieces. Now that the threat of him is gone, she's starting to smile like she did in pics from five years ago. Wearing her own face on stage is doing wonders for her confidence. She got a friend from Monroe to cargo-ship a trunk of her old performance costumes; watching her shimmy through a crowd in sparkling hot pink, her beautiful smile lighting up the room, puts a warm feeling in my chest that I think might be *pride*.

I'm not delusional enough to expect her to feel the same. I know she's already got something going on with Gaby. Besides, what do I have to offer to a Monroe celebrity? When boiled down to my essentials, I'm nothing but a literal leech, using botanical experimentation and meaningless flirting to spice up the monotony of my pointless immortal life. The only reason she hasn't told me to go pound sand yet is because I have a nice...face.

The other thing I can offer is my knowledge of Hades and my decades of experience as a vampire. So I'm selfishly using that as an excuse to spend time with her, knowing she'll eventually get bored. Part of me hoped that hooking up with her would get it out of my system, but my system hasn't got the message yet.

I watch her watching the night sky as we walk back toward the resort. The moons above us shine bright, with a scattering of stars behind them. Seeing her experience this planet for the first time makes me appreciate it anew.

"Dance with me," I say on impulse.

She turns to me with a surprised laugh. "What, right now?"

"Why not?"

"Well, all right then," she says, taking my outstretched hand and spinning into my embrace.

The distant howls of nightbirds are our only music as I lead her into a shimmying, swaying dance I learned back when the resort used to offer lessons. She's a great dancer—of course she is—and follows my lead effortlessly, adding her own flair to the movements.

I spin us away from the reaching grasp of a lure vine and see the lump on the ground just in time to lift Lea away from it. She senses my sudden shift and looks down. "What is that?"

And then she gasps, because what it *is* is a dead animal.

Specifically, it's a spiger, a six-legged, many-eyed, furry, warm-blooded land creature that mainly hunts birds and simian tree-dwellers. Running across one in the wild can be a tense moment. Humans aren't their normal prey, but they'll attack if threatened.

This one's got an obvious bite wound on its throat.

I crouch, ignoring the cooked, rotting smell that tells me this thing's been dead at least a full day-night cycle. The spiger doesn't have many natural predators. Anything that could prey on something of its size wouldn't leave a body this intact. A tree would swallow it whole; an avian hunter would carry it away to a nest; if a pack of smaller creatures took it down, they'd tear it to pieces. This body is pristine other than the neck wound and a certain gaunt, deflated look that I've come to associate with exsanguination.

"That bite mark came from a human mouth," I say softly.

Lea has her hand over her mouth, possibly trying not to be sick. "I thought you said that wild animals give us stomachaches."

"They do," I say. "I can ask around, but I highly doubt one of the Midnights made this kill. They know better than to leave evidence. If we kill wildlife, we feed the body to a lure vine."

Having said so, I grab the creature by one of its paws and start dragging it back to the lure vine we just avoided.

Lea watches me, still looking a bit nauseated. "But if it wasn't the Midnights, who else comes out here?"

"Officially, nobody." As the lure vine quests toward me, I back away and let it begin the process of scooping up the spiger corpse. "Unofficially, there are at least a few dozen infected people who are employees of the resort. Most of them have moral objections to taking blood from tourists, so they're on the med center ration. Maybe one of them got hungry enough to come out here and…supplement." I wipe my hands on a patch of moss. I kinda want to take Lea's hand again, but touching a dead animal ruined the moment. "It shouldn't be a problem if they do it discreetly, but I should let the Chief Ranger know. She doesn't like it when people sneak out."

"What about us?" Lea asks.

I laugh. "Oh, she'll be flared off that we were out of bounds, too. But I don't answer to her."

We're close to the hidden entrance to the network of lava tubes that leads back to the Midnights' cave. As we step out of the cover of the trees, Lea takes one last look up at the sky and gasps.

She catches my arm and points up. "What's that?"

A huge shadow blots out two of the moons at once. My heart starts to pound.

"That's a behemoth." And it's going for the beach, which at this hour is no doubt teeming with tourists. "Run for the tunnels. I'll be right behind you."

GABRIELLE

I'm hiking in the jungle with Romeo,> Lea messages. <*Be back before dawn.*>

I click off my keycuff, dismissing the messages with annoyed finality. So they're off together again. Fine. Cool. I wouldn't want to take casual trips out to the wilds anyway. That's a recipe for getting eaten.

Or, apparently, vampirism.

My mood stays foul through the rest of the night's patrol. There are a bunch of new arrivals getting drunk and causing problems, like shoving each other into burning hot sand, or (for indiscernible reasons) trying to roll and smoke one of the bioluminescent mushrooms illuminating the walkway. By the time we're doing the final-hour rove, my tolerance for unsafe behavior and general dumbassery is at an all-time low.

And that, of course, is when the breach alarm sounds.

"Ugh, what *now*?" bursts out of my mouth, but I'm already making eye contact with the other rangers, searching their body language for an indication of where the threat is.

They're all looking up.

I tilt my head back in time to see an enormous shadow cross in front of the moons. My mouth goes dry. There've never been any confirmed sightings of this mega-avian predator, just rumors. We call them *behemoths*, but no one's ever given them a scientific name. They're basically cryptids. That means we have almost zero reliable data on their behavior.

Also, they're fucking *huge*. If this creature's wingspan was a beach umbrella, we'd only need two for this entire beach.

My mopey mood evaporates, replaced with sheer adrenaline. "Everyone get below," I yell, flapping my arms at a couple of dumbstruck tourists gaping at the sky. "Go! Now!"

I'm not far behind them. A creature the size of a mass transport starship isn't something even a ranger has the ability to handle. Once we herd the guests below, our protocol for this threat level is to get down there after them like our asses are on fire.

I yell at a slow-moving couple to ditch their beach towels and cocktails. "What part of emergency do you not understand?"

They're still straggling behind the rest of the crowd. The hulking shape dips lower, thin segmented limbs like bug legs beginning to extrude from its belly.

"RUN!" I yell at the guests, falling back to cover their asses. If they get me killed, I'm suing.

I crack off a couple of shots into the sky. Although the blasts hit the behemoth's belly, they do fuck-all against its thick feathered hide. It's still coming on fast, and now its creepy spindle legs are aimed directly at me as it swoops—

A distant, high-pitched shrieking shatters the air.

I wince and close my eyes, bracing for pain. But all I feel is the sharp whoosh of air as something narrowly misses me. I stagger and fall backward, my eyes flying open.

The behemoth has apparently lost interest in the beach and is turning inland, gaining altitude again. Heading for something beyond the wall. *Stars, tell me it doesn't have a mate.*

I scramble to my feet and sprint the last few meters to get below. The rest of the rangers follow me down. Someone slams a fist against the lockdown button that seals the hatch.

"Beach is closed for the day, folks," my colleague Bree announces, cupping her hands around her mouth to be heard over the nervous murmur of the milling crowd. "I recommend the Underworld Lounge for some quality entertainment. The rangers will notify you when it's safe to go topside again."

There's a general groan of disappointment, but it doesn't take a lot of convincing when almost everyone saw the behemoth's arrival.

Once the tourists have dispersed, my fellow rangers and I huddle up to decide our next move. We'll have to rely on air traffic control to track the creature's movements. Bree and Jason head to the control tower to monitor in person because they don't trust the bots, leaving the rest of us to complete our patrol shifts below ground.

As soon as I'm sure nobody's watching, I change direction and head for the Midnights' tunnels. They have some secret exit into the wilds, and that's most likely where Lea and Romeo will return—if they return.

No, *when*. They're both smart enough to avoid a giant bird. The jungle's abundant flora will have provided them ample cover to keep safe.

I hope.

It kills me to admit it, but even though Romeo has been my longtime rival and is handily stealing the affections of the woman I want for myself, I don't actually want him dead. Now that I'm certain he isn't behind the disappearances of Hades tourists, we've built a flimsy bridge of trust, with Lea's well-being as its main support. That's one thing we can both agree on: we care about Lea and want her safe.

And I guess he's not so bad, either. Maybe. Ugh.

The vampires obviously hear me coming, because when I stumble out of the dark cavern maze into their community gathering area, a handful of them are already there waiting for me. I recognize two: the man called Benito and the woman I've heard Romeo refer to as Jules. They're the ones who helped me to the med center after I was exposed to the sunrise.

"Where's Romeo?" I ask immediately.

Benito has his feet up on an empty crate. He smirks at me and says, in a mock high-pitched tone, "Hello, Beni, how are you?" Then, switching to his regular voice, "Yeah, I'm all right, you?" And back to the voice I'm assuming he's using to imitate me: "Well, the stick up my ass is getting a little bendy these days, but it's still there."

"I'm not interested in small talk," I snap. "Is Romeo back or not?"

"Clearly," says Benito, still smirking. "And no, he's not. He and your girlfriend went out exploring hours ago. He was gonna show her the hot springs, if you know what I mean."

He's trying to push my buttons. I refuse to give him the satisfaction of a response. "Listen, asshole, this is serious. There was a breach alarm a few minutes ago. A fucking behemoth almost swooped up a couple of people." *Me included.* "So excuse me if I'm a little worried about my friends."

"Oh, *friends*? 'Cause I thought—"

"Beni, cut it out." The voice that interrupts Benito's drawl is deep and familiar.

A faint thrill runs down my spine as I turn toward a side tunnel and see Romeo and Lea there standing side by side. They look sweaty but unhurt. Relief floods through me.

"Just givin' Miz Ranger a hard time, boss." Benito grins unrepentantly.

"We've been trying to message you, Gaby. Didn't you see it?" Lea says.

I check my keycuff, then remember I muted my messages in a fit of jealousy. "I was...uh...busy."

"We saw the behemoth coming for the beach," Lea says. "Romeo was amazing. He knows how to imitate their mating call."

My eyebrows shoot up. "That shrieking sound—that was you?"

Romeo gives a little bow.

I'm not going to tell him he saved my life, because I don't want him holding that over my head. But I'm filled with a grudging respect for a man who took the risk of calling the creature's attention to himself to divert it from innocent tourists. It wasn't only my life he saved. Dozens of beachgoers could have been eaten if he hadn't distracted it.

Is it possible I might be a little too harsh on him?

But then he casually puts an arm around Lea, and now I'm right back to hating his guts. "Did you have something you wanted to talk about?" he asks.

I deflate. "Just wanted to make sure you two didn't get eaten. You're alive and well, so...I'll go."

I spin on my heel and stride into the dim tunnel, willing myself not to trip on the uneven ground.

"Gaby, wait," Lea calls after me. But I don't turn around.

Chapter 19

ANGELIQUE

My Underworld performance that night is packed, but the crowd is restless. I guess I can't blame them; no one pays for a room in a luxury resort only to stay cooped up underground. A couple of fights almost break out over table space.

Luckily, the Midnights are there, smoothly interrupting the belligerents and redirecting their attention. As I croon a down-tempo cover of a popular musical number, I watch Romeo tap a teeth-baring, fist-shaking saurian man on the shoulder and murmur something in his ear-hole. The saurian looks startled, then adjusts his swim top and strides over to a sleek, red-scaled saurian woman at the bar. I have to swallow a grin as I watch it play out. Romeo clearly used his mind-bending power to suggest that the man's time would be better spent picking up women rather than picking fights. *Smooth—and effective.* By the end of the song, the two lizard-humanoids are laughing together, and the man's buying the woman another drink. The dispute with the other tourist has been forgotten.

I catch Romeo's eye across the crowded room. He's drinking a glowing purple cocktail, which he lifts in a toast to me. This time, I can't hide my smile, which is inconvenient when I'm trying to sing a melancholy song.

I'm just winding down the show, ending on a wistful but hopeful oldie that's always a guaranteed crowd pleaser, when movement in the doorway catches my eye. I look up and am startled to see four soldiers in red jackets have just entered the lounge, to the not-entirely-hidden consternation of several guests. Hades being an Authority-free zone makes it a popular vacation destination for people who aren't strictly operating within the confines of the law.

Not to say everyone on Hades is a crime lord—but a non-zero number of these tourists probably are.

I glance over to where the Midnights were sitting, looking for Romeo's reaction, but he and his crew have already managed to disappear. I imagine they're none too pleased about this development.

I take my bows, say good night, and run offstage to call Gaby and ask if she knows anything.

She doesn't take my call.

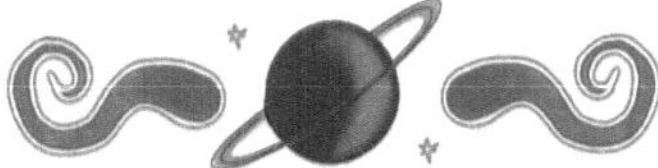

GABRIELLE

C hief Ranger Han is fuming. I've worked with her long enough to see the signs, although I'm pretty sure the Authorities currently standing in her office can't tell. The flat mouth, stiff posture, and overly formal tone of speech are plausibly deniable as professionalism.

The other three rangers chosen to join her during this interview stand against the wall with me, watching her clasp the lead Authority's hand in a firm shake. "Chief Ranger Korrie Han, at your service," she says. "It's an honor, Captain...?"

"Penn," the lead Authority says. "Captain Jothan Penn. Pleased to finally be here. My wife's been bothering me to take a vacation here for years. After our business is concluded, maybe I'll fly her and the kids out."

"Business. Yes," says Chief Han. "Unfortunately, we were not briefed before your arrival. How can my team assist you?"

"Well..." Captain Penn scratches his ruddy beard. "We've had a few reports. Disappearances. Attacks. Individually, they seemed like things your team could handle, so we've remained hands-off for a number of years. But it does unfortunately seem to be an ongoing pattern. After the latest report, it was decided that an official safety review of your operation was in order."

Chief Han's face remains perfectly blank and composed. If I was on the receiving end of that stare, I'd be shitting my shorts and wishing I'd updated my will.

"I'm happy to show you through our incident response records," she says after a long pause. "You'll find, I hope, that we handled each of them in keeping with Imperial legal standards, despite not receiving any official government support. We take guests' safety very seriously."

"I'd appreciate that, to start with," says Captain Penn. "My team will also be touring your various facilities over the next few days and observing operations. If there are any concerns, I'll bring them to your attention immediately. I'm sure you'll be eager to rectify any oversights. None of us want this facility shut down."

"Absolutely, sir. On that, we can agree." Chief Han wakes her wallscreen and begins logging into the confidential records archive. "Rangers Lopez, Barnes, Germaine, and Qureshi, return to your duties. I'll call if we need assistance."

As I bow, I note the slight tremor in the hand that types her passcode. Our boss is worried. And with good reason. The records she's about to show Captain Penn may not mention vampires in so many words, but the pattern of attacks will paint a very clear picture. I know, because up until a few months ago, I myself thought the Hades resort housed some kind of elusive monster savaging people from the shadows. Or a serial killer with a penchant for exsanguination.

Now that I know the truth, I understand why it would be disastrous for the Authorities to learn it, too.

Hades would be abandoned. The parasite would be deemed a dangerous life form, much too pervasive to be eradicated. Every last uninfected human would be evacuated, the resort shut down.

And the vampires? *Lea?*

They'd be left behind. Probably with no supplies. Quite possibly slapped with a ban on supply ships landing to bring them aid. They'd be marooned, their potentially eternal lives spent in total estrangement from humanity.

Now that I know them, I can't watch it happen and still sleep at night. I doubt Chief Han will, either.

But the misdirection and stonewalling that worked on me, her subordinate, isn't guaranteed to work on an Imperial Authority. They're bound to stumble across something that leads them to the truth, and when they do, the whole resort is in danger.

Including—perhaps *especially*—Romeo and Lea.

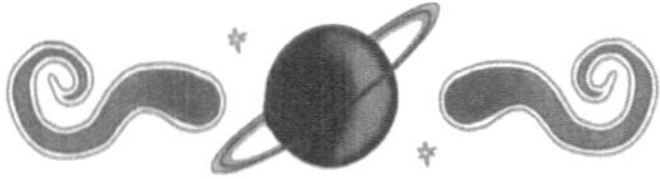

ROMEO

Benito is swearing a blue streak, threatening to pack his shit and light out for the wilds. Julia keeps trying to calm him down, but she's freaked, too. The whole gang is. I can't blame them.

This is exactly what we've feared for so long. If the Authorities figure out we exist and what we are, the next step is them trying to eradicate us.

I *can't* let it happen, and that's what I'm trying to say to reassure everyone. But I'm not sure any of them can hear me over all their shouting.

What's more, while I can promise I'll fight to protect them, I can't swear I'll be successful. Dealing with the Imperial Authorities is a whole different flyball game to dealing with the rangers. There were infected people joining the rangers from the start, shaping their policies to create careful loopholes that carved out space for us to exist in the resort's fringes. Chief Han put in the work to rise up the ranks, and now the rangers are controlled by a vampire. Chief Han and the Midnights aren't exactly buddy-buddy, but I know she'll do everything she can to keep our secret. It's her neck on the line as well as ours.

The Authorities have no such tie to us. They also have expensive tech, top-tier military training, a practically infinite budget, and won't hesitate to kill us all if it means containing a contagious infection.

The worst of it is, we vampires can't even flee the planet. We live or die here, on the black sands of Hades.

"Can everybody just calm down a second?" Mercedes bellows. "Romeo's trying to say something!"

They all gradually fall silent and turn to look at me. My blood feels like it's turned to syrup, my pulse throbbing thick against my throat.

Be a leader.

I take a deep breath and say, "Everyone is to stay out of the main resort until further notice. Greg and Nan, you two go block up the entrance to this tunnel. We're going to put a round-the-clock guard on it. If any other vamps come looking for sanctuary, we let 'em in, but carefully. If they're being followed, we go full lockdown. I'd rather one person gets caught than all of us."

I hesitate before continuing. This next part is going to be unpopular, but it has to be said. "Strictly no—and I mean absolutely NO—feeding from humans while the Authorities are here."

Several cries of protest. Nan says, "Where are we supposed to get food from, if not from the hospital and not from the tourists?"

I grimace. "Hate to tell you this, friends, but I think we're going to be hunting wild for a week or two."

The whole gang pulls a face en masse. "Romeo, no," Vi protests. "I got the worst burning shits last time—!"

"I know, I know, I know!" I yell over the rumble of dissent. "I've been experimenting with a couple of herbal supplements that should cut down on the bellyache. I'll hand those out later today. I'm aware that wild blood comes with teeth and claws a lot of the time, so everyone hunt with a partner for safety. Hopefully, this is going to be a week, two max, before the Authorities get bored and leave."

"What if it isn't?" Benito asks, his voice quiet and flat. "What if they post a permanent guard here?"

"Then we'll start making alternative plans," I say. "Listen, Midnights. We joined together because we all realize our normal human lives are over. We wanted to take our second life on our own terms without crumpling ourselves up to fit in the resort's box. I'm not about to give up what we've built for ourselves just because a couple of redjackets got bored and decided to take a leisurely few weeks toasting their buns on the beach while calling it an investigation. If they won't leave, we'll fuckin' *chase them off*. And that's a promise."

"Blazin' right," says Greg, punching a fist in the air. "This is *our* planet."

I pump my fist right back at him, even though a cold pit in my stomach reminds me that it *isn't* our planet, not really. And until we change that, we'll never be truly safe.

Seventh Episode

Chapter 20

ANGELIQUE

I 'd been hoping the Authorities were just passing through, but here they are again in the Underworld lounge for my morning show. It's hard to miss them; they're conspicuous in their bright-red jackets and full-length trousers amongst a crowd of bikini-clad beachgoers.

The rangers announced at sunset that the behemoth has been observed winging its way back toward the southern mountains. They're using some kind of satellite data to track it, but as long as it doesn't turn around, they're allowing use of the beach again. Thank stars for small favors. With the Authorities sniffing around and the subterranean resort packed with cooped-up tourists, this place was starting to feel like a pressure cooker.

Romeo and Gaby both messaged me last night. Romeo said he's sequestering the Midnights in their cave, and Gaby said she's going to be busy with ranger business all day—which I took to mean she's got to babysit the Authorities and make sure they don't see anything.

When I visited the med center for my blood ration, the healers made me consume the whole thing in a storage closet with the lights off. "Chief Ranger's orders," they said. I can guess why. Everyone's walking on eggshells, worried that something they do will call Imperial wrath down on the entire resort.

That includes me. I'd rather not be the one who blows it for everyone else. But with Gaby and Romeo variously occupied, I'll go stir crazy if I don't do *something* to help.

So, after I get offstage, I go into the locker room and change into a bikini top that accentuates my assets, with a flowing, nearly-transparent skirt to cover the bottom half. And I do something I don't normally do: I exit into the lounge itself, chatting and waving and accepting photo requests.

Now that I'm out of hiding, various reporters have "coincidentally" arrived to vacation on Hades, hoping to scoop an interview about what I've been doing for the past two years. I've been declining these requests gently but firmly. Maybe a time will come when I'm ready to tell the story of what Jude did to me, but it's going to be *very* far in the future.

I'm not opposed to interacting with fans, but it's been jarring to try to fit back into my persona from before I disappeared. I'm not that Angelique anymore. She was carefree, flirtatious, daring, a bit conceited, a ton of fun. Me? I'm...well, I *want* to be all of that. But all the fearful solitude has turned me more cautious and introspective. I have a lot of healing to do before I'll be the Angelique Azalea who sparkled at parties and flitted from lover to lover like a butterfly.

Maybe I'll never be her again.

Still, I make my best effort as I work my way through the lounge, pausing to sign a fan's collarbone in lipstick and make kissy faces with a trio of teen girls. In the old days, this would've been mindless fun for me.

Today, it's purposeful.

I weave ever closer to the Authorities, who are just about to finish their second cups of coffee. Just before they rise to go, I "accidentally" stumble and catch myself on the edge of their table, jostling their plates. One soldier's coffee cup tips and spills. There's only dregs left in it, but a few drops still make it onto his pristine red jacket.

"I am *so* sorry," I exclaim. "Clumsy me! Excuse me, server? We need a cleanup here!"

The serving bot whisks over to spot-clean the soldier's jacket, while I help mop up the spill. As I do so, I make small talk, asking them if they enjoyed my show, wondering if they'd heard of me from Monroe. Only one of them admits it.

"What brought you here, if I may ask, Miz Azalea?" he asks.

"Oh, me? Well, things were just getting a little intense over on Monroe, you know? A little too much of the spotlight!" I affect a high-pitched giggle. "I missed the days when I would perform in bars and lounges where no one knew my name, just the quality of my music. So I went on a little incognito tour of the galaxy, and turns out I liked it here the most!"

"You like it here?" The soldier looks dubious. "We saw that safety brochure. The dangers are…significant."

Ha! If only he knew. I roll my eyes and toss a hand carelessly. "Nothing the rangers can't handle. Why, just yesterday, a huge bird came swooping down over the beach…but not a single person was hurt! They got us all down into the resort so quickly, you'd think it happens every day!" I flash them a winning grin. "Lucky thing it doesn't, hmm? I've been here a few months, and I've only heard of two wildlife incursions. And of course they're very careful about clearing the beach before sunrise. Wouldn't want anyone to get sunburned."

"Sunburn. That's one word for it," the soldier snorts.

I hold out my hand to him. "I'm Angelique. What's your name, sir?"

He takes it and bows. "Etric. And these are my colleagues, Jorge and Stieg."

"A pleasure to meet you." I bow back. "If you don't mind some advice…" I drop my voice. "It's far too warm for those jackets. I'd get a swim set if I were you. Wouldn't want you to spend your vacation sweating!"

"We're working, actually," says Etric. "Investigating. There've been some safety concerns with the resort. Our captain will make sure it's all seen to, but in the meantime, you'll see us around."

"Oh, wonderful!" I paste on a grin. "For a few days? A week?"

"We aren't sure," says Jorge. "It could be longer, depending on how many, ah, *concerns* there are."

"Well, feel free to stop by the lounge anytime!" It's becoming a strain to keep my voice bright and cheery. *Longer than a week? How will Romeo's people get fed?*

"Wait. One more thing," Etric says, seizing my hand again. "The informant who tipped us off about this place mentioned some strange...*paranormal* happenings here. Monster attacks, but *inside* the resort where there aren't any wild animals. Have you ever seen anything like that?"

I shake my head, my heart pounding. "Paranormal?" I let out a high-pitched giggle. "Are you sure that someone didn't patch a few too many mind-alts while they were enjoying themselves on the beach?"

Who alerted the Authorities? The Midnights and the rangers each have vested interest in the Authorities ignoring them. So it had to have been a tourist—some bystander who saw too much, just like I did when I first arrived.

"Well, if you ever do see anything strange, let us know right away," says Steig. "That guy's report read like a holo-drama episode, but he seemed way too articulate to be patching."

"Was it even a local?" I ask. "You'd be better off asking someone who lives here. They see more than any tourist." *And are all compelled to lie about it.*

"Not sure. The weird thing is...his location pinged outside the resort. But that had to have been a mistake." Etric laughs. "No way this Judah Andrews guy was hanging out in the wild jungle. That'd be a death sentence."

My blood turns to ice.

"When did you say you got this call?" I choke out.

"Oh, about a week ago..."

Long after Jude was supposed to be dead.

Maybe they were wrong. Maybe he'd sent it before that tree ate him, and the soldiers are misremembering the timeline or the message somehow skipped a few uniweb syncs. That *has* to be it, right? Because if not...

Then Jude's still alive.

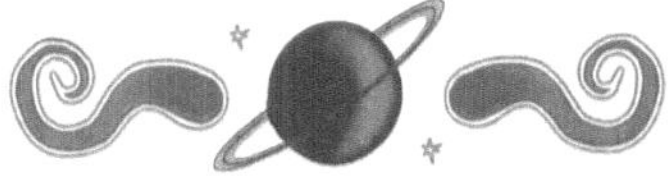

GABRIELLE

"Ranger Lopez. May I have a moment of your time?"

I lower my thermal-vision binoculars and look down from my perch atop the lifeguard stand.

Blast it, it's Captain Penn. The one person I can't reasonably say no to, even if I'm literally in the middle of a lifeguard shift.

Faking a cheery smile, I say, "Happy to, sir, if you can grab one of my colleagues to cover the stand for me." Better the request comes from him than me; my fellow rangers would rib me for shirking a job that we all consider simultaneously stressful and boring.

The captain comes back a moment later with Barnes, who raises her eyebrows at me behind Penn's back. I don't dare make a face in reply, so I just climb down from the stand and pass off the thermal binocs. "Be right back," I assure her, even though I have no idea how long Penn is going to monopolize me.

I follow the captain to a corner of the beach right next to the perimeter wall, out of earshot of any tourists. He pulls up a couple of beach loungers and offers me a seat.

"Thanks, but I prefer to stand while on duty," I say. It's not strictly true—I was literally just sitting on the lifeguard stand—but I don't want to get too comfy. Whatever Penn wants, I need to keep my wits alive and answer carefully.

"Suit yourself." Penn stretches out on the lounger. He has to be boiling in that Imperial uniform; the man hasn't even taken his jacket off. "I've been going over things with your Chief Ranger, and your name came up," he says.

"Oh?" is all I can manage.

"Don't worry, nothing bad." Penn waves a hand jovially. "Quite the contrary. One of your colleagues mentioned in passing that you'd taken a personal interest in investigating what you perceived to be a pattern of disappearances here on Hades. Is that true?"

Shit. Shit, shit, shit. "Yes, sir," I reply.

"And?" He tilts his head up at me. "Did you find anything?"

"Not so far, sir. For a time, I thought maybe we had a resident wild animal, something really good at hiding. But I've searched the place high and low. Nothing."

"I had a similar thought when I read through the incidents," says Captain Penn. He gives me a look I might describe as *approval*. "What are your other ideas, then? Tell me how far you've gotten."

I swallow. "Well, sir, there's the possibility we might have a serial killer. But..."

"But?"

"It'd have to be someone who lives here all the time. Or a regular who vacations here often. There's no pattern to the incidents, except that there were a lot of them right when the resort opened, and then a cluster about eight years back. Otherwise, they're spaced out randomly and usually months or even years apart."

"Question is..." Captain Penn snaps his fingers. "What happened at the beginning, and then again eight years ago?"

I'll admit, that had been a focus of my investigation. Romeo told me a lot about the founding of the resort while Lea was in the hospital, but I still haven't worked up the courage to ask what the fuck was going on during the second wave of attacks. Back in 3720, a year before I came to the resort, a series of bodies were found ripped apart. Young women, all of them, and mostly tourists. After about three months of utter terror, during which tourism to Hades dropped drastically enough that the newsies picked it up and the governor threatened to close the resort, the attacks stopped abruptly. Then it was back to the occasional report of a disappearance or two.

I think it's past time Romeo came clean about it. Because I'm almost certain Chief Han knows the truth of what was happening back then. If Penn's resorting to pumping me for conspiracy theories, then she must be stonewalling the blazes out of him. Which means it was serious enough to spell disaster if I accidentally trip into helping Captain Penn solve it.

"Wish I knew, sir," I say, hands on hips. "The trail went cold right after the second murder spree. Usually, an escalation like that, there's no coming back from. I'm guessing either the perpetrator left to terrorize another planet, or…"

"Or they're dead?" Penn suggests.

"Or that." I shrug. "Can't lie, I hope that's it. Even if it means we never know the truth, I'd hate to think they're still out there somewhere."

"I can't let this case rest until I confirm it," says Penn. "It was seven years between the initial flurry of disappearances and the second bloodbath. If that's a pattern, and the killer's still out there, then we've just come due for another escalation."

A chill runs down my spine, despite the oppressive humidity.

Yeah, I *definitely* need to talk to Romeo.

Chapter 21

I need to talk to you.>

I send the message to both Romeo and Gaby. Normally, I'd be spending my off hours on the beach, but I've locked myself in my room as I try to breathe through an oncoming panic attack. It's been threatening to consume me since I talked to the Authorities earlier.

And both Gaby and Romeo have been blowing me off all day. I'm guessing the arrival of the Authorities rattled them both, but I can't help but feel a little hurt that they haven't responded to my messages. It's not as though I'm officially dating either of them, but them leaving me on read is unusual.

This time, however, I'm relieved to hear the chimes of responses arriving—two in quick succession.

Gaby: *<Have you heard from Romeo? I think we all need to talk.>*

Romeo: *<We should discuss safety measures while the Authorities are here. Can you come to the Midnights' cave? Make sure you aren't followed.>*

I shoot back another message to Romeo, asking if I can bring Gaby. When he agrees, I reply to Gaby's message and ask when she'll be off duty.

A few hours later, we meet up outside Underworld. She's changed from her ranger gear into a pair of loose shorts and a tight, cropped halter top.

She's ponytailed the front section of her chin-length hair at the crown of her head, giving her style a cute, youthful twist.

I smile, but her face stays grim.

"What's wrong?" I blurt, before mentally kicking myself. "Never mind. I have a couple of guesses."

"If one of them wears a red jacket, you'd be correct," Gaby says in a low voice. "Come on. Let's not talk here."

I hold out my hand, and she takes it, though I get the sense it's more because it makes us look like an innocent pair of tourists on a date than because she wants to hold hands right now. Mindful of Romeo's warning, I lead us at a wandering pace along the touristy shops and eateries, avoiding the corridor leading to the Midnights' hideout. It's obvious that Gaby is getting annoyed with the meandering, but I wouldn't put it past the Authorities to have plainclothes spies among the tourists right now.

Eventually, I steer us down the right corridor, getting touchy and giggly as if we're looking for a place to hide and make out. I stop a couple of times, listening carefully for footsteps behind us, but the KEEP OUT signs are doing their job. At last, we're free to find the crevice in the wall that leads to Romeo's cave.

It looks different now. If I hadn't squeezed through that seemingly blank stretch of wall a dozen times by now, I might not have been able to find it. Someone's built up a blind wall to partially seal the crack, making it look like a dead end until I'm already most of the way inside.

A sharp voice says from the shadows, "Who's there?"

I jump. "It's me. Angelique. Lea. I brought Gaby, uh, Ranger Lopez with me. Romeo asked us to come."

A torchlight flicks on, illuminating first my face, then the speaker's. It's Nan, one of the Midnights. "Were you followed?"

"I don't think so."

She gestures ahead with the beam of the torchlight. "Go on, then."

I drop Gaby's hand, but keep pace with her as we make our way into the maze of caves. Quietly, I say, "Sorry we had to take the scenic route to get here."

"I get it. You don't want the redjackets following." Gaby brushes a hand across my back. "I'm sorry, too. I'm just in a bad mood from my interview with Captain Penn. Seems like he's already figured out Chief Han isn't telling him everything, and he thought he'd try me. I'm scared I'll tell him the wrong thing and blow your cover." She sighs. "Romeo can help us both get our stories straight."

"Thank stars," I say. "I was worried you were angry at me for hanging out with him too much."

Her mouth twists wryly. "Maybe I was a bit jealous. I'm trying not to dwell on it."

I want to tell her she has nothing to worry about—I *really* like her—but the thing is, I like Romeo too. They're completely different people, and maybe that's why I can't choose. I'd struggle to commit to *only* eating pizza or *only* eating ice cream for the rest of my life, because who the fuck makes that an either/or choice? They're both glorious, and I love them equally for different reasons.

Not that I'm using the L word yet.

And pizza and ice cream can't get jealous of each other when I take too long to decide what to snack on.

Ugh.

As we approach the Midnights' lair, I hear a low rumble of voices echoing off the cave walls. "Romeo?" I call out, not wanting to startle them. "It's Lea. Gaby's with me."

"Come join us!" yells back a voice that I recognize as Benito's.

We round the corner and find the Midnights gathered in their makeshift lounge. Romeo's there, but he's squinting at the scroll unfurled on his lap, clearly distracted.

I make my way over and perch on the crate next to his. Gaby shadows me but remains on her feet. She still seems uncomfortable among the Midnights, who, judging by their sidelong glances, are equally wary of her. I wish I had the confidence to assure her they're all harmless, but trusting Romeo doesn't mean I can say the same about his entire posse. Vi still gives me the creeps.

Romeo looks up from his scroll, and I see that he's been messaging a name I don't recognize. From a quick glance before I politely avert my eyes, it looks like he's trying to reassure them to keep their head down and wait for the Authorities to leave.

If only that was our biggest problem.

"Hey, Lea," he says, forcing a smile. His tired eyes tell me he hasn't been sleeping. "Gaby."

Gaby finally gives in and sits on the crate next to me so she can look Romeo in the eye. "What happened eight years ago?"

Romeo blinks. "Excuse me?"

"Captain Penn has zeroed in on the spike in attacks happening right when this resort opened, and then again eight years ago. I assume the ones at the beginning were you all figuring out what you were and how to control it. So what about the second wave of attacks?"

Before Romeo can answer, Julia speaks up. The rest of the Midnights have fallen silent listening in, so the word falls loud in the heavy silence. "Wright," she says.

The other women in the group hiss through their teeth, as if she's uttered a vile curse.

"Tell me," Gaby says, her voice low but loud enough to echo through the suddenly silent gathering. "Because I'm trying to keep your secrets, but I can't misdirect the captain if I don't know what to steer him away from."

Romeo rubs his forehead. "It's more the women's story than mine. They were the ones who took care of him."

Gaby transfers her attention to Julia. "Took care of who?"

Julia's knee bounces as she twists her hands in her lap. "He never should have been turned. It was a mistake."

Inez jumps in. "He came here as a tourist. Somehow he found out about us—I think maybe Francine bit him and forgot to wipe his memory. Or tried and failed. Either way, once he knew, he started flirting his way into the Midnights' circle. At one point, about four of us thought we were dating him. He wanted to be turned. Most of us refused, but I guess he finally got exposed to our blood somehow. Might've been Francine, but she's not alive to defend herself, so we don't like to assume." She shakes her head. "Once he was a vampire...the mask fell. He said he preferred to hunt alone and left the group."

"Then the bodies started piling up." Julia's voice shakes. "He was using compulsion to lure women and do...who knows what to them, before leaving their bodies ripped apart in very findable places. It was a power trip to him. We assume he'd always had the urges to hurt people, but once he was infected, he thought he could get away with it."

Mercedes jumps in. "He thought wrong. The Midnights' women he'd tricked got together and trapped him. Once we had him restrained, we dismembered him and fed each piece to a different tree in the forest. That's as close to dead as you can get, for a vampire." She grins savagely. "Me, I hope those scattered bits of him are still conscious, being slowly digested. It'd serve the bastard right for all the pain he inflicted on innocent women."

My stomach churns. "Um...in possibly relevant news..."

Romeo's eyes find mine. "What, Lea? You look like you've seen a ghost."

"Maybe I have," I mutter. "I talked to some of the Authorities in the Underworld today. They said Jude's the one who called them in. He's...maybe still alive?" I squeeze my eyes shut. "I guess feeding someone to a tree doesn't always kill them."

Shocked silence all around. It's broken by Julia getting up and running into the network of cave rooms, a sob echoing in her wake.

"Stars, I hope you're wrong, Lea," says Benito grimly. "You've just giv-
en Julia nightmares for fucking weeks. Wright was the one who turned
her—she was the survivor of his last attack."

He follows his partner into the maze.

Romeo exhales loudly. "Well, this just makes a bad situation worse,
doesn't it? For the record, though, Wright's definitely one hundred percent
dead. If he could have come back, he would've before now. So I don't want
to hear anyone spreading rumors that *he's* alive, *got it?*"

That's for the benefit of the other Midnights still listening, not me,
although I feel the sting of it. I didn't mean to reopen an old wound for
them—I was too busy reeling from that story scraping open my own very
recent scab.

"Jude's another issue entirely," Romeo continues, snapping his scroll
shut. "If that asshole really is responsible for bringing the Authorities
down on us, I'll give him the Wright treatment myself. Lea, have you seen
him since...?"

I shake my head. "Maybe he hasn't found a way back into the resort yet."

"Good," says Gaby, "because if it was that easy, the rangers' safety pre-
cautions would be failing." She frowns. "I should tell Chief Han to beef
up our security just in case. How'd he find out about the disappearances
to report them to the Authorities? I'm worried he's hacking our systems."

"He might just be reading newsie pages," I point out.

She nods. "Every time someone goes missing, the old *Death-tination
Vacation* tag trends on the uniweb. And I'm sure he has a lot of time on
his hands, trapped out there. Wonder how he's charging his tech without
the solar battery frying."

I shiver. "So do we definitely think he's infected?"

Romeo grimaces. "That dead spiger says yes."

"And he's probably figured out he can't be the only one. Do you think
he told the Authorities about *that?*"

"If he did, he's more of a quarkbrain than I thought. No, he didn't tell them his location or request a rescue. I bet he guessed enough of what's going on and decided to get rid of competition before he moves in." Romeo folds his arms, turning his attention to Gaby. "Speaking of blabbing to the Authorities, you absolutely can*not* tell anyone other than Chief Han what we've talked about here." His eyes flash orange.

I elbow him. "No compelling Gaby! She's our ally."

"And she's under scrutiny by the Authorities right now," Romeo snaps back. "I'm taking zero risks."

"You don't have to worry about me," Gaby says. "Compulsion or not, I have Hades' best interests in mind. I'm not going to spill any of this to the Authorities." She turns to me. "But we have to do something about Jude, if he's really out there."

"I think we should hunt him down." I'm surprised by the words coming out of my own mouth, but once they're out, I realize I mean them. Jude's an active danger, not just to me, but to everyone. This stunt he pulled, calling in the Authorities, has endangered every infected resident of the resort. I'm not interested in waiting around politely to see what he does next.

I especially dread turning around one day when I least expect it and seeing his face again. I'd rather surprise *him*.

Bonus: he'll never see me coming. Because he's only ever known me as the beaten-down version of myself who'd wait for him to make the first move. That isn't me anymore, and I plan to prove it.

Gaby and Romeo both give me surprised looks, but they're tinged with approval. Gaby jumps to her feet and says, "I agree. We can't give him any more opportunities to fuck with us. I'll lead the search party."

"Oh, no, you won't," Romeo cuts in, standing to face her. "I remember what happened last time. You were lucky not to get killed by the sunrise. *I'm* leading this hunt, and if I order you back to shelter, you'll blazing well go."

"You're not my commander." Gaby's getting up in his face now, glaring into his eyes, and—oh, my. Do I detect a little spark there? Would it be wrong of me to want them to kiss right now?

Yeah. Probably. *Unless...*

Romeo clears his throat, looking away first. "I may not be your boss," he says, "but I'm an experienced leader, and my goal is bringing everyone home alive. So stop acting like I'm your enemy, will you? We're on the same side here."

Gaby looks down, letting out a sigh. "We are. For the moment."

They both look at me.

"You're not going to tell me I can't participate out of some misguided need to protect me, are you?" I ask.

Gaby laughs. "I wouldn't dare."

Romeo says, "I was about to ask for your help, actually. You know Jude best. Where should we start?"

Warmed by their new confidence in me, I say slowly, "He mentioned finding a cave. We were trying to get there when I fed him to the tree, and then I couldn't find it in time to shelter from the sunrise. Honestly, I thought he might've been bullshitting me and the cave never existed. But maybe he *did* find something, and that's where he's been sheltering." I turn to Romeo. "Do you have a map of the wilds at all? Know any areas near the crash site that have another network of lava tubes?"

"Nothing written down," Romeo says, "but most of us do love hiking. If we all put our heads together, I think we could come up with an approximate sketch of landmarks in the surrounding area. Maybe we should take a recon jaunt tonight and scope it out."

"No!" I say quickly. "What about that dead spiger we found? Jude's out wandering the jungle too. In fact, we're lucky we haven't already run into him." I shudder to imagine him watching us from the trees while we bathed in the hot spring, or as we danced near the lure vines.

Romeo cracks his knuckles and bares his teeth. "I can take him."

"Just—don't engage, if you find him," I plead. "I don't want you getting hurt."

Romeo nods. "Better to let him think we aren't onto him yet, anyway." He glances at Gaby. "You two shouldn't be seen going back and forth between these caves and the resort. We're in a lot of danger if the Authorities find this place. But I want you both to stay in touch. Message me anytime you find out something new...and stay safe. Please." He runs his hand lightly down my arm, leaving tingles in the wake of his fingertips. "Protect each other."

"We will," I promise.

Gaby just looks at me, eyes troubled. I know she's thinking of my panic attacks the last time Jude stalked me. I'd like to reassure her those are behind me. That's what I've been telling myself these past few months. That I'm healed, now that I'm an immortal being with the ability to rip a man's throat out if he looks at me wrong.

I'm not so sure anymore. Because if it's Jude—if he's truly back from the dead—I'm afraid the shame-heavy spell he held over me might still bind. I'm stronger, more confident, but I'm not magically trauma-resistant just because I drink blood.

Maybe Gaby and Romeo are right to worry about me.

Chapter 22

GABRIELLE

I walk Lea back to the Underworld lounge, where she has one more show later. She tries to convince me to stay, but I lie that I have a work shift tonight.

Truth be told, I'm free until tomorrow. But if Romeo's going trekking in the wilds to look for Jude, my gun and I are coming with him.

I message him as soon as Lea disappears into her dressing room, telling him I'll meet him by the rangers' garage. Predictably, he tries to talk me out of coming. *<It's safer out here for infected people. We're harder to kill,>* et cetera.

<Do you think I'd've become a ranger if I was scared of a little risk?> I shoot back. *<I'm going out there. Meet me or don't.>*

When I sneak into the garage and let myself through the contamination-control airlock into the jungle, sure enough, Romeo's there. His arms are folded across his chest, and he looks flared off.

"I assume you checked to make sure you weren't followed?" he challenges.

"I did, thanks for asking." I hold up my keycuff. "I even got Chief Han to give me a guest ID to scan when leaving, just in case the Authorities decide to check the door logs."

Grudgingly, Romeo tilts his head, inviting me to come along as he begins trekking into the jungle.

Other than our frantic search for the crashed ship a few weeks ago, I've almost never been outside the resort perimeter. A few quick trips to haul dead monster parts into the jungle, where they can peacefully decompose without drawing more wildlife into the resort, don't really count. Romeo, however, seems to be a lot more casual about hiking through the alien jungle. I stick close as he dodges lure vines, avoids touching poisonous plants, and picks a sure path through the overhanging foliage like he's tramped this way a thousand times.

If he's been here since the building of the resort, he probably has.

"What you did the other night, with the behemoth," I say tentatively. "How did you know...?"

"They come sniffing around here once every decade or so," Romeo says. "Last time, it was a mated pair, and I heard the sounds they made to communicate with each other. I don't think they have enough of a preference for humans to bother us. I bet we give them the same stomachache that they'd give us if we tried to eat 'em. My guess is they only come looking for easy prey when they have a nest full of young and the hunting's scarce. Easy to draw them off, though."

He's so casual about such an important discovery, I want to shake him. "You should be reporting things like this! Our database of knowledge about Hades native life forms is way too sparse. Training the rangers on behemoth mating calls could save a life if you're not around."

"Oh." It's like the thought has never even occurred to him. "Well, sure, I'd be happy to write down what I know. Don't expect me to go out and record a behemoth call, though. I stay far away from their nesting grounds."

"But you know where they are! That's more than the rangers know." I groan. "What else have you Midnights been keeping secret?"

"Well, I've done quite a bit of botanical research..."

I start to roll my eyes at the reminder of Romeo's side hustle, but then stop to consider that he's right. His trials of the various effects of consuming Hadesian plants could speed up scientific discoveries on the planet's native species by decades.

"Only problem is, I can't explain my methods for finding out all that stuff," he says. "Unless you want me to write down that I just put shit in my mouth for fun because I have a parasite that won't let me die of poisoning."

"Fair point," I say. "But you could at least point the med-center researchers in the right direction for discovering sources of natural medicine."

He hums in his throat, tilting his head. "Maybe I could, yeah."

There's a short silence as we tramp onward. Then I say, "Don't take this the wrong way, but I always assumed you were just a loser who bummed around conning tourists."

"Oh, I'm certainly not taking *that* the wrong way," Romeo says dryly.

"Shut up. I'm trying to tell you that I was wrong, all right? And I'm...I'm sorry. You're an intelligent man and a good leader. I think you could be a huge asset to the Hades community if you were willing to work with us."

"'Us' being the rangers?" Romeo sounds skeptical. I suppose we deserve it for being so blatantly antagonistic toward him and the Midnights all these years.

"I'm not saying we should just ignore all the history." I trot to catch up with him. He's avoiding my gaze, his face impassive as he weaves through the foliage. "What I *am* saying is that I'm willing to start building bridges and...I'm going to fight to change my colleagues' minds. Because I think you've always been an important member and founder of our community, and you deserve a lot better than the way we've been treating you."

He stops, looking at me, and for a second I think I might be getting through to him. Then, in one quick motion, he seizes me by the waist and lifts me off the ground, spinning me away from the lure vine that has just pounced where I was standing a split second earlier.

My pulse pounds in my throat. I stare into Romeo's eyes, mesmerized by the green that looks so very human. I've seen those eyes flash orange when he's compelling someone—like me—and I know I shouldn't trust the smoke screen that is his handsome face.

"Th-thank you," I choke out, taking a step back. He lets his hands drop from my waist, though the warm imprint of his palms lingers on the skin under my shirt.

"This way," he says, his voice rough, and sets off again.

ROMEO

*B*e careful, man, I tell myself sternly. *Gabrielle Lopez isn't your friend.*

Though if what she just said is true, maybe she's trying to be. I don't totally buy it. With the Authorities looking for a scapegoat, I'm still afraid that the rangers will decide it's worth the risk to themselves to throw the Midnights under the subtrain. I don't know if I'll fully trust anyone—even my fellow vampires—until the redjackets are gone.

But I'm surprised at how much I *want* to trust Gaby. With the silent tug-of-war we've been playing over Lea's heart, I expected to do nothing but resent her. But she's saying all the right things, blast it. Recognition and respect from the wider Hades community, not just my little group of outcasts, is tantalizing bait for my ego.

And, all right, when I had her in my arms...for a split second, I understood what Lea sees in her.

If I'm gonna be perfectly honest, it's not the first time the thought has crossed my mind. I'm not completely oblivious; Gaby Lopez is hot. But there're a lot of hot rangers, and I'd never consider hooking up with any of them, because I'm not into self-harm. Either they know what I am and hate me, or they have no idea, which is setting myself up for drama when they inevitably figure it out.

But Gaby knows I'm infected now. And she…doesn't hate me?

I think I could see us becoming friends. At the very least, we've called a truce.

I hide a smile as I duck between hanging vines. And then the smile freezes on my face.

There's a ragged blue shirt fluttering in the breeze, draped across the branch right in front of me. The fabric looks like it's been shredded by something with teeth. I brush my fingers across it. Still damp.

There hasn't been any rain tonight.

"What—" Gaby cranes to see over my shoulder. "*Oh*."

"Looks like our guy needed to do laundry." I keep my voice low. "This hasn't been here long. He's close."

"What do we do? Hide out and wait for him?"

"I'd like to get eyes on him, but without him seeing us," I murmur. "His cave must be nearby." I check my scroll for the rough landmark map the Midnights put together. "We're not far from the coast. There are some rocky cliffs to the southeast. Let's head that way."

That's when we hear it: a howling cry, not unlike the one I used to draw the behemoth away yesterday. Chills creep up my arms despite the heat. It sounds close. Too close.

"It came back?" Gaby whispers. "But the trackers said…"

"I don't think it's a behemoth making that sound."

Was Jude watching us when I used it the other night? Is he watching us now? The call could be meant to scare us off…or it could be an attempt to bring the beast down on us.

I say, "I changed my mind. Maybe we should get back to the resort."

Gaby rubs her arms, her eyes darting between the shadows surrounding us. "Maybe we should," she says.

As she strides into the jungle, I notice her hand stays near the holstered weapon at her side.

Eighth Episode

Chapter 23

The next morning, during my first show, the Authorities cruise through the lounge. It's obviously freaking people out, seeing redjackets here. There were quite a few hasty departures in the night as folks who were here on not-so-savory business packed up and found another vacation spot.

They throw me off a bit, too, and I'm not even doing anything wrong. Other than drinking weekly rations of human blood from the med center, and I don't even think that's illegal. Just kinda messed up.

I doggedly continue my show despite them, though I stick to the stage more than I usually might. Sometimes it's fun to work the crowd a little—I get nicer tips if I do it—but with four guys in red jackets wandering between the tables and glaring into people's downcast faces as they try to enjoy their omelettes, my turf's been taken.

When I exit the stage to tepid applause, I breathe a sigh of relief. The dressing room backstage is quiet and dim, a welcome respite, but I wish I had a coworker here to complain to. Boris will be in later. Maybe I can catch him before the show and we can snark about the redjackets cockblocking our tips.

As I'm shrugging on my beach robe, I hear the door swish open. I hurriedly make sure I'm fully covered before turning around.

Two of the Authorities have just entered via Karina's office. The Underworld manager hovers behind them, giving me an apologetic grimace behind their back.

I recognize the two soldiers as Etric and Jorge, the ones I talked to yesterday. They don't return the tight smile I offer.

"What can I do for you?" I speak brightly to cover the sinking feeling in my stomach.

"Miz Azalea, would you meet with us in Miz Karina's office? We have a few questions for you."

"Of course!" Mentally, I'm cursing up a storm. What did they find out? *If they've gotten in contact with Jude, he could've told them anything...*

They guide me into the manager's office. Karina pretends she has urgent business to take care of in the kitchen, leaving me alone with the two Authorities. Etric plants his ass on Karina's desk, knocking her holo projector askew. I lower myself onto the edge of a chair and brace for whatever they're going to throw at me.

"Miz Azalea," Etric says, "we've been investigating a person of interest in the disappearances here on Hades, Mas Romeo Mezzanotte. Multiple witnesses claim that you've been spending a lot of time with the man. Is that fair to say?"

Fuck. I nod, trying to keep my expression innocent. "He was one of the first to welcome me to the resort. I'd call him a friend."

"And what do you do with Mas Mezzanotte when you spend time with him?"

My mind flashes to the two of us naked in the hot spring, and a blush heats my skin. "We get drinks, hang out on the beach, go for walks together..."

"Is there a romantic aspect to this friendship?"

I fold my arms. "Sorry, sir, but I don't see how that's any of your business."

Etric stares down at me with hooded eyes. "We're just trying to get a picture of who this man is. What he spends his time doing, and with whom."

"He likes plants," I blurt out. *Oh, stars, don't tell them he samples psychedelic fungi for fun.* "He's...kind of a scientist. And he's an Underworld regular. He and his friends are always hanging out there."

Jorge, who's been lounging in Karina's wheelie chair, takes his feet off the desk and leans forward. "Does he disappear at odd hours? Show too much interest in strangers?"

"He's pretty outgoing." *I really don't like where this is headed.* "I mean, I was a stranger until he 'showed too much interest' in me. Now we're friends. That's how that works. What are you suggesting, exactly?"

Etric ignores the question. "And about how long have you known Mas Mezzanotte?"

"Two months, give or take. We met shortly after I arrived here to take this job." And I'm now realizing I didn't even know his surname until the Authorities said it.

"So you barely know him at all," Jorge says, somewhat snidely.

The words hit home. My temper kindles. "I know enough," I snap. "He's a kind person who takes care of his friends. He loves this planet, this community. I know he'd never do anything to put it in danger."

"Do you, now?" Etric says, eyes locked on my face, which feels hot enough to melt my makeup. "So you've discussed the killings with him? You know he was here during every single one, right?"

Careful, Angelique. "Yeah, I know he's lived here a long time," I say. "We haven't talked about that stuff in detail. Just that it was a bad time." I have half a mind to tell them about Wright so they have a different lead to chase. But I'm afraid of what other conclusions that story might lead them to.

"I think you should ask him about it next time you see him," Jorge says. "If he tells you the truth about what happened, this could all go away."

"This? This what?" I narrow my eyes. "Are you accusing him of something? Or are you accusing *me*?"

"We know you can't have been involved in the attacks," says Etric, waving a hand. "You've only been here a short time. But you hardly know this guy, even though you obviously think you're in love with him."

The flush is full-body now. I'm burning up. "No one said I was in love."

"Keep telling yourself that, doll." Etric smirks. "So maybe you don't know anything. But we think your boyfriend *does*, and if you help us figure out what, then we won't need to arrest you for obstructing our investigation."

I gasp in outrage. "I haven't obstructed anything! I've been helping you!"

Jorge gets up from his chair and approaches mine, leaning down to murmur close to my ear, "It *will* be obstruction, if you don't cooperate with the directive we just gave you."

I really can't explain why I do what I do next. I bare my teeth at him and *hiss*.

He spooks, stumbling backward. "Your eyes," he chokes. "They—they—"

I bet I know what they're doing. I've seen it on Romeo—the orange glow that means the parasite's taking over.

"We're done here," I say, enunciating it deliberately, making sure to keep my eyes locked on Jorge's. His practically glaze over. I turn my gaze to Etric and repeat the same to him: "We're done. Leave me alone."

Both of them seem frozen in place as I jump to my feet and stalk toward the door. They don't stop me.

I wait until both the office door and the door to the corridor outside Underworld are slammed closed behind me before I let out a shaky breath, my hands starting to tremble. I'm already tapping Romeo's call code into my keycuff.

Except he doesn't answer. I try twice more, but he's not picking up.

As my head cools, I wonder if it's enough of an emergency to bother him. After all, I handled it. I didn't tell the Authorities anything, and I got them to back off. Why bug Romeo just to tell him baby did her first mind control?

But the cold pit in my stomach refuses to subside.

"Lea, what's wrong?"

I look up from where I've been sitting on my beach lounger, arms wrapped around myself as I mentally process the interview. Gaby's standing over me in ranger uniform.

"I'm fine," I say, too quickly.

She sits on the edge of the lounge chair next to me. "You've been hugging yourself and rocking back and forth for ten minutes. Something happened, didn't it?" She leans in close. "Jude didn't contact you, did he?"

I hold my expression steady. "It wasn't Jude."

"Then what?"

Reluctantly, and in a low voice, I give her a quick recap of what the Authorities said.

Her lip curls in a snarl. "They tried to get you to rat on Romeo? Typical redjacket bastards."

"And they threatened to arrest *me* if I don't." I brace my elbows on my knees and stare at the sand. "Then I accidentally compelled them. Or not. I'm not sure how successful it was. What if they come after me anyway? I might have put us all in worse danger."

Gaby cracks her knuckles. "Let them come. They'll have to get through me if they want to arrest you."

"Please don't do anything rash," I beg. "I don't want to see you get in trouble over this."

She laughs wryly. "Girl, I'm already friends with two vampires and covering up your unsuccessful murder attempt on your ex. Talk about trouble! I'm in it up to my neck."

"Friends with *two*...?" I raise my eyebrows. "Are you and Romeo friends now?"

I'm pleasantly surprised to see Gaby blush at that. "He's not so bad, I guess."

Grinning, I poke her with my elbow. "Careful, you're on your way to the dark side."

Her smile fades. "The only dark side is the one that hurts and harasses people for fun. I once thought Romeo was on it, but he's done a lot to protect this community from it."

"So have you." I brush a lock of her hair back and tuck it behind her ear. "I'm glad you two aren't enemies anymore. I like both of you so much."

"I like you too," says Gaby.

I lean in to kiss her cheek, but she turns her head and catches my lips with her own. My eyelids flutter shut. With her hand on my cheek and mine at her waist, the kiss heats up fast. I try to ignore the faint sensation of hunger; I've already had my blood ration today.

It's Romeo's fault my body thinks lust and blood-thirst are connected.

Gaby pulls away first, flushed and giggling. "I'm still on duty," she says guiltily. "Let's put a pin in that, yeah? Want to meet me in the gym after I'm off tonight?"

"Absolutely."

I wonder if Romeo is as cool with this arrangement as he pretends. Jude always got screamingly jealous if I so much as glanced at another man. (For some reason, he never cared about women. I think he thought they "didn't count," even though in my opinion they absolutely do.) I guess I assumed any man would hate my affections being split two ways.

But it doesn't *feel* bad, especially now that Gaby and Romeo are finally starting to get along. It feels giddy, exciting, wonderful. Gaby makes me fizz all over like a glass of champagne, and Romeo is somehow safety and danger all rolled into one. And after that are-they-going-to-kiss moment in the Midnights' hideout... The idea that they could both be into *each other*, as well as me, piques a curiosity I've never explored before.

I'm annoyed to realize it *now*, when Romeo's told us not to visit his hideaway until the Authorities leave.

Also, he still hasn't responded to my call from this morning. He almost never ignores me like this. I'm starting to worry that he went looking for Jude without telling me.

<*Call me back as soon as you can,*> I message him.

ROMEO

We had almost no warning before the Authorities found our hideout. Just a ping from Julia, who was on lookout duty, saying that someone was in the corridor outside. The next thing I knew, she was sprinting toward us, making frantic hand gestures.

"They spotted the entrance and sent a scout in!" she whisper-yelled as we crowded around her. "Redjackets are gonna be here in minutes. Grab your stuff and run!"

We had protocols in place for this kind of thing. Benito had sculpted and painted huge pieces of fake rock to cover the tunnels leading to our sleeping spaces. We slotted them into place in record time. There was no hiding our common area; the awning and crates would take too much time to move. We left them and fled, grabbing only backpacks of our most prized possessions on our way to the hidden back tunnel that leads to the surface.

The lava tubes are winding, wet, and infuriatingly echoey. Despite our best efforts to pass in utter silence, our footfalls and breaths are deafening. My keycuff buzzes with messages; I ignore them and focus on moving onward and up.

When we finally arrive at the hatch that seals our cave off from the surface, all twenty-four Midnights are sweating from more than just heat. We're all anxious the Authorities will track us, or worse, break through the false front to pillage our rooms. I'm already bracing myself to find my pharmaceutical stash confiscated. The idea of restarting the foraging and drying process from scratch makes me want to scream.

"How long are we gonna have to stay out here?" Vi mutters, waving off a curious insect before finding a boulder to perch on. "If they aren't going to leave by sunrise, we need to find shelter."

I've got motion-sensing cams near the cave entrance that should tell me when the Authorities leave, but I have no idea how long they're planning to poke around, or if they'll come back later. "Shelter's a good idea," I tell her. "There are some dead-end tunnels not far from here. Let's hole up there for now. No lighting fires or making a lot of noise, yeah? The Authorities probably won't think to look outside the resort perimeter, but just in case, I don't want to make it easy for them to find us."

Plus, there's the problem of Jude.

I haven't shared my plan to eliminate him with the Midnights yet. Better I just quietly handle it myself.

Being stuck out here makes it all too convenient. I'll wait close to dawn, tell the camp I'm scouting, and run back to where I found evidence of Jude's camp yesterday. If the man has half a brain, he'll be holed up in his own cave shelter against the oncoming sun. I'll corner him there and put an end to him, swift and clean.

Gaby and Lea will be flared off at me later. Gaby didn't want me to go alone, and Lea...well, if I told her I was going, she'd probably say the same. Maybe she'd even want to deal justice by her own hand.

But right now, I'm focused on keeping everyone safe. Since we're forced to shelter out here in the wilds, safety means that I can't wait around for the perfect time to dispatch Jude. There are two dozen Midnights depending on me to protect them. From wild animals, hungry and poisonous plants...and from the man who tried to bring the Authorities down on us.

Who knows what he'll do, given this chance to mess with our heads?

I won't wait to find out.

It has to be now. Tonight.

Chapter 24

ANGELIQUE

When I show up at the gym, Gaby's already cleared out a corner for us and set up a punching dummy. She hands me a pair of boxing gloves. "This is what I do to blow off steam when I wanna murder someone," she says. "It's good self-defense practice."

I grin. "My dad was big into self-defense when I was a kid. He would've loved you."

"Wish I could've met him," says Gaby. "He raised an amazing daughter."

My smile turns goofy as my insides melt. I take the gloves and pull them on.

After about an hour of doing more flirting than working out, I'm sweaty and a little bit sore, but buzzing with energy. A dozen little touches in passing, a few play-wrestling matches, and a kiss or three have worked together with Gaby's aura of safety and strength to ignite my libido. I'm about two horny heartbeats away from suggesting we shower together in the gym locker room, even though that is a very dangerous idea if we don't want to get arrested by one of Gaby's colleagues.

Thankfully, Gaby saves me from myself by leaning close and whispering, "Want to skip the shower and come back to my place?"

"Never wanted anything more," I choke. She nips my earlobe in response and I nearly jump her right there in the overly-bright locker room hallway.

Somehow, despite stopping to make out in a couple of quiet corners, we find ourselves back at her apartment in the rangers' block. This is the first time she's brought me into her own space, and I can see why: it's even smaller than mine. Gaby's made every effort to cheer up the place with strings of paper lanterns, a coat of soft yellow paint, and a bunch of animated posters of holo stars (including, I note with amusement, a shiny new Angelique Azalea one—a sexy shot from an old photoshoot where I've got one strap of my bedazzled dress drooping low on my shoulder as I wink and blow a kiss).

I barely have a minute to admire the place before Gaby's tackling me to the mattress of her single bed. Giggling, I tangle my legs with hers and turn my face to accept her eager kisses. Obviously, she's just as needy as I am. She grinds against my thigh, her breaths coming fast. I nip at her lower lip, careful not to break the skin, and then move my mouth to the sensitive skin under the curve of her jaw.

Gaby tugs at the hem of my tank top, lifting it up and off to reveal my sporty, flattening breastband. She deftly unhooks it and flings the garment over her shoulder. "Stars, yes," she breathes, circling my nipple with her thumb.

I'm just as eager to get at the rest of her, but she catches my wrists and holds them to the bed on either side of my head, dipping to flick her tongue against my areolas. The sensation heightens my burning arousal. "Gaby," I moan. "Please."

"No," Gaby murmurs against my skin. "You're going to have to be patient." She guides my hands to the wooden bedframe, curling my fingers around the slats in the headboard. "Hold that," she commands. "Do not let go."

"Yes, Miz Ranger."

She shoots me a heated look through her lashes, and wow, I think I'm going to die.

Gaby works her way down my belly to the waistband of my leggings and begins slowly peeling them down. I wriggle restlessly, hoping to speed up the process, but she just smacks the side of my ass gently and says, "Bad girl. Stay still."

By the time my leggings and unders are all the way off (again, flung into the abyss of Gaby's bedroom floor; retrieving my clothes later is going to be a struggle), I'm panting and needy. But Gaby decides now is a great time for a striptease and starts taking her own clothes off in a similarly unhurried manner.

"You're doing this on purpose," I moan.

"You're blazing right I am," she says, and gives me a saucy wink to rival Poster-Angelique.

As she slides her tight shorts down her muscular thighs, revealing the luscious curve of her ass, a strangled moan bursts out of me. "Gaby, you're so fucking hot, baby."

"So are you." Her eyes meet mine, and she licks her lips. "Can I sit on your face?"

"Fuck, yes, *please*."

She straddles me, facing the foot of the bed, and lowers her pussy to my mouth. The first taste of her is heaven, musky and hot and already dripping wet.

She leans down, breasts skimming my abdomen, and I feel the tease of her tongue against my folds. My hips jerk, but she holds me down, and I lose myself in the glorious sound of her moans as I get to work driving her as wild as she's driving me.

My fingers dig into the bedframe harder and harder, until finally I can't take anymore and let go, allowing my hands to roam the shapely curve of her ass. She's moaning into me and I can tell by the tension in her thighs that she's as close as I am. I keep circling my tongue steadily, pushing her closer to the peak, feeling the same delicious clench tightening in my own belly. Dimly, I notice a wet feeling and a slight twinge in my palm as I slide it down her thigh, but I'm too far gone to care.

She comes first, shuddering and gasping and dripping gloriously, and I'm not far behind her. She rolls next to me, and for a moment it's nothing but the glow and aftershock of pleasure as we pant together.

And then I realize what the moisture I was smearing across her thigh is. It's a drop of blood.

My own blood, I realize, as I bring my hand up to my face and see the small cut that a splinter from the bedframe has opened in my palm. It's nothing horrible—probably won't even require more than a quick spritz of wound sealant—but my stomach drops as I realize it's not just blood anymore.

I could infect her.

Horrified, I scramble out of bed and dash for Gaby's en-suite washroom. "Don't move," I yell. "Stay still, don't—"

"What's wrong? Is there something on me? A bug?" Gaby sits partway up and spots the smear. "Oh, don't worry, it's just a little bit of—"

"Don't touch it!" I scream.

I watch as it finally clicks. Her face pales. "Shit," she says. "There are antiseptic wipes in my top drawer. But it should be fine, right? I didn't swallow any, and I don't have any open wounds."

Blazes, I hope so. I retrieve the wipes and clean her up as quickly as I can, then tend my own scratch. For good measure, I disinfect the bedframe, yanking out the splinter that cut me. After hunting to make sure no blood got on her bedsheets, I finally relax.

"I'm so, so sorry," I say, when she beckons me back to bed to cuddle. "I wasn't even thinking." I let her enfold me in her warm arms, her sticky skin pressing to my back.

"I've been studying the risks," Gaby says calmly. "As long as I don't lick your blood or get it on an open wound, we should be fine."

"But what if—Gaby, Romeo told me that sex has a risk of transmission too. Low, but still there. What if that happens? I couldn't live with myself. Maybe we shouldn't do this anym—"

Her hand comes up to cover my mouth. "Don't even. If it makes you feel better, we can use protection. But I've been thinking about it a lot, Lea. The idea of being a vampire. I...I'm not going to say I'm ready to go out and do it on purpose right now. But..." She lets out a shuddering breath. "My mom died in a mining accident a few years ago, and I don't talk to my dad anymore. Hades has been my home for almost a decade. I don't see myself leaving. So being stuck here forever wouldn't really ruin my life." She kisses the curve of my shoulder. "I could get used to the idea of drinking blood, I guess. You said it didn't taste bad once you turned?"

"Like a fruit smoothie." I laugh shakily. "But it's more than that. It's living *forever*, Gaby. Isn't that...I don't know, don't you think it's a huge commitment, giving up a natural death?"

"Giving up disease and aging doesn't sound so terrible," says Gaby. "The only thing that would make immortality awful is not having anyone to share it with."

I roll to the side so I can meet her eyes. We don't say anything. There's nothing *to* say. I can't promise we'll be together forever, because we've only known each other for a few months. Much as I like her—and Romeo does, too, I think—promising each other an immortal eternity together so soon feels foolish.

"Well, you're still human for now," I say finally. "You have a lot of time to decide. Honestly, I...I wish I'd thought it through more."

"Given the circumstances, I'm glad that you did what you could to survive," says Gaby, leaning in to kiss my lips softly. "After all, it bought me more time with you."

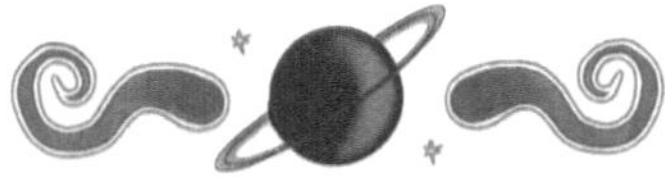

Romeo

Dawn is rapidly approaching by the time I manage to slip away from the Midnights' cave encampment. I curse under my breath as I slip through the underbrush, feeling the intensifying heat that heralds the approach of the sun. Without a hovercycle to speed my trip there and back, I'll be trapped in Jude's cave until dusk.

Which means, for better or for worse, one of us has to die before the sun comes up. And I'm going to make sure it's him.

Given where we heard and saw the signs last night, I'm almost certain he lives east of the resort, close to the beach. Traveling alone, without Gaby or Lea, I'm able to move quicker and quieter, approaching the area in near perfect silence. With any luck, he'll never see me coming.

I pass the spot where we saw the shirt hanging on the branch yesterday. It's gone now. I step closer to the branch, reaching out to run my fingers across the smooth green treeskin...

And step right into a snare.

My leg jerks above my head before I can get out even a single-syllable curse. As my head spins, I scrabble frantically for the knife I carry at my belt anytime I leave the resort perimeter. *I can cut myself down. This is fine. I can—*

Low, sardonic laughter chills me as Jude steps from the shadowy trees.

Rough living hasn't agreed with him. He looks gaunt and filthy, his skin shiny with burns that even the parasite must have struggled to heal after his deep dive into the carnivorous plant's belly. His blond hair and new-grown beard are disarrayed and matted with...*ugh, probably animal blood*. His clothes are rags.

"Thought you might be back," says the asshole. "You got a little too close for comfort, sneaking around with that glitch Ranger last night. Glad my preparations paid off."

"I'm gonna fucking kill you," I grit out, fumbling to cut the vine holding my leg.

"Wait," says Jude, smirking. "I thought that was *my* line." And he whips out a little hollowed-out reed, puts it to his lips, and blows.

Something hits me in the chest, stinging like a motherfucker. *A blow dart? What is this guy, a former Junior Imperial Scout?*

"This planet has all sorts of interesting ways to hurt you," he gloats. "One of those blasted dragonfly bugs stung me on my second week out here. Paralyzed me for hours. I just about cooked before that shit wore off and I could drag myself to the cave."

The knife falls from my hand as my limbs start to seize. My muscles spasm painfully. *Bloodstinger venom.* The carnivorous insects pack a nasty paralytic sting, but finding a good insect repellent was one of my first experiments with local flora. I haven't had the displeasure of getting stung in years.

I can't believe this dickhat found a way to use the bugs as a weapon.

Curled in a stiff knot of pain, I'm still fully aware as Jude cuts me down from the snare and ties a vine around me to drag my dead weight off to his lair.

I said one of us was going to die before dawn, didn't I?

Off in the distance, the resort's first dawn alarm sounds.

I have a horrible feeling that it's going to be me.

Season Finale, Part One

Chapter 25

ANGELIQUE

It's been more than a day now, and Romeo still hasn't responded to any of my messages.

Waking up in the same bed as Gaby should have been a soft, joyful, shy-smiles-and-coffee type of morning. Instead, I woke to the sound of her murmuring voice as Chief Han debriefed her over vid-call. Last night, the Authorities found the Midnights' hideout, and they've spent the daylight hours ransacking the place. Chief Han is doing her best damage control, but she needs Gaby and several other rangers on hand to ensure the Authorities don't jump to the wrong (*correct*) conclusion about the Midnights.

As soon as I figure out what's going on, I message Romeo, *<Are you all right?>* Anxiously, I wait for a response, but minutes roll past and he hasn't even read it. I get ready for my morning show, curling my hair and doing what basic makeup I can with products I borrow from Gaby. And still nothing.

"Gaby," I call, sticking my head out of the washroom to where she's hopping on one foot to pull on one of her boots. "Did Chief Han mention if the Authorities captured anybody?"

She shakes her head. "They didn't. No one was in the Midnights' hideout when they got there. And no one's seen them in the resort, either."

"But messaging still works outside the perimeter, doesn't it?"

"It should," says Gaby. "Why?"

I bite my lower lip. "Romeo hasn't contacted me since yesterday. He's not even reading my messages. I'm getting worried."

"They'd have to get pretty far away from the resort for messages not to go through." Gaby wrinkles her brow. "Did Romeo mention any other places he and the Midnights go to hide? Maybe deep in the lava tubes? If he's really far underground, the signal might be blocked."

"Yeah, you're right. That's probably it." But worry still gnaws at my stomach. Romeo wouldn't drop completely off the grid without sending at least a quick warning, would he? Especially not if he saw my panicked message from yesterday. We may not be officially dating, but until now, he's been in contact every day. He checks on my hunger levels, gives me advice about the biological changes my body is undergoing, and frequently invites me to spend time with him and the Midnights. I care about him, and his behavior is not what I would expect from someone who could ghost me without warning.

Not that I think he *would*, even if he was that sort of person. We're both immortal and tied to this planet, potentially forever. You don't want to burn bridges with someone who's guaranteed to be your eternal neighbor.

I let myself enjoy Gaby's sweet goodbye-for-work kiss, then head for Underworld as she sets off for the beach for her lifeguarding shift.

The lounge is packed as usual, breakfast smells making my stomach growl. Boris is already inside the locker room, humming to himself while shining his dress shoes.

As I'm touching up my makeup in the washroom, my keycuff chimes with a message. I drop my lipstick in the sink. *Romeo?*

The ID displays his name. "Thank stars," I whisper, tapping to project the message in a glowing holo above my wrist.

<Hello, Angel. Don't you worry about your boyfriend. I'm keeping him safe for you.>

My blood chills. *That isn't Romeo.*

Another message follows a second later. *<If you don't want me to tell the Authorities what he is, you're going to need to do exactly as I say.>*

<Jude?> I type back, my fingers shaking.

<You're smarter than you look.>

I tamp down the impulse to reply with a recording of myself flipping him a rude gesture.

<I owe you a little pain for letting that tree eat me,> Jude messages. *<Here's what's going to happen. You're going to get a starship and fly it out of the resort alone. Land on the beach outside the perimeter and I'll meet you there. Don't try anything with the Authorities or that ranger glitch. If I see anyone besides you coming, I'll cut off your boyfriend's head.>*

<If I do what you say, will you let him go?> I ask.

<I won't kill him,> is Jude's response. *<But he won't be free until you and I are far away. I'm not giving him the opportunity to attack me again.>*

I begin typing, *<We can't leave the planet now that we're vampires, you dumbass,>* but pause and decide to delete it. Jude hasn't had the (relatively) easy transition that I had. No one's explained to him what's happening to his body. He craves blood and doesn't know why; he goes through hideous torture and doesn't die.

And he still thinks he can leave Hades.

What was it that Romeo told me? *The parasites thrive on the sun's radiation. If you try to leave, they'll take over your mind and stop you.*

Maybe that's exactly what I need to happen. If I can push him to the point where the parasite takes over, he'll be distracted and I can gain the upper hand.

<All right, I'll come. Just don't hurt him,> I send.

<I didn't promise that,> comes the chilling reply.

"Bastard," I whisper under my breath.

Then I tap Gaby's call code straight away. Because I *am* smarter than I look. Smart enough not to go off to meet a deranged kidnapper without making a plan first.

GABRIELLE

I can't decide if it's good or bad luck that Chief Han happens to be in the room with me when Lea calls.

"Jude has Romeo," Lea blurts as soon as my audio connects.

The look on my face must be a study. Chief Han waves my other colleagues out and closes the door behind them as Lea continues to babble about Romeo being kidnapped and some plan to trap Jude.

"Lea, Lea, hold on a sec," I interrupt. Han's mouthing, *Is that Angelique Azalea? What's going on?* I switch my audio to include the Chief Ranger in our conversation. "Where are you? Are you safe?"

"I'm in Underworld. Jude messaged me using Romeo's tech." Stars, she sounds distraught. "He's threatening to kill him if I don't meet him alone on the beach. But I can't go without someone knowing where I am."

"Fuck no you can't!" I burst out. Chief Han gives me a raised-eyebrows look. "I'm coming with you."

"Hold on, hold on," Han interrupts. "Hi, Miz Azalea, this is Chief Ranger Korrie Han. We haven't been formally introduced yet, but Ranger Lopez tells me good things. Now, let's think carefully about this situation. What did Jude say exactly?"

Ten minutes later, Chief Han and I have cobbled together a seat-of-our-pants plan to help Lea and—hopefully—capture Jude. Once Lea clicks off the call, she's going to head for the hangar and fly her personal ship out to the beach to meet Jude. Meanwhile, me, Han, and a couple of snipers will set up a stakeout in the jungle. If Jude makes a single wrong move, we'll shoot his ass.

Much as I resent the Chief sticking her nose in, it's nice to have a little backup.

By midnight, we're crouching in a hastily built blind, propped up to the height of the average jungle plant and disguised with fake foliage. Chief Han's night-vision binoculars are trained in the same direction as mine: the glowing tideline crashing onto black sands, where, silhouetted, a standing figure paces back and forth along a prone one.

On either side of us, the rangers' two best snipers have their guns trained on Jude, ready to strike him down if he makes a wrong move.

"Angelique just landed and disembarked," says Chief Han quietly. "She's climbing down the rocks now."

I adjust my angle and catch sight of Lea. My heart thumps wildly. Snipers notwithstanding, she's still very much in danger. I'd have argued harder against letting her go to him if I thought she'd listen to me.

Plus—much as I hate to admit it—I'm worried about Romeo, too.

"Hold," I tell Germaine as he follows Jude's movements through his scope. "Don't shoot yet. Let's watch how this plays out."

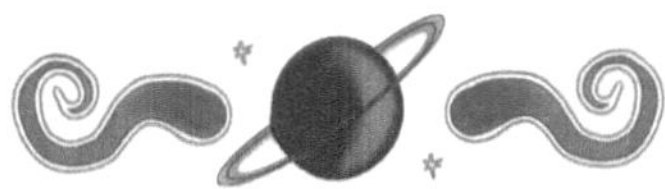

ROMEO

The starship that lands on the bluff above us is Lea's, the same one she flew in on months ago. My heart sinks. I was hoping she wouldn't come.

Jude's been stabbing me with these cursed insect stingers every few hours for an entire day. If I hadn't built my pain tolerance by taste-testing alien plants that would liquefy a human's insides, the excruciating pain of cramping muscles might've broken my mind.

But not today, motherfucker. Not this vampire.

It's been about four hours since my last dose. I'm starting to feel the effects loosen up a bit. Still can't move much, but I could maybe get out a couple of strangled words if I put in the effort. Still, when I see Lea emerge from the treeline, alone and carrying only her bedazzled blaster, all I can do is grunt a panicked scream.

Blast it, if Jude hurts her because she came to rescue *me*, I'll never forgive myself.

Jude's makeshift knife, made from a spiger claw, pricks at the underside of my jaw. "Did you come alone?" he asks Lea.

She holds her blaster pointed at the ground, but maintains a two-handed grip on it, tense and ready. "You said you'd kill him if I didn't. So here I am. Let Romeo go."

Jude wavers. For a moment, I think he might actually release me. But then he laughs. "Not until you drop that ridiculous little accessory and come beg on your knees."

Lea's eyes meet mine. I try to shake my head, but only manage an uncoordinated jerk that digs the claw deeper into my skin. Warm liquid trickles down my neck, and Lea sucks in a sharp breath.

"Don't," I croak. "Leave me. Run."

She wavers. Then the blaster drops from her fingers to the black sand, and my heart sinks.

GABRIELLE

I t's a struggle holding my binoculars steady as I watch Lea drop her gun.

"Now, Chief?" Germaine asks. "I have a clear shot."

Chief Han bites her lip. "He's got a knife at Romeo's throat. If he gets distracted and his grip loosens, *then* I want you to take the shot."

"You got it, boss."

Chief Han's keycuff chimes. She drops her binoculars, cursing. "What *now?*" Surely anything going on back at the resort can wait until we've taken care of Jude...

As soon as she answers the call, Han's expression freezes. "Yes, sir," she says crisply. "I apologize for missing our check-in. An emergency came up. I took a team outside the perimeter to deal with it." A pause. "Yes, some local wildlife got a little too close for comfort. We're, ah, hunting it right now. No, no, we have it under control. No need to send help."

In the chaos, I'd nearly forgotten all about the Authorities being here. The last thing we need is their "help."

Chief Han curses emphatically. I tear my eyes away from the binoculars again to see that she's frantically trying to reconnect the call. "He hung up on me! Blast it, those tourist-ass redjackets are probably going to barge in now. We need to wrap this up."

"I lost the shot," Germaine grumbles. "Should've let me take it while I had it."

Han rubs her forehead. "Just get him back in your sights and—"

"Uh, Chief?" the other sniper, Barnes, says slowly. "We've got another problem. Look just there. West of the target."

Chief Han aims her binoculars in the direction of Barnes's pointing finger. I do the same, and catch sight of what Barnes saw an instant before the Chief does.

People moving through the underbrush, dressed all in black. They're moving with the confident stealth of predators well-accustomed to their environment.

Their faces aren't visible from here, but I'd bet my last credit that those are the rest of the Midnights, come looking for their leader.

"Shit," I hiss. "If Jude sees them coming…"

Chief Han meets my eyes and tilts her head in their direction, a clear order. "Go quietly," is all she says as I clamber down to the jungle floor.

I wish I'd picked up Romeo's ease navigating the nighttime forest. Sadly, I haven't; I get snapped at by two lure vines and nearly put my foot down a burrower hole before the Midnights hear me coming. They surround me so silently that, if they were Hadesian predators, I'd already be a meal.

"Well, well, well," says that glitch Violetta, stepping out of the bushes in front of me. "If it isn't Gaby Lopez, our favorite pain in the ass."

It's the same ten of them who volunteered to help us search for Lea after the crash. I only remember a couple of their names, but they all sure seem to think they know me.

"I came over here to warn you." I keep my voice just above a loud whisper, because I'm nervous that we're close enough to be in Jude's earshot. "Don't interfere. We have things under control."

"Do you?" says Benito. "Because Greg went scouting this morning and found Romeo being held captive by some asshole none of us have ever seen before. Wanna explain that?"

I sigh, continuing to hold my hands up in a surrendering gesture. "That's Angelique Azalea's ex. How much time d'you got?"

ANGELIQUE

I take a step toward Jude, my stomach churning. Romeo's screaming now, his voice croaky and strangled from whatever Jude used to paralyze him. It's too bad the parasite doesn't give us telepathy. Romeo will understand eventually, after my plan works.

I hope.

"You want me?" I say, my voice low and tight. "Fine. Take me and let Romeo go. The ship's waiting."

Jude tightens his arm around Romeo's neck, still digging the claw into his skin. "I believe I said *beg*."

Swallowing, I glance at Romeo. I wish he didn't have to see this. The look on his face already makes me feel even more like a piece of shit.

I let myself fall forward, knees hitting the scorching sand. "Please," I grit out. "Please, Jude. I'll go with you. I'm...sorry I left you before."

Sorry I left without cutting off your dick first.

"That's more like it," Jude purrs. In a lightning-fast movement, he drops Romeo and transfers the threat of his claw weapon to my throat instead.

Romeo's screaming in the background as Jude forces me to my feet, digging the claw into my neck. "Let's go," he murmurs in my ear.

And that's when the searchlight of another starship sweeps the sand, illuminating our fucked-up little tableau.

An Imperial fighter.

"Redjackets," Jude hisses under his breath. For an instant, his eyes blaze bright orange. "You *glitch*. I told you to come alone! Now your boyfriend's gonna die."

"No!" I yank at his arm, trying to pull him back toward my starship. "I didn't call them! I don't know how they knew to come looking for me, I swear! Jude, please!"

The pilot of the Authorities' ship says through a loudspeaker, "In the name of His Majesty the Emperor, drop any weapons and put your hands up."

Jude's face switches from fury to calculating calm. Slowly, he opens his hand and drops the claw weapon.

The fighter lands next to my ship and disgorges five Authorities, who quickly slide down the bluff and surround us. "What's going on here?" their captain demands. "We were told that this was a wild animal hunt. Nothing that should involve civilians."

Jude shoots me a poisonous look, but then schools his face into his usual charm. "I'm sorry that you were misinformed," he says smoothly. "The rangers must be working to cover it up so they don't look bad. The fact is, I've been investigating here for months, and I've finally caught your murderer."

He points at the pathetic heap of Romeo lying on the sand.

"It's him," Jude says, meeting my eyes with a triumphant sneer. "Romeo Midnight."

Chapter 26

The Authorities have Romeo in magcuffs before I can even protest. He's an easy target for the accusation; he can't fight back, and can barely speak.

"It wasn't him," I keep saying, but no one will listen to me. And honestly, why should they? I don't have any proof.

But neither does Jude. And I'm not letting that human-shaped pile of shit get away with this.

Captain Penn vidcalls Chief Han to say, "You can come out now, Korrie. What gives with all the secrecy? You could've just said you had the murderer in your sights."

"Be there in a moment," is all Chief Han says. "Don't assume anything, Captain."

But Penn doesn't *have* to do any assuming; Jude is feeding him the narrative, and he's eating it up with a spoon. Something about how Jude is a private detective hired by Hades' governor to solve the myriad disappearances, how he was chased out of the resort by Romeo's minions for daring to investigate, and how he's been scraping by a meager existence in the lava tubes, pirating our uniweb connection to do his research.

I believe *some* of that last part, but the rest is obvious bullshit. If Captain Penn bothered to do even a cursory background check on Jude, he'd see that none of it adds up. But every time I open my mouth to say so, Jude elbows me hard. After the third time, he leans in and whispers, "I'll tell them you were fucking the murderer, Angel, and get you arrested right along with him."

Futile anger burns me up. I don't trust the Authorities to be on my side. They've *always* chosen to believe Jude over me. So I have to stand there and listen to Captain Penn commending him on the citizen's arrest and even offering him a reward. Jude modestly pretends to refuse, letting the captain "insist." It's nauseating to watch.

Ten excruciating minutes later, Chief Ranger Han comes crashing out of the woods with another ranger holding a sniper rifle. I worry a little when I don't see Gaby with them, but Jude's furious glance in my direction reminds me that I have more pressing problems.

"I think there's been a misunderstanding here, Captain," Chief Han says. "Apologies for the lie, but we felt your involvement would only complicate things, which, by the way, it *has*. The man we were hunting is the one you've just been shaking hands with. He's a person of interest in a stalking case involving our lovely resident singer here."

She gives me a significant look. I yank my arm out of Jude's slimy grasp. "I kept trying to say you've got the wrong person," I tell them, taking a giant step away. "Jude is my ex-partner. He's been stalking me for two years. Two months ago, he attempted to kidnap me and crash-landed our ship outside the resort perimeter. The rangers rescued me, but we all thought Jude was dead until a few days ago."

"What she says is true," Han puts in.

Captain Penn folds his arms. "That's all immaterial. I'm here to discover the murderer, not investigate relationship disputes."

"What I mean, sir, is that Jude's lying about *everything*. Including that," I say. "He has no evidence at all for Romeo's involvement. He's just accusing my...friend...to hurt me."

"Well, if this Romeo man didn't commit the murders, who did? We've been running a background check, and the person identified as Romeo Mezzanotte was last known to be a construction worker on this planet fifteen years ago. He was reported deceased after the project reached completion. A great cover for a killer working off the grid."

I glance at Romeo. "Fine, then. I'll tell you the truth."

Romeo makes a sort of yelping sound, but he doesn't need to worry—I'm not fool enough to tell them the *whole* truth.

"Eight years ago, there was a man named Wright. A serial killer. He hunted here for a few months before the locals took care of him, vigilante-style. It was never reported because the people who took him out were worried they would be labeled murderers too. Romeo can tell you more. He was there."

It's a bit of a gamble, telling them that much. They might assume Romeo was accomplice to killing Wright (true) and arrest him for *that*. I'm hoping, though, that the Authorities will decide not to prosecute anyone for doing what should've been their job.

The Authority standing next to me is busily tapping something into his tablet. "That actually checks out, sir. A Monrovian man called Wright Bullen vanished after taking a flight to Hades eight years ago. His disappearance coincides with the rash of deaths around that time."

"What about the incidents before that? Just after the resort was built?" Captain Penn raises an eyebrow at Chief Han. "Surely a similar pattern of attacks can't be explained away so easily?"

"I've told you, we concluded those attacks were the result of a wild animal finding its way into the resort tunnels," says Chief Han. "After that, we put in a lot of effort to fully map the tunnels and wall off any openings."

"Hmm." The captain consults his own scroll, seemingly reluctant to believe us. "Judah Andrews, was it? Your uniweb profile suggests you are not, in fact, an Imperially-sanctioned private detective as you led me to believe. Lying to an Imperial soldier is a crime punishable by a hefty fine. What do you have to say for yourself?"

Jude's eyes dart back and forth. Now that Penn's run a check on his history, he's out of lies to tell. His final actions before being reported missing—kidnapping me and crash-landing in the wilds—are all well-documented in Chief Han's files. Gaby wrote the report herself.

Then I see his eyes flick to the claw weapon he dropped in the sand. It's too far away for him to reach before the Authorities stop him, but—

Oh, fuck.

Somehow, Jude's managed to arrange himself so that he's a mere arm's length away from my sparkly blaster, which has been forgotten in the shuffle.

He lunges for it, turning the motion into a sideways roll and coming up braced on one knee with the blaster pointing directly at me. The Authorities draw their own blasters, but Jude yells, "Don't, or I'll shoot her!"

Then he begins backing away, making for the ships parked on the bluff.

"Captain?" Etric says, voice strained as he holds his gun steady. "Want us to fire or not?"

Captain Penn, tight with fury, says, "Hold."

And then a sniper shot from the trees blows the blaster out of Jude's hand.

Jude howls. Even in the dim moonslight, I can tell that his hand is a bloody mess. He takes off running, dodging a couple of the Authorities' late-timed shots, and pulls himself up the rocks toward my starship.

The Authorities' blasters and whoever's sniping from the forest pepper my shiny ship. I wince. It's going to take thousands of credits in repairs to make her spaceworthy again...but I already knew I was never leaving this planet.

Jude isn't either. Whether he knows it or not.

The ship takes off with the wobbly trajectory of a pilot steering one-handed. The lights disappear into the distance all too quickly.

"Well, I think we're done here," says Captain Penn.

Chief Han rounds on him. "What? But he got away!"

"Chief, we riddled that ship with enough holes that it won't make it out of atmo. If he returns to the resort by morning, you'll arrest him. But there aren't any other civilizations on Hades, and I doubt he'll find another convenient cave to hide in. Once the sun comes up, he's fried."

"But your investigation—?"

Penn gestures at Romeo. "We'll stay long enough to get the full story from Mas Mezzanotte here. If what Miz Azalea says is true, and the murders were the result of a serial killer who's no longer active, then I'm satisfied that the resort is once again safe for tourist visitation."

"Oh," says Chief Han, looking somewhat gobsmacked. "Well, then, let's get back to the resort, shall we? I don't think it's wise to linger out here with no protection."

"Agreed," says the captain. "May I offer you a lift?"

GABRIELLE

"Fantastic shot, G," I murmur, watching the Authorities load Chief Han, Lea, and Romeo onto their transport.

Germaine grunts. "Shoulda been aiming for his head."

"What are the redjackets gonna do with Romeo?" Violetta demands. Lest I forget that the reason I'm hiding here in the woods, and not down on the beach with my boss and my lover, is because Chief Han ordered me to babysit the Midnights and make sure they didn't fuck up this whole situation.

I type a quick query to Chief Han, who responds tersely, *<They're going to question Romeo. All fine. I will supervise.>*

"We gotta rescue him!" yells the vampire whose name I think is Mercedes.

"No!" I hold up my hands in a "settle down" gesture. "Chief Han has this under control. We need to wait until we get more information. Where are you all staying? Let's go hole up there until—"

"I'm sorry, Miz Ranger, you don't give the orders here." That's Benito. "With Romeo out of action, I'm the Midnights' leader, and—"

"And you don't want any of your people getting injured or killed, right?" I fire back. "I'm not gonna challenge your leadership, Beni, but I am gonna stop you from kicking a bloodstinger nest. The Authorities just agreed to leave. Let's not give them any reason to stay. Chief Han will make sure they don't take Romeo with them. In the meantime, we wait." Benito opens his mouth to argue, so I huff and rephrase. "It would be *a wise leadership move* to wait, but it's up to you, *boss*."

Benito looks like he wants to strangle me, but he can't refute my point. After a moment of opening and closing his mouth repeatedly, he finally says, "Well, I don't want to sit around and wait for dawn. You got access to all the ranger data, don't you? Can you figure out where Jude went?"

I pull out my scroll-tablet and check. Sure enough, Chief Han hasn't remembered to revoke my air traffic control log viewing privileges. Lea's ship was flagged as an unauthorized departure, highlighted in red, with her beach landing flagged as a high-priority anomaly. I snort, remembering how the system didn't even register the crash landing a few months ago. I guess unless a ship forgets to register its flight plan, traffic control bots aren't programmed to care.

The ship's second unauthorized flight is still in progress. Jude appears to be flying vaguely south, though his wandering flight path makes it clear he has no fucking clue where he's going. In fact, he looks like he's headed straight for the mountains, which is probably a bad idea—

Flight data lost, says the system suddenly.

It's unlikely he flew out of range or managed to turn his tracker off, so...most likely the ship crashed into something.

Shame. It was a really nice vehicle. I hope Lea wasn't too attached to it.

"The tracker just lost him somewhere in the southern mountains," I tell the Midnights.

"He crashed again? Fuck yeah. Hope it hurt," says Vi.

Nan looks at Benito. "So we going to get him or what?"

"Yeah," says Julia, cracking her knuckles. "Nobody fucks with the Midnights. He tried to hurt Lea and Romeo, so we make sure that crash was fatal. Right, Beni?"

"Whatever my girl wants." Benito pretends to leer. The vampire women shriek with laughter, bloodlust sparking in their eyes.

"No way!" I blurt. "It's way too far, even on a hovercycle. You'd never make it there and back before the sun comes up."

"But he got there in a starship in less than fifteen minutes," Benito says, scratching his chin. "Anyone we know who has a spare starship...?"

They look at me.

I shake my head. "Oh, absolutely not. I don't have a personal starship, just borrowing privileges for the rangers' shared vehicles. And Chief Han will never agree to this."

Benito waggles his eyebrows. "Does Chief Han have to know?"

Blazes. Can't believe I once thought *Romeo* was annoying to deal with.

"She's going to kill me," I say, "but if it keeps you all out of the Authorities' way..."

Chapter 27

GABRIELLE

Germaine's invested in keeping his job, so he opts out of helping the Midnights chase down Jude. We part ways as soon as we park our hovercycles in the rangers' garage.

"I'll wait an hour before I report you to Chief Han," he tells me gruffly, which I take as a personal favor. If he wanted to stop us, he'd have already messaged Han and told her everything.

As he's walking out of the hangar, his rifle case slung over his shoulder, I call, "Thank you!" after him. He turns around and gives me a nod, his eyes glowing briefly orange.

Ah. There it is. I'd been wondering, but didn't have the guts to ask.

The rangers' small fleet of starships wouldn't fit in this lower garage; they're parked in the main hangar alongside all the guests' personal vehicles. I hop on the lift to the upper level and mash the buttons, impatient to get moving.

By the time the lift drops me off, I've already put in the request to borrow our largest ship, the one that seats twenty. Since I'm in good standing, the system automatically approves it. I scan my ID at the keydrop to pick up the starter ring, then head to the berth where the ship is anchored. She's old, but still in decent shape. Most importantly, there's a robust solar shield installed, just in case.

"Gaby!"

I nearly jump out of my skin before I recognize the voice. "Lea?" I exclaim. She's jogging over from the welcome kiosk, pausing at the fence that separates ranger vehicles from civilian ones. I hurry over to unlock it and let her in. "What are you doing down here?"

"The Authorities took Romeo for questioning, and Chief Han went with them." Lea shrugs. "Guess they kinda forgot about me. I was asking your coworker over there if he could track where my ship went. You know, just in case Jude's coming back..."

"We think he crashed," I blurt.

Lea winces. "*Again?*"

"He's hard on starships, that guy." I gesture at the twenty-seater behind me. "I was just about to pick up the Midnights and go out hunting him."

A whole array of emotions flicker across Lea's face. Fear and worry, but also a flash of vicious determination.

"I'm coming with you," she says.

I stroke my hand down her arm. "Are you sure? It's going to be danger-ous."

"How am I ever going to sleep at night unless I *know* what happened to him?"

She sounds scared more than anything, but it's the violent glint in her eye that convinces me to say, "All right. Come on."

No one on this planet wants Jude dead more than Lea does. And that's exactly the sort of energy we're going to need.

Flying in a straight line, steering with both hands, makes the trip a lot easier than it must've gone for Jude. The ranger starship isn't as fast as Lea's sleek two-seater, but in twenty minutes, we're circling Jude's crash site looking for a safe landing area.

There's not a lot on offer. I don't know what Jude was thinking flying out to the mountains (most likely he *wasn't* thinking), but even here in the foothills, everything is either a sheer, impassable cliff or a slope tangled in thick jungle flora. Half this area hasn't even been explored except by satellite. Hades wildlife has been classified as level orange on the Imperial regulatory board's green-to-red scale for galactic exploration. Meaning you won't die instantly from vicious bacteria...but you stand an extremely high probability of getting eaten without serious protective gear.

We finally manage a perilous landing on the very edge of a cliff. The Midnights raid the ranger ship's supply storage and pull out grapples and rope to help us descend to where Jude's wreckage lies. But I already have a sick feeling that we're not going to find him in it. The man's too slippery to die in a crash, or he'd have done it the first time.

Sure enough, by the time we rappel down the cliff face and hack our way through maybe a kilometer of jungle, the crumpled wreckage of Lea's ship is empty of its pilot. All that remains is a puddle of his blood.

Lea hisses through her teeth when she sees the mess. She strokes the side of her ship mournfully. "Poor baby. Look what he did to you."

Benito indulges in a curse, but then turns to the Midnights. "All right, everyone. Romeo's taught us what to do. We track this asshole until the sun comes up."

"Ideally until twenty minutes *before* the sun comes up," I interject, "at which point I will be flying back to the resort with or without you."

"Yeah, yeah, Miz Ranger," says Beni. "Midnights, follow the blood scent. Yell if you see anything!"

I tag along behind the vampires as they sniff their way through the undergrowth, keeping a close eye on Lea. She's alert, eyes darting between shadows, but I think I might actually be more scared than she is. She seems at home in this jungle. Maybe it's all those hiking trips with Romeo.

"Must've wrapped his wound," Julia mutters. "No more drips to follow."

"But he's a clumsy hiker," laughs Mercedes. "Look, he put his foot right through a mushroom there. I could track him in my sleep."

Benito scales a large boulder and, from the top of it, scans the path ahead. "Looks like he's making for the cliffs over that way. Probably searching for shelter." Dawn is only an hour or two away; he'd be a fool not to.

Vi snatches my night binoculars and clambers up beside him. "There's a huge overhang up on the bluff, just southeast of here," she reports.

Beni nods. "His trail heads right to it. I wonder if he saw it from the air as he crashed. Well, Midnights, what are we waiting for? Let's get after him!"

A grueling thirty-minute trek later, we arrive at the base of the cliff. I expected us to catch up with Jude before now, but he's nowhere in sight. With a wounded hand, I don't see how he could've already got up to that overhang, unless he found an alternate path that we missed.

But the Midnights swear this is the path he took. And the pool of fresh blood we find, swarming with insects, seems to prove they're right.

The gory spill turns my stomach, but the Midnights gather around it with intent expressions bordering on hunger. I recall with unease that it's probably been a couple of days since any of them fed, and I'm the only human in the party.

Can vampires drink each other's blood? I decide I don't want to know.

"No sign of his body, but this is a lot of blood," Julia says. "D'you think an animal got him?"

Greg shrugs. "Or he just stopped here to retie his bandage before climbing up."

"If it's bleeding that badly, I doubt he has the strength to climb," says Lea.

I nod. "Question is, if an animal took him, is that enough to assume he's dead?"

"Depends on the animal," says Benito. "We know this fucker can kill and drink a spiger. So it'd have to be something even nastier than—"

A chilling screech splits the night.

We all freeze, staring at each other in the gloom.

Nan whispers, "That sounded like…"

"Uh-huh." I'm already moving to put my back to the cliff, eyes to the sky. Because I've just remembered that the southern mountain range is the behemoths' supposed hunting ground.

"It's coming down from the cave!" Benito whisper-yells. "Get to cover!"

Blast me. We're in deep shit now.

Then we all hear another sound, faint and distant but still instantly identifiable.

"HELP ME!"

"Shit, I think that's Jude," I mutter. "It's coming from the overhang up top."

Julia bares her teeth. "So the creature swooped him and took him to its nest for a leisurely meal?"

"That's sure what it looks like."

"Think we can count on it to finish him off?"

I shake my head. "I'm not assuming he's dead until I see it with my own two eyes. Getting eaten didn't kill him before."

"Ugh." Mercedes folds her arms. "You mean we have to go *rescue* the dickhead?"

"Only if no one else gets eaten," Beni says quickly. "I don't want to have to explain that shit to Romeo."

"I think I might have an idea," I say. "But, uh, it's not gonna be fun…"

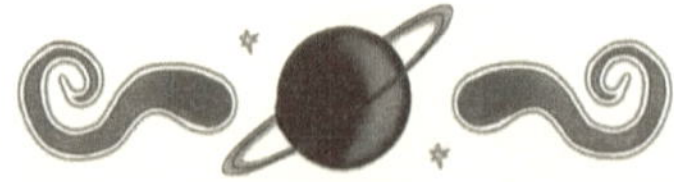

Of course nobody wants to be the bait.

"Why don't *you* do it?" Vi challenges me.

"I'm the only uninfected human here!" I remind her. "Slower than all of you, plus a lot easier to kill!"

Lea says tentatively, "I could—"

"Don't you dare," I hiss back.

The argument is taking longer than we can spare. Glancing at Benito, I say pointedly, "If Romeo was here, *he* would…"

"I'll do it." Benito sounds like he'd rather gnaw off his own arm, but a volunteer is a volunteer.

A few moments later, he's sprinting off at top speed through the jungle, screeching in an imitation of the behemoth cry. The creature lets out an earsplitting response, then swoops after him, dropping from the cliff into a low glide over the treetops. Its graspers quest downward after its prey.

"Run fast, Beni," Julia whispers.

As soon as the beast is far enough away, I snap, "Let's not waste time. Grapples up."

The Midnights beat both me and Lea to the top of the cliff. Mercedes is waiting at the cliff's edge with an outstretched hand to haul me up. A couple of months ago, I wouldn't have trusted her not to shove me off and watch me splatter on the rocks. Now, I grab her hand without question.

I glance over and see Lea reaching for Vi's hand. That's one vampire I still don't trust, and from the look on Lea's face, she feels the same. But Vi pulls her to safety anyway, steadying her as she stumbles.

Lea mutters, "Thanks," as she dusts herself off.

"Hey," says Vi quietly. "I know I've been rough on you, but you saved Romeo's ass back there, and you stuck your neck out to do it. We don't forget shit like that in a hurry."

They make eye contact, and Lea nods. I catch that fierce gleam in her gaze once more.

"Let's go," she says, turning to reach for my hand.

The behemoth nest takes up the entire overhang, which is shallow but wider than the resort beach. The nest appears to be made of plant matter, chewed to a pulp and molded into a massive bowl shape.

As we approach, Jude's screams grow louder. Under his noise, I can hear something else. A high-pitched chirping, almost like...

"Oh, blast me." I turn to Lea. "I think there are babies."

We clamber over the lip of the nest and peer into the dim, musky-smelling recess of the cave. Sure enough, there are two lumps in the middle of the nest, fat larval forms with vestigial limbs waving in distress. They're easily three times my size, but they look newborn, too young to do anything without their mama around to help them.

Then Lea draws in a sharp breath. She's seen Jude.

My stomach rolls. How the blazes is this guy still alive? The behemoth must've been tearing pieces off him to feed her young. He's missing an arm and most of a leg. There's enough blood soaking the nest around him that I have to wonder if he's got any left.

"Well?" says Vi, coming up behind us. "Are we hauling him out? Or do we wait for the monsters to finish eating him?"

I open my mouth to answer. Then I close it, because this is morally messy in a way I didn't expect.

I'd hoped to find him already dead. Barring that, I figured we'd have to fight him, and if we ended up killing him, *oops, oh well*. But murdering a guy who's helpless and in pain doesn't sit right. Not even a man as awful as Jude.

"Maybe we should take him back to the resort," I say tentatively. "Chief Han will want to put him on trial..."

The Midnights unanimously start yelling variations of "No!" "Absolutely not!" and "You've got to be kidding me."

"Yeah, right," says Vi, with a derisive snort. "C'mon, Gabs, imagine for two seconds that we take this asshole back and hold a trial. What happens if he gets acquitted somehow? You want to put him back on the streets? Or say he gets convicted—we'd have to stick him in a prison forever and waste a bag of blood on him a week. Plus, unless the court recognizes his immortality and gives him an *eternal* life sentence, he'll get released someday and go right back to being a danger to society."

Julia nods. "I say we put him out of the misery he should have been released from when Lea fed him to a lure vine. He's already supposed to be a dead man. We're just finishing what the tree should've."

"Lea," I say, turning to her. "What do you think we should do?"

She's staring at the ruin of Jude, her face a mixture of pity and loathing.

"I agree," she says slowly, "that it feels wrong to kill him when he's like this. But I also don't think prison will be enough to keep us safe from him." She wraps her arms around herself, glancing at the larvae behind us. "I think...I think we have to..."

She's right, blast it. Doesn't mean I have to feel great about it. I just have to back her up.

"Well, then. Who wants to do the honors?" I ask, gesturing at Jude, who's now moaning incoherently.

There's a moment of silence as we all wait for someone else to volunteer. A silence that's broken by the behemoth's piercing screech.

"That didn't sound far enough away," Nan whispers.

Julia runs to the edge of the nest and hoists herself up, binoculars raised. "It's coming back!" she cries. "Stars, Benito, you'd better be all right, or I'll..."

I make a snap decision and run toward Jude. Someone's gotta do it, and we're out of time to play rock-paper-scissors. The knife I carry in my utility belt feels cold against my clammy palm. I yank it out and scrunch up my face in disgust as I lean over him. *It's just like gutting an animal*, I tell myself, even though it's nothing like that whatsoever...

Jude lunges.

I have two seconds to think, *Blast it, the fucker was faking,* before my head is wrenched to one side and his teeth are buried painfully in my throat.

Chapter 28

It happens too fast. The behemoth's getting closer, and I turn my back for one second, and suddenly Gaby's screaming.

I whip around to see Jude sitting up, his one good hand fisted in Gaby's hair. She's got a knife and keeps stabbing him with it, over and over in the side and back and stomach, but it's not stopping him. His teeth are dug deep in her neck. Blood drips down her collarbone and stains her white shirt.

Greg yells, "Stop!" and rushes forward, trying to wrench Gaby away from Jude's hungry grasp. Jude growls and hangs on. Mercedes comes around behind Jude and grabs him by the hair, yanking him backward. Gaby screams as a mouthful of her skin comes away in his teeth.

Jude, eyes orange and frenzied, slams his head backward into Mercedes' knees. She swears and stumbles, losing her grip on him.

Anger rips through me. *No more.* Jude doesn't get to hurt anyone else. I'm done standing by.

"Let her go, Jude," I say calmly. "Wouldn't you rather drink me instead?"

That penetrates the haze of feral bloodlust. He spits out Gaby's flesh and turns those glowing orange eyes on me. "Angel," he says, with a bloody smile that chills my spine as it mirrors the kind, charming man I once was convinced I could love. "Come here."

I take a step. Then another, until I'm at his side. I can smell the blood on his breath, horrifyingly mouthwatering.

Greg pulls Gaby a safe distance away as soon as Jude's grasp loosens. Jude reaches for me in her place, his burn-scarred hand catching my sleeve and yanking me closer.

He dives for the pulse racing in my neck. But I'm done letting him do whatever he wants to me. *Angelique Azalea LaRue is a fighter,* my dad's voice whispers in my head.

And then it's joined by an image of Gaby yesterday, boxing gloves held up in front of her, urging me to punch harder. *Like you mean it.*

I curl my fist in the shape Dad taught me and punch Jude right in the throat.

As he's choking, I duck under his arm and twist, forcing him to release my shirt as his arm torques painfully. Mercedes comes in from behind, wrestling his arm behind his back and pinning it there, while someone behind me holds down his flailing legs.

"Do it!" Mercedes yells. "The knife's right there!"

Jude snarls, snapping at Mercedes as he writhes to free himself from her hold. The hatred burns in his eyes just as bright as the parasite's orange flame.

My hand curls around the hilt of Gaby's knife.

It's one thing to say out loud that I think this man needs to die. It's entirely another thing to be the one who kills him.

But the behemoth is coming, and Gaby's hurt. Later, there will be time to feel the horror.

Right now, there's only time for action.

With all my new vampire strength, I slash the knife across Jude's throat.

I only manage the one cut before I stagger back, revolted at the warm gush of blood over my hands. Mercedes grabs the blade and finishes the job with ruthless efficiency, severing Jude's head and tucking it under her arm.

"We can leave the rest of him for the babies," she says. "As long as the head's buried somewhere else, he's not coming back. Now let's *go!*"

I remember only flashes of what happens next. Hiding in a dark niche, waiting for the behemoth to forget about us and go back to feeding its babies. A blur of trees. Greg hacking vines with a machete.

Gaby's unconscious over Vi's shoulder. The Midnights bandaged her up, but there's a lot of blood. My mouth waters at the scent. Then the hunger response to my girlfriend's pain turns my stomach sour, and I stop to dry heave.

When we finally make it back to the starship, Benito's there waiting, scratched up and sweaty but otherwise fine. "Took you long enough," he calls. "We only have ten minutes left until dawn. Everyone accounted for? I'm gonna need to take off, like, *now.*"

"All accounted for, and the mission was a success." Mercedes lifts Jude's head triumphantly.

I suppress another gag. "Can you put that away?"

Mercedes shoves the head under her passenger seat, which isn't much better, but at least I don't have to look at it.

Beni fires up the engine. Greg and Nan have the first aid kit out and are doing their best to treat Gaby's neck wound. She's still alive, thank stars, but she's lost a concerning amount of blood for someone who's not a vampire.

I lean back in my seat and close my eyes, battling nausea and flashbacks of Jude's face right before I killed him.

His looming thundercloud over my life is gone. I'm free.

I thought I'd feel more relieved. Right now, all I feel is dirty.

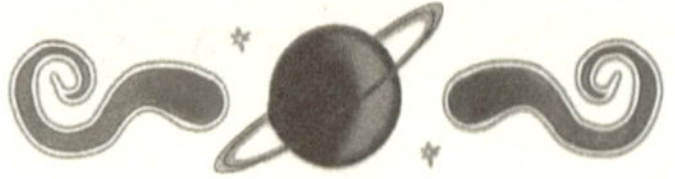

ROMEO

The bloodstinger venom starts to wear off during the Authorities' interrogation. My limbs loosen and the pain eases a little, allowing me to finally think straight about the story I'm spinning.

I tell them as much of the truth as I can, peppering in a couple of nasty details about the aftermath of Wright's murders. I'm careful not to name any of the women who worked together to end him, and I'm frank about my refusal to do so. "They did the community a service," I say bluntly. "This place is already dangerous enough. Wild animals, paralytic insect stings, deadly solar radiation. The last thing we need is for people to get the idea that we're a haven for killers."

"Some would argue that you and your friends are criminals, too," says Captain Penn testily. "The way you hide in some off-the-map cave, don't hold jobs, don't contribute to the local economy..."

"I think you'll find that none of that is actually a crime, Captain," I say, fighting to keep my face neutral. *Elitist glitch.*

"We asked some of the locals about you. Several mentioned drug dealing."

"An interest in local flora and an enthusiasm for sharing my discoveries with my neighbors? Not a crime, either. Particularly when said substances are unknown to the Imperial Institute of Scientific Research, and therefore not regulated or controlled. I'm happy to provide samples to the IISR for further testing, if they're interested."

Captain Penn is starting to get a strange look on his face, like he's confused about whether to be angry or not. "That should have happened long before you decided to sell any of it," he says finally, "but I'll reach out to the Institute and have them contact you for follow-up."

"Excellent," I say, flashing him a one-sided smirk. "Appreciate the favor, Captain."

They release me not long after. Captain Penn seems flustered and more than a little annoyed that he has not only failed to accuse me of anything he can prove was illegal, but also possibly hooked me up with some new and useful connections in the scientific world. After a quick word with Chief Han, he and his soldiers pile onto their ship and depart into the unforgivingly harsh daylight.

I'm just about to disappear off to the Midnights' hideaway and start cleaning up whatever mess the Authorities made of it, but one of Chief Han's rangers catches me and blocks my path. "Chief wants to talk to you."

"No rest for the wicked," I mutter, but allow her to lead me to the med center.

She nods to the nurse on duty, who allows us back to one of the private rooms. The ranger taps on the door and then slides it aside, ushering me in.

I stop dead in my tracks.

Chief Han sits in the visitor's chair next to a hospital cot. Several Midnights are gathered around the foot of it, looking not unlike a gang in a musical who are about to break into a song-and-dance number about kicking their rivals' asses. (I'm so proud.) Lea's there too, leaning against the far wall with a hollow, haunted expression. She smiles when she sees me, making my heart leap.

Then it drops again, because it's Gaby lying in the cot. Her uniform is torn and filthy, her face shiny with sweat, a huge bandage wrapped around her neck. I've never seen her so pale.

At the foot of the bed, right between her feet, is an object the rough size of a bowling ball, swaddled in what looks like a body bag.

"What happened?" I blurt.

Chief Han folds her arms. "Your Midnights talked Ranger Lopez into taking a ship to look for Jude's crash site." She gestures at the round object at the foot of the bed. "They found him."

Suddenly, I have a sinking feeling that I know what's in that body bag. I step forward and unfold a corner of the plastic sheet. Lea turns away, pressing her hand to her mouth.

Yup. Exactly what I thought. I grimace and quickly wrap Jude's head back up.

The Midnights start telling me the story, each of them contributing details, until they get to the part where Jude attacked Gaby. I glance at Lea and see tears streaming down her face.

"Lea," I say softly, "what happened then?"

"I...he wasn't going to stop hurting people, so I...I killed him." A huge shudder goes through her, and she begins to sob. "I hate him so much. I wanted him to die. Why did it have to feel so bad?"

I cross the room and offer my arms to her. She steps into them, burying her face in my shoulder.

"It feels bad to kill because you're not like him," I tell her, stroking her hair. "It's *supposed* to feel bad. But it had to be done, and it's over now." I rest my chin on the top of her head as she shakes in my arms.

The rhythmic beeping of Gaby's monitor comforts me a little; it proves she has a pulse. I glance at Chief Han. "He didn't infect Gaby, did he?"

"It doesn't look like it. The healers want to do more testing after she heals, though. She lost a lot of blood, but she's going to pull through, thanks to your Midnights. They did a stellar job of administering first aid."

Relief floods me. "Well done, all of you. I couldn't be prouder."

I'll yell at them later for going after Jude without me.

"We just did what you taught us," says Benito. "Glad to see you up and walking, man."

"I'm just barely managing it," I admit. I can't wait to suck down a bag of blood, slink back to the safety of my cave, and knock out. "Why don't we all go get some rest? We'll decide what to do with the...um...*that* tomorrow." I gesture at the swathed head.

"Take it with you for now," says Chief Han. "It's a biohazard to the non-infected healers."

Much as I'd rather not sleep with a severed head anywhere nearby, I have to agree she's right. I nod at Greg, who picks up the bundle and carries it out.

"Benito?"

"Yeah, boss?"

"Can you contact the group who are still sheltering outside the perimeter and tell them it's safe to come home?"

"Happy to." Benito looks just as exhausted as I am, maybe more, but he still manages a genuine grin.

I attempt one in return. This is a win for us, after all. Authorities gone, Jude dead, everyone else alive. Our turf is our own again.

But it feels different now. Every weakness of our current system has been tested, and we barely passed. Tomorrow, I'm going to have some tough decisions to make.

But for tonight...

"Lea, sweetheart," I say gently to the pop star who's still clinging to me. "Will you let me take you home?"

Season Finale, Part Two

Chapter 29

ROMEO

I wake with Lea in my arms, and for a long moment, all is right with the world.

As I hold her tight, reveling in our shared warmth, my soft mattress, and the candle-like flicker of my string lights as the battery wears down, the previous day's events begin to trickle in.

It was hard to convince Lea to leave Gaby's side last night. Chief Han had to promise to stay and keep watch before Lea would let me take her back to my cave.

The mess from the Authorities' incursion was less than I expected. The false stones seem to have fooled them. Our caves remain untouched, though we did find a couple of hidden cams in the common area, which we promptly disabled.

That was all we had energy to do before we fell straight into bed. There was no question of doing anything *but* sleeping. Lea begged me for a dose of dreamspice, fearing nightmares, but even dreamed sex felt like a toe over the line when we were both so shattered. I dug up a tea blend I'd created to induce dreamless sleep instead.

Careful not to disturb Lea, I tilt my wrist to check the time. We've slept all day and halfway through another night. I must've oversteeped that tea...or maybe we were really that exhausted.

I could stay here forever, holding her while she breathes slow and even, but I can't leave the Midnights to do all the cleanup themselves. Dropping a kiss on Lea's forehead, I extract my arm from under her head and tuck the blanket around her.

I'm halfway out the door before I second-guess leaving her. How to reassure her if she wakes alone? I scan my trinket display for a token to leave, and settle on a dried flower I preserved from one of my jungle hikes. As the petals dried leather-tough, it lost its glow but retained its color, magenta deepening to a mysterious maroon.

I've kept it for years as a reminder that becoming a vampire toughened me up, but kept me sexy. Smiling, I retrieve the flower and place it on the pillow next to Lea's tangle of brown hair.

"You better not tell the Midnights I'm this sappy," I whisper.

Then I duck under the curtain and make my way out to our common area.

Someone's put the head, still partially wrapped in its body bag, on a crate in the center of the space. Benito's drinking coffee with his feet up on the crate, his bare toes wiggling in the head's face.

"Aw, c'mon, Beni, that's so gross," Julia's complaining as I walk up to them. "Romeo, don't you think so?"

"Yeah, man, you don't know what fuck-ass diseases he had," I say. "At least put some shoes on."

Over to the side, a group of the Midnights who weren't involved in the hunt last night are listening to Mercedes retell the story, complete with dramatic sound effects. She's getting good at imitating the behemoth cry.

I remember what Gaby said to me the other night: *Training the rangers on behemoth calls could save a life.*

She was right. I've done what I can to prepare other infected people for surviving the Hades jungle, in case we're ever chased out of our home. But my focus has always been too narrow. The rangers, both infected and not, have to deal with this planet's wildlife too. And, while tourists will probably never care about Hadesian botany, the vendors and service workers on this planet have a right to know what they can do to protect themselves.

"Coffee?" Greg offers. There's a pot brewing on the camp stove behind him. "You look like you could use it."

I accept a mug from him. "Thanks. I'm still a little out of it."

"But you're feeling all right now?"

"Yeah." The muscle pain from the bloodstinger venom is gone, though I've got an itchy bump in each spot where Jude stabbed me with his homemade darts. "I just wanted to say...thank you all for getting the job done last night. You should have waited for me, and believe me, I'm still flared off about it. But *I* went off without *you* first, and I just about got killed for it. So...lesson learned. The Midnights work better as a team than solo. I'm proud of you for realizing that."

"Hear, hear," Benito murmurs, annoyingly smug.

"Beni did a great job of leading us, too," Julia says loudly. "*And* he volunteered to be the bait."

"You did good," I tell him. "Really, really good. But listen. No matter how well this all turned out, it easily could've gone the other way. And I can't say for sure that there won't be a next time. The Authorities could come back. Some other sadistic asshole could get infected somehow and go on another rampage. We're going to need to set ourselves up to deal with that."

Inez calls from across the room, "What do you have in mind?" The various clusters of chatting Midnights have all paused to listen to me. I suddenly realize I'm giving a speech I haven't prepared for at all.

Except I *have* been thinking about it, ever since Lea brought up building a new settlement for vampires a few days ago. The more I think about it, the more I'm starting to wonder if all the obstacles are in my head. Sure, the governor won't like it, but enforcing his building ban would be so expensive and annoying that it's possible he wouldn't bother. As long as we don't interfere with the resort and fund the project ourselves...

"To start, we're going to need a judicial system for what happens when a vampire goes rogue," I say. "We can't wait until they start kidnapping or murdering people. I think we should work with Chief Han..."

ANGELIQUE

Whatever Romeo put in our bedtime tea worked wonders. I stretch and yawn, wincing at the soreness in my muscles. If I was still human, all that climbing I did yesterday would've flattened me for a week. As a vampire, I still feel it, but it's healing fast.

So is the emotional soreness, I think. Sleep has taken the edge off of yesterday's trauma. I'm still going to need to research therapists who take offworld clients, but I'm functional again today.

The flower on the pillow puts a smile on my face. I brush a finger over the petals. *Such a gentleman.*

After a long, languid stretch, I check my keycuff and message Karina to tell her I'm going to need another day off. She's not happy with me, of course. I tell her that Chief Han will write me an excuse note if I need one. After all, I was the victim of an attempted kidnapping yesterday.

Officially, Jude died in a starship crash while fleeing the Authorities. Chief Han's already filed the report and sent a copy to Captain Penn. I doubt they're planning to investigate, but just in case...

I swallow a sudden surge of sick dread. We have to get rid of the head today.

When I wander out of the cave into the Midnights' common area, Romeo's in the middle of giving an impassioned speech about building our own space and securing a blood source that doesn't exploit nonconsenting humans. I lean against a crate and listen for a few minutes until he notices me.

As soon as he does, he breaks off and quickly throws the plastic sheet over what I belatedly realize is Jude's head in their midst.

"Sorry about that," he says. "How are you feeling this morning, Lea?"

"Better." I smile at him. "I thought you'd decided we had to wait on building Vampire Town."

"We're *not* calling it Vampire Town!" Benito yells.

This place is kind of trashed after the Authorities tossed it around. Romeo nearly trips on a crate in his hurry to cross the room and give me a hug.

"I've been rethinking a lot of things," he says. "I'm going on a hike this morning to get rid of the—" He gestures over his shoulder at the bag-wrapped head. "Want to come with me, and we'll talk about it?"

I nod. It'll be a relief to have the last remnant of Jude gone.

Then a voice echoes from the other side of the cave. "You'd better not be going anywhere without me!"

I watch Romeo's eyes light up as we both say, "Gaby!"

Now it's my turn to trip over crates as we rush across the Midnights' common area to meet our favorite ranger, dressed in a fresh and unstained uniform. Her neck is still bandaged, but the color's returned to her face.

"Are you sure you should be out of bed yet?" I ask, kissing her cheek.

She groans. "I was getting so *bored*. Really, I'm fine. The nanites are almost done healing up my wound, and they've been making me drink some nasty solution that's supposed to help with blood loss. Apparently they see a lot of that here. Go figure."

"I don't think the healers would want you to go hiking." Romeo sounds severe, but the almost-smile tugging at the corner of his mouth betrays his relief at seeing her upright.

"Tough. I'm going." Gaby crosses her arms. "I wanna help bury this glitch for good."

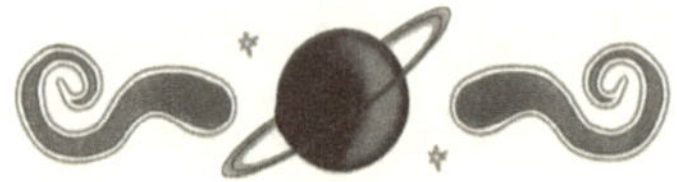

GABRIELLE

Hiking is more of a strain than I expected, but I refuse to admit it. I'm not about to let Romeo and Lea send me back to the resort to nap through my convalescence like an old lady.

The spot Romeo chose is a cliff overlooking deep water, a half-hour's hike to the north. He and Lea pause several times to rest, and I get the sense that it's not just for me. The past day—really, the past several—have put us all through the wringer. Romeo made us practically bathe in bloodstinger repellent before we left.

Despite him promising to tell us whatever it was he was soapboxing about with his gang, Romeo's quiet on the hike out. I can tell he's deep in thought, and it kinda seems like Lea is too, so I keep my mouth shut. But it makes me a little antsy.

Once we arrive at the top of the cliff, Romeo slings his backpack down and stretches his back with a groan. "Dude's head is heavy as blazes," he complains.

Instead of getting rid of it right away, however, he sits down on the edge of the cliff and takes a few deep breaths. I join him on one side, Lea on the other, and we take a moment to breathe in the humid night air, full of the scent of an alien jungle's mingled growth and decay.

"Do you want to say anything?" Romeo asks Lea finally. "Like, a funeral rite, or...?"

She grimaces. "Ugh. Not really."

"I will," I say, reaching behind us to grab the backpack. It *does* weigh a ton. "Here lies Jude Andrews, who, despite having every opportunity in the galaxy to do the right thing and mind his own business, chose to be a piece of shit to the very end."

Then, with a great heaving swing, I let Jude's head fly out across the black depths of the water below. The waves churn as a shoal of sea creatures converge on the bag and tear into it.

Lea lets out a shuddering sigh. "It's done. It's over. He's really gone."

"He was gone the moment it happened, Lea," Romeo says softly. "I've never seen someone come back from being beheaded. This part is just...an abundance of caution."

"Still." She leans into him, and he snakes his arm around her waist. "This feels...final."

"It's called closure," says Romeo, "and I think we all needed some."

We sit there a moment longer in silence. I'm trying not to overthink their embrace, but it's increasingly obvious that Lea has feelings for Romeo as well as me. They even spent last night together. It makes my heart twist to think of them together without me, but I really don't want to be the glitch that makes her choose a side.

I'm not even sure there are sides to choose. Not when I'm starting to feel a spark of something new, something nebulous and confusing, whenever I see Romeo smile. It's not what I feel for Lea, not even close, but I think it's something that could grow if I let it.

Romeo stretches again. "Oof. Maybe coming out here so soon *was* a bad idea. I don't normally get this sore."

"Me, too," Lea groans, rubbing her calf. "Hey, how far is that hot spring?"

He lights up with a smile, and my stomach does that weird little flip again. "Just a short detour on our trip back."

"A hot spring?" My own muscles haven't recovered from all that climbing and running yesterday. "Say no more. Let's go."

ANGELIQUE

Gaby slides her arm around my shoulders as we make our way down from the cliffside. I lean into her, craving comfort. The relief of this all being *over* is finally sinking in.

When Romeo pulls a little ahead of us on the trail, she stops and tugs on my hand to pull me into her arms. I make a throaty noise of encouragement and slide my hands around her waist, pressing my lips to the side of her neck that isn't bandaged.

"You care about Romeo, don't you?" she asks quietly.

"Gaby, I care about *you*."

She gives me a tiny smile, cupping my cheek in her palm. "That's not what I asked, sweetheart. Listen, I'll go first if it helps: Romeo's hot as blazes, and I maybe don't hate him as much as I thought I did. And right now, I'm feeling *really* glad that we're all alive." She bites her lower lip. "Am I totally off base in thinking you have similar thoughts? And that you'd maybe like to fuck him about it?"

"*Gaby!*" Heat flushes into my cheeks, but it's *good* heat, relief and arousal at hearing her voice the wish I've been keeping locked in my daydream vault for weeks now.

"Yeah," I say in a low voice, feeling shockingly shy for my age. "I care about Romeo. *And* you. And I'm...very open to having you both at once, but only if you and he are comfortable with it."

"Well, you've got my vote," says Gaby with a little smirk. "Should we go find out what he thinks?"

Chapter 30

ROMEO

My sore muscles are screaming for relief by the time I shove aside the last trailing frond and lead Gaby and Lea into the clearing where the hot spring pools lie. Surrounded by soft moss and glowing fungi, they make a tantalizing sight.

I'm halfway through pulling off my clothes before I remember that Gaby's here with us this time. With my shirt dangling from my hands, I turn, searching both women's faces. Lea has been with both of us. Is this going to put her in an uncomfortable position...?

Lea strides toward me, a determined look in her eye, and surges up to kiss me on the mouth.

Eyes open, I watch Gaby's face. Do these two have some kind of arrangement? Lea said she only wanted me as a friend with benefits. What does it mean that she's willing to kiss me in front of her girlfriend?

She steps back and slides an arm around Gaby, meeting the other woman's eyes. Gaby presses her lips together, her gaze flicking between Lea and me. Then, deliberately, she leans in and presses a kiss to Lea's lips, slow and sensual.

I take a step back. *This is clearly some kind of territory-marking, and I'm not interested in stealing her girl. I'll get out of the way...*

Then Gaby's hand shoots out and grabs my wrist. Breaking off from Lea, she pulls me in and captures my bottom lip in a bruising bite of a kiss that literally knocks me off balance.

I yelp into her mouth and just barely manage not to fall into the pool. She releases my lip, but goes in for another taste. It's my blood-hunger more than anything else that has me responding with a growl, sweeping my tongue across hers.

She releases me and steps back, looking at Lea first. Our beautiful singer nods, smiling tentatively.

"We were just talking," she says, reaching out to take my hand. "And we...would you...Romeo, would you spend the night with us?"

If they're asking what I think they're asking...arousal surges through me, as hot and sharp as blood-thirst. But I can't resist a little bit of teasing.

"Aren't I already spending the night with you?" I look up at the dark sky, scattered with stars. "Or are you interested in a more specific activity?"

"I think you know what we mean." Gaby takes Lea's other hand, leaning in to nibble her earlobe. "So are you going to finish taking off your clothes, or what?"

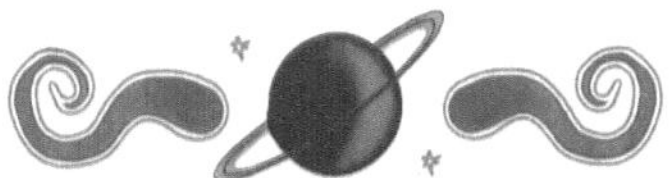

ANGELIQUE

Romeo doesn't hurry taking his shorts off. Now that he knows we both want him, he's gone annoyingly smug. He steps down into the pool, treating both of us to a half-lidded smirk. "Well? Are you two planning to join me?"

Gaby shrugs out of her orange jacket. Her white top and shorts follow quickly after, leaving her glorious brown skin on display.

Romeo's already sitting up and paying attention—as is his cock, dimly visible beneath the surface of the pool. I take a little more time disrobing, letting my filmy swimsuit cover flutter to my feet before slowly peeling off one strap, then the other. I push the skintight suit down over my thighs, making sure to bend over and give them a good view of my ass.

"Lea," Romeo says in a strangled voice. "Get in here."

Gaby's already waist deep in the pool. She holds up a hand to help me in, her eyes eating me up. I let her guide me into the water, then lift her chin for a long, slow kiss.

Romeo watches and waits. I'm conscious of his rough breathing, which catches as Gaby's hands wander and one of them closes over my breast.

I enjoy tormenting him for a moment longer, then tug Gaby along the rim of the spring, where we kneel on either side of Romeo. I nibble his ear while she claims his lips, her fingers drifting down to pinch his nipple.

Romeo turns to kiss me next. I lose myself in the stroke of his tongue and the soft exploration of his fingers making their way from my hipbone to the inside of my thigh.

Gaby straddles his lap and rubs up against his cock, making him break our kiss with a moan. "I want you first," she tells him, hand at his collarbone. "Lea already got to have you. It's my turn now."

Hearing her act bossy turns me on so much. Romeo's fingers find my opening, and as he slides two into me, Gaby slowly lowers herself on his rigid cock. I lose my breath with the erotic wonder of it, watching the two of them in ecstasy together with me.

Gaby begins to ride him, and he fucks me with his fingers in the rhythm of her hips. His thumb strums against my clit. I let out a breathy moan, and Gaby moans too, leaning over to pull my face to hers for a kiss.

"Stars, woman, I'm not going to last like this," Romeo groans. "I...oh, fuck..." His fingers falter in my pussy as his hips grind up to meet Gaby's. "Pull off now if you don't want me to come in you," he gasps.

"Ugh, yes, do it. *Now.*" Gaby's lips trail down his jawline.

"But I could infect—"

"Lea and I already had this talk," she assures him. "If it happens, it happens."

Romeo groans. Then his hips arch up as he pistons into her, making her throw back her head and scream with delight. I watch both their faces as he comes, awed and envious and desperately horny.

Gaby seizes him in a searing kiss as his body comes down from the high, relaxing into a puddle of a man on the hot spring ledge.

Unsated, she turns to me. "Lea, sweetheart, you're squirming over there. Come sit up here for me." She pats the lip of the spring next to Romeo's head.

She doesn't have to tell me twice. I hoist myself to the edge and let my legs fall open for her.

"Oh, yessss," she whispers, rubbing her thumbs up either side of my labia before pressing an open-mouthed kiss to my clit. Already sensitive from Romeo's ministrations, I nearly fall backward as my back arches, legs trembling.

Romeo watches her eat me out for a few moments. His eyes meet mine, and his fingers brush my hand clutching the edge of the pool. Then he grins and dives under the surface, and Gaby gives a yelp of surprise against me. Then the motions of her tongue and lips are interspersed with breathy moans and cries.

"That's...some skill, Romeo," I gasp as she drives me higher and higher. "How long...do you think he can hold...ahh!...his breath?"

Gaby doesn't respond, except by circling my clit with her tongue in such a sweetly perfect rhythm that I teeter on the edge of climax.

"I'm going to...ah, Gaby, I'm coming!"

She growls a throaty laugh as I fall apart. Then it evolves into a high-pitched cry of pleasure as Romeo does something underwater that must be truly fantastic. Her eyes close and her mouth drops open in what I've learned is her close-to-coming face, little whimpers escaping her throat in staccato, until with a shudder she comes hard with her face between my thighs.

Romeo resurfaces, spitting water and looking far too pleased with himself. He's hard again, and I crook my finger to invite him to join me on the edge of the pool before sliding in and taking his cock in my mouth.

"Ah, yes, Lea!" he cries. "Gaby, oh, stars—" Because she's just squeezed between his legs with me and is cupping his balls. I pull off and let her lick his shaft with me, our tongues tangling against him.

"Fuck, fuck, fuck," he gasps. "I need—"

"Lea, your turn," Gaby says in my ear. "I want to watch him fuck you."

"I don't think that's what he needs," I say. "Listen, Gab, this might be gross to you, but…"

"Ohhh." She raises her eyebrows. "Sexy biting? I could be into it. Why don't you show me how it's done?"

I pull Romeo back into the water with me. He presses me back against the edge of the pool, his eyes asking for permission as he notches his cock at the opening of my pussy. I nod and wrap my legs around his hips as he slides in.

"Do you want me to bite, or you?" I murmur as he closes his eyes and moans out a breath.

"You…bite me…please."

I'm more than ready to meet his demand. I lick the vein in his neck and then sink my teeth in, quick and sharp to spare him the most pain. He gives a guttural groan and his hips slam into mine. I feel Gaby's hand caressing my arm and see out of the corner of my eye that she's touching herself with the other hand as she watches us.

Romeo's blood flows bright and delicious across my tongue. Pleasure surges through me, the indescribable tandem joy of tasting blood and having my pussy wrecked at the same time. Another orgasm starts building, the sight of Gaby's head thrown back in ecstasy spurring it along.

But it's Romeo's rough gasp as he comes a second time, burying his teeth in my shoulder as he does, that pushes me to new heights. I release his vein, my mouth dripping red, and scream his name as I explode into stars.

In the aftermath, after we clean and bandage our wounds, we bask together in the water and cuddle, all three of us. For a long time, it's companionable silence and soft caresses.

Then Romeo says, "I've been thinking a lot about our future."

The last time I asked him about building a community of vampires out here in the wilds, he had a whole list of reasons why it wouldn't work. But going up against the Authorities seems to have emboldened him. Now, he can't stop pouring out new ideas.

"The Midnights have a fair chunk of rainy-day credits saved up. I'm thinking we work on building a compound out here first, with what materials we can source locally, and then once we have a secure perimeter, we bring in some livestock with blood that wouldn't make us sick. Earth-descended creatures like horses, cows, pigs. We could grow them ourselves from incubators to save on shipping costs. We'd figure out how much blood we can safely drain from them per week, and build up enough of a herd so that we could rotate the blood loss."

"Uh, just don't tell anyone that's what you plan to do with them," Gaby says. "Animal safety activists won't like it. They'll tell you to synthesize blood instead of getting it from animals."

"Oh, yeah, that'll be another project we can work on long-term," Romeo says. "That's a lot of expensive machinery, though. We're going to need to build up some kind of money-making business."

"I have some savings I could contribute," I offer.

Romeo kisses me. "That's really generous of you, sweetheart, but you might need that money someday. I'm thinking we start a business. What about jungle tours?"

Gaby laughs. "Chief Han is never going to go for that."

"No? Not even after I've taken you out into the jungle how many times and brought you back safe and uninfected?"

"Oh, so yesterday was a fiasco just because you weren't there?" she teases.

"Now you're getting it." Romeo smirks. "If Chief Han doesn't like the tour idea, I can build a greenhouse and grow parasite-free strains of local plants to sell off for science purposes. Captain Penn promised to put me in contact with the right people."

"Oh, I love that idea!" I squeeze his arm. "Maybe you can start growing some human-safe foods too, just in case the governor or the Authorities ever decide to quarantine us and cut off our supply runs."

"My thoughts exactly," says Romeo. "And before you ask, Gaby, no, I'm not going to ask the governor's permission for any of this. He'll just say no. But what's he going to do, send the Authorities out into the wilds to arrest us? They were nearly shitting their pants just talking to Jude on the beach. Imagine if they saw one singular spiger. Or had a lure vine come for them."

"They could bomb you from orbit," Gaby says seriously. "If they thought you were enough of a threat, they wouldn't hesitate."

"Then I'm going to make sure we look as nonthreatening as possible. A little village with some farm animals and a greenhouse? If they ever roll up asking what we're doing there, we'll offer them some fresh fruit and let them pet our horses."

There's a tiny insect skating along the surface of the water. I cup my hand under it, letting it settle onto my palm before gently lifting it away from us. The insect repellent Romeo made us rub into our skin will only poison it if it tries to bite us. Better it finds its meal somewhere else.

"What if they try to take us offworld?" I ask. "Or want us to come meet with the governor in person? He still does technically rule this planet. He can summon us if he really wants to, but the parasite won't let us leave."

Romeo looks at Gaby, smiling. "Actually, I've thought about that. There are a couple of people, like Gaby here, who aren't infected but know about vampires. I think someone like her would make an amazing ambassador."

"Whoa," says Gaby, throwing up her hands with a laugh. "I didn't sign up to be a *diplomat*. I still want to be a ranger." She leans her head on Romeo's shoulder. "Besides, I might want to become a vampire someday."

"Doesn't have to be you. But someone trustworthy like you."

My heart swells at the way they're smiling at each other. Given the way they hated each other when I first moved here, I never could have foreseen them like this—but it makes me ridiculously happy.

"Anyway, I'm interested in this little village you're going to be building," she says lazily. "Are regular humans going to be allowed there? And will you be hiring any rangers to help with your jungle tour business? Assuming, that is, that Chief Han lets you do it. Because I'd like to spend a *lot* more time with you both, and that's going to be tough if we aren't living in the same town."

"Anyone's going to be welcome," I say, before Romeo can open his mouth. "No exclusions, and no requirements either. Vampires can keep living and working in the resort if they want. I sure plan to."

"You'll keep singing at the Underworld, then?" Romeo asks.

I laugh. "Jude chased me across the galaxy for two years and kept finding me because I couldn't stay out of show biz. If that asshole couldn't keep me away from my music, then nothing can."

"All right," says Romeo, snaking an arm around my waist. "Looks like I'm going to have to figure out a safe way to commute daily between our new village and the resort. Because I don't want to sleep another day without you."

His words send a thrill through me. I've never been someone to throw around the word "love" lightly; there was a time in my life when I thought I might be incapable of feeling it.

But meeting these two changed my mind. Gaby's optimism and drive for justice, the way Romeo cares deeply for both this planet and the people around him, and *both* of them caring and supporting me through all the shit that's happened…I'm relieved I don't have to choose between them, because I'm not sure that I could.

"I love you," I say softly. "Both of you. So much." I lean in for a kiss, first with Romeo, then Gaby. "I can't wait for the rest of our lives together."

"Young and hot forever," says Romeo with a smirk. "And this planet will keep us on our toes."

"Speaking of which…" Gaby draws her knees up to her chest. "Does anyone else feel something slimy tickling their feet?"

"It's just the algae," I say confidently.

Then a questing tentacle caresses my ankle, and I rocket out of the spring so fast that I scrape my leg on the rocky ledge. Gaby's not far behind me.

Romeo climbs out after us, laughing his ass off. We berate him for not warning us about the tentacle monster as we clamber damply into our clothes and set off for home.

And it *is* home, I realize, squeezing my partners' hands intertwined with mine. A last resort, turned into a dream future.

I belong here, on the black sands of Hades.

ROLL CREDITS

End

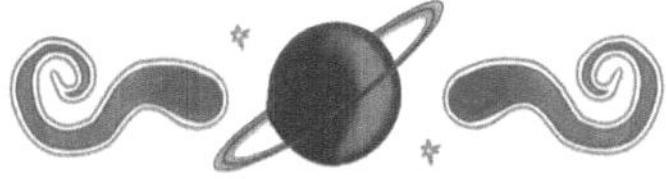

Thank you for joining me on another Halcyon Universe adventure! If you enjoyed this book, please leave a review. Turn the page to subscribe to my newsletter so you can stay updated on future books in the series!

Free short story with newsletter signup!

Pirates shouldn't mess with the grandmas who feed them...

Welcome to Grandma Rae and Grandma Toni's cafe, where delicious home-cooked comfort food is served up daily on an asteroid pit stop for long-haul starship pilots. The Waystation's thriving businesses might look like a juicy target for a pirate attack, but watch out! When the grandmas' livelihood is threatened, they won't go down without a fight.

This short story takes place in the Halcyon Universe series after the events of Petrichor Blooms. It can be read standalone.

Sign up for Mindi Briar's newsletter and receive this FREE story in your inbox! Visit www.mindibriar.com to find out more.

Acknowledgements

shrug Listen, sometimes you just gotta write what basically amounts to a fanfic of your own book series, and hope other people have as much fun with it as you did.

I'm gonna keep this one short and sweet, so... all my gratitude and love to the following people:

Skye Kilaen, J.E. McDonald, and Lila Gwynn for beta reading!

My online support system: Skye, for weekly accountability check-ins. The Discordant Owls, for being indie publishing badasses and inspiring me every day.

My IRL support system: Joe, for neverending creative encouragement and for being my favorite person. Chelsea, for keeping up the weekly writing sessions. The Four Four-Eyes, for supporting every single book release.

And last but not least, I owe thanks to many authors of books that depict queer, polyamorous love stories, for inspiring me as I wrote this one. Here are just a few that I recommend:

Space For More by Emily Antoinette

Shake Things Up by Skye Kilaen

The *Venora Mates* series by Octavia Kore

Road To Ruin by Hana Lee

The Thread That Binds by Cedar McCloud

A Fae's Two Alphas by jem zero

The Orchid and the Lion by Gabriel Hargrave

Wicked Beauty by Katee Robert

Iron Widow and *Heavenly Tyrant* by Xiran Jay Zhao

Also by Mindi Briar

HALCYON UNIVERSE: THE DRAGON-TOUCHED SEQUENCE

Petrichor Blooms
The Invisible Bright
The Taste of Lies

HALCYON UNIVERSE: SIDE QUESTS

Adrift in Starlight
The Black Sands of Hades

About the author

Mindi Briar's favorite book as a child was "Commander Toad in Space," an early sign that she was destined to become a gigantic nerd. She lives in the Seattle area with her husband and three cats, two of whom are named after punctuation marks. She will be your friend if you offer tea, or if you want to talk about Star Wars.

She is the author of the Halcyon Universe sci-fi romance novel series. Her short stories have also appeared in four anthologies.

www.ingramcontent.com/pod-product-compliance
Lightning Source LLC
Chambersburg PA
CBHW030429160726
47991CB00005B/1653